Maximo slapped the chisel on his leathered thigh. "I pay you. You find me good hands! Not *idiota*!"

"I'm sorry, Maximo. He's gone. You'll never have to work with him again."

"Good."

The great artist's gaze slid over Emily. His eyes stopped at the white-knuckled hold she had on the large black portfolio.

He waved a hand toward her. "What are you?"

Emily's throat slammed shut.

"A new intern possibly," offered Dante. "She's here from the Stoddard School of Art."

Deep brown eyes the color of rich coffee, no cream, speared her beneath frowning brows. He flipped his hand toward the portfolio. "Come. Show me."

Emily shot a look to Dante. He gave her a tiny nudge, like a parent pushing a frightened child toward Santa's lap.

"Come, come, come." He snatched the portfolio from her numb fingers, unzipped it and laid it open across a crowded worktable. He used the rag in his hand to wipe the sweat from his lip as he flipped through photos and sketches of her latest works.

"Nice. Hmm. No." A nod for this one. A shake of the head for another. "Yes. This one is good. Good."

He looked away from her sketches and gave her a hard stare before looking down the full length of her and back again in a slow appraisal. Emily released the breath she was holding.

"Let me see your hands."

Rock Solid

by

Lisa A. Olech

The Stoddard Art School Series

Rock Solid

Cover Art by *Angela Anderson*

The Wild Rose Press, Inc.
PO Box 708
Adams Basin, NY 14410-0708
Visit us at www.thewildrosepress.com

Publishing History
First Champagne Rose Edition, 2014
Print ISBN 978-1-62830-605-7
Digital ISBN 978-1-62830-606-4

The Stoddard Art School Series
Published in the United States of America

Dedication

To the best of the bests:
Kathy,
Sue,
and Alice
Better than sisters,
Closer than friends.

Acknowledgments

It takes many hands to turn a rough stone into a polished gem, just as it takes many ideas and talented readers to turn an idea into a story, into a novel, and bring that novel all the way to publication.

I want to thank Krissy, Shannon, Kat from A Day to Remember, Suzanne, Tim, and Jon, who all got caught in the creative brainstorming of this story.

I also need to thank Kathy for her tireless support and encouragement, my agent, Dawn, and her team, my editor, Cindy, and The Wild Rose Press, who all helped smooth out the rough edges and gave this book its glossy finish.

And last but certainly not least, to the brilliant Bartlett Bunnies who helped me bring the extra facets to this story to make it sparkle!
I love you all!!
~Lisa

Chapter One

"*Non si ha il cervello in testa! Idiota!*"

The volume of cursing increased as Emily Baskins held a death grip on her portfolio. "I don't speak Italian."

"He's telling someone they have no brain in their head."

"I understood the 'idiot' part." She nodded. More yelling and crashing echoed through the immense studio. Tall industrial ceilings added to the monumental scope. "Should I come back another time?"

The man standing next to her smirked, gave a little snort, and shook his head. "No. It's fine. He's just in a mood."

A tall, lanky young man covered in dust rushed from a curtained section of the huge open space, a pair of safety goggles pushed back on his forehead. He released the ties of his leather apron, wrenching it over his head, knocking the goggles and the apron to the ground in his wake. He skidded to a stop before the studio manager Dante Rizzoli, who had just greeted Emily and welcomed her to the Vega Studio.

"He's insane! I don't care who he is. He can't treat people like…like…"

More crashing before the "he" stormed toward them. Maximo Vega. "The Sculptor for the New Generation." Emily's mother had a framed copy of the

New England Journal of Art with his image on the front. And here he was. Dark eyes shot daggers at the young man doing his best to hide behind the studio manager.

"I said, OUT!" He pointed an arrow-tipped chisel at the door. He threw up his hands and swiped the dusty cloth from his head. His hair was jet black, each wave as shiny as polished onyx. "Four days wasted. FOUR DAYS!" Maximo spun around and aimed his chisel at Dante. "I see him, never again." He spit out the words.

"Yes, Maximo." Dante turned to the young man. "Go."

And he went. Like he was being chased by wolves.

"Ruined! The piece, she is ruined!" His English was halting and thick with a hot Italian accent. He threw up his hands "*Incompotant sciocco!*"

Maximo Vega gathered his composure. He wore a black T-shirt, gray across the shoulders with dust, worn jeans, and heavy boots under a thick leather apron that reached to his knees. Hanging his head and bracing his hands on his hips, he was a study in frustration. The sleeves of his shirt hugged defined muscles of steely arms. And his hands...they were artist's hands. Sculptor's hands. Beaten by stone and scarred by tools. They spoke of years of rugged, blistering work.

He was tall. His shadowed jaw, rigid with anger, cut sharply against the tanned column of his neck. Maximo slapped the chisel on his leathered thigh. "I pay you. You find me good hands! Not *idiota!*"

"I'm sorry, Maximo. He's gone. You'll never have to work with him again."

"Good."

The great artist's gaze slid over Emily. His eyes

stopped at the white-knuckled hold she had on the large black portfolio.

He waved a hand toward her. "What are you?"

Emily's throat slammed shut.

"A new intern possibly," offered Dante. "She's here from the Stoddard School of Art."

Deep brown eyes the color of rich coffee, no cream, speared her beneath frowning brows. He flipped his hand toward the portfolio. "Come. Show me."

Emily shot a look to Dante. He gave her a tiny nudge, like a parent pushing a frightened child toward Santa's lap.

"Come, come, come." He snatched the portfolio from her numb fingers, unzipped it and laid it open across a crowded worktable. He used the rag in his hand to wipe the sweat from his lip as he flipped through photos and sketches of her latest works.

"Nice. Hmm. No." A nod for this one. A shake of the head for another. "Yes. This one is good. Good."

He looked away from her sketches and gave her a hard stare before looking down the full length of her and back again in a slow appraisal. Emily released the breath she was holding.

"Let me see your hands."

She held them out and he grasped her wrists and examined first her palms before turning them over. "Cold," he said just loud enough for her to hear.

The smell of the heat of his body and the spice of soap drifted past her.

"Nervous."

He lifted a quick eyebrow. "Good."

Maximo nodded to Dante as he handed Emily back her portfolio. He looked around the studio. "WORK!"

He disappeared like the Wizard behind his curtain. Artists, assistants, and models jumped at his command and the studio strained with forced activity.

"Looks like you're in. Welcome to hell," muttered Dante. "Come with me."

Emily followed Mr. Rizzoli into a tidy, yet miniscule office. Rows of clipboards hung along one wall, holding invoices and orders. A large calendar graced the other wall. Every single block bore a name or notation. He picked up a file and extracted a letter. Emily recognized the Stoddard School of Art intern requirement forms.

"Mr. Rizzoli, I—"

"Dante, please."

"Certainly, Dante, I can't tell you how excited I am. This is such a huge opportunity. I'll work harder than any intern you've ever seen. I'll do anything. Clay prep, apertures, I'll even sweep. Anything."

"I appreciate your enthusiasm, Ms. Baskets."

"Baskins. Emily Baskins. You know, like the ice cream people but without the Robbins. My dad always used to say, 'Wish we had their money, or at least the lifetime supply of ice cream.' He loved ice cream. Chocolate, chocolate chip. It was his favorite. We couldn't keep it in the house. Mom would buy it and it'd be gone the next day. She'd yell at him, 'Oliver! You could have saved some for the rest…of…'"

Dante rubbed his temples.

Oh, God, he thinks I'm a lunatic! "I'm sorry. It's Baskins, Emily. Everyone just calls me Em. I never talk this much, I swear. Shouldn't have had that fourth coffee. I'm…I'm a little nervous. Or maybe it's excitement. I mean, you've gotta agree this is pretty freakin' amazing. Right? Me! Little Emily Louise Baskins from Stoddard, New Hampshire, working alongside the great Maximo Vega! My mother—oh my God, if you think I'm crazy thrilled, she is going to freak out. She loves him. She has one of his early statuettes. Saved for months to buy it. Says it speaks to her. I mean, *really* speaks to her. She's a little odd, but nice." Emily's eye twitched. "I'll stop talking."

"Promise?"

Emily clamped her lips together. "I'm sorry. I don't know what's the matter with me." She slapped a hand over her mouth.

"Ms. Baskins…" He started to close the file, shaking his head. "I'm not sure this is going to work out."

"Oh *please*, Mr. Rizzoli, you'll see. I'll be as quiet as a kitten in a pillow factory. You'll never even know I'm here. My mother always says—"

At his raised eyebrows she made the sign of locking her lips and tossing the imaginary key over one shoulder. If she didn't shut up, she was going to blow the biggest thing that had happened in all her twenty-four years.

Dante opened his top drawer and pulled out a king-sized bottle of aspirin. Em grimaced as he ate two. Just chewed them, no water. He looked at her, shook his head, and chewed another.

"All right, two weeks. I'm taking you in on a trial basis. Not that I think you'll survive that long." He scribbled his signature on her paperwork. "Now, there are rules. You will follow them to the letter. The most important is you *never* speak to Vega. *Never.* You never enter Vega's space or ask him questions.

5

Anything you produce for us is the property of Vega Studio and will not receive his signature if it does not meet his exacting standards.

"The studio is open twenty-four hours a day, three hundred and sixty-five days a year. Vega works all hours of the day and night when he's preparing for a show or working on any midnight inspiration he might have. You may be asked to be here at odd hours.

"Today's display of temper was nothing. A snit. Anger Vega and you'll be on the other side of the door faster than you can say, 'My career's over!' But, if you survive the next two weeks and the rest of the time scheduled for your internship, there's a good chance you'll be hired on after you graduate. If not, simply adding the Vega Studio to your résumé will open a lot of doors."

Em could barely sit still. Keeping her mouth shut was torture, but she knew if she opened it, there was no telling what would fall out.

"This is one hell of a break you're getting here. Maximo Vega never lies. If he looked at your work and said, 'Good,' then you can take that to heart." He gave her a hard look. "Please don't make me regret this, Ms. Baskins."

"Oh, Mr. Rizzoli—Dante—you can count on me." Emily jumped to her feet and thrust her hand across the desk to seal the deal. Her pinkie caught the top of the open aspirin bottle and knocked it off the desk, shooting hundreds of round, white tablets all over the floor.

She stood in wide-eyed shock. *Oh, NO! I can't believe I did that!* "I'm…I'm so sorry. Don't worry. I'll clean it up. I can be such an incredible klutz sometimes." She scrambled to her knees and scooped handfuls of the pills and returned them haphazardly to the bottle. "Please, Mr. Rizzoli, don't change your mind. This was just an accident. Can my two-week trial start tomorrow?"

"Stop. Enough!" He grabbed the bottle. "If you leave this instant, I'll let you start first thing in the morning."

"Oh, thank you, thank you." She stood and brushed off her knees. The soles of her shoes ground a half dozen aspirin into dust. "Oh, sorry. Really."

Dante held his head with one hand and waved her out of his office with the other.

"I'll be here bright and early. You'll see. I'll be great!"

"Great," he muttered looking at the sea of pills all over the floor.

Emily tipped him a smile and a quick shrug before snatching her signed internship form and rushing out. As the heavy door to Dante's office made the slow sweep to close, he called, "Wait! Did you say klutz?"

She knew better than to stop and answer.

Em pulled her Jeep into the driveway of her mother's house. Funny, she still thought of the little, pale pink Cape Cod as Mom and Dad's house even though she'd been living there for the last year. Little had changed, yet *everything* had changed. She was here. Dad was gone. No more Frank Sinatra blaring through the house. No more dancing in the kitchen. No more midnight ice cream cones. God, she missed him. Especially today.

Given her news, he'd have lifted her in a big bear hug and spun her about in their own private happy dance until she was dizzy. He was her number one fan. She still loved him no matter the mess he left behind. He'd done it all for her.

After Em's dad passed away—almost three years ago now—things for Mom had been tough. 'Course her ever-stoic Yankee mother would never admit it. Em had seen the signs though; no more cable, no Chinese takeout boxes in the fridge, and last November she caught her mother wearing three sweaters and four pair of socks because she'd turned the heat off to conserve oil. Even with the income from her beauty salon, Trixie's Pixies, Trixie Baskins was in trouble. Emily's schooling was beyond anything she could afford now.

Em was forced to leave her exciting, big-city life at the School of the Art Institute in Chicago and return to the tiny town of Stoddard, New Hampshire, and enroll in the Stoddard School of Art Master's program to finish her degree. At times it didn't feel like she was here to help her mother with the bills. It felt like she'd failed. But the money she'd thought was there for her education wasn't. Her father had neglected to mention how much he owed. The savings and life insurance Trixie believed to be there were gone. All had been cashed in to keep Emily in Chicago.

She had no choice but to move back into the room where she spent her teenage years. The same room where she dreamed about leaving the small, rural town behind. But she was back, and the room was exactly the same, with posters on the walls and fuzzy purple and orange pillows on the bed.

At least the boy band posters had been replaced with Emily's favorite art prints: *Flaming June*, *Starry Night*, *Water Lilies*, *The Kiss*, and from Maximo Vega a photograph of *Fame*, his most famous sculpture of a woman bound, gagged, and blindfolded. It was a striking commentary on his struggle with celebrity. Everything Emily read about him talked about his elusiveness. Somehow it only added to the man's charisma. And now she had front row center on the great Vega mystique. Perhaps small and rural could turn into the big time after all.

Emily couldn't help but let her enthusiasm carry her away. Inside, she was in a full swing happy dance all on her own, even without her father's bear hug. Wait until Trixie heard the news.

Her mother was in the driveway before Em could get out of the car.

"Well?" Trixie chewed her thumbnail.

"Well, what?" Em made a grand show out of closing and locking the car door.

Her mother planted her hands on her hips. Her face flushed. "Emily Louise Baskins! You know damn well—"

"I'm in!"

Both women screamed little-girl screams, grabbed hands, and jumped up and down.

"Oh my, God!" Trixie covered her mouth with a shaky hand as her eyes filled with tears.

"Jeez, Ma, don't cry."

"Tears of joy, baby girl," she sniffed. "Your father would have been so excited."

"More than you? I doubt it. You think Maximo Vega is up there with Picasso or Elvis."

"He is. They say he's a direct descendent from Michelangelo." Trixie was still bouncing on the balls of her feet. "Tell me everything. What was the studio like?" She peered down. "Oh! Look at your pants." She pointed. "That's *Vega* dust! You can't wash those pants, ever."

"Ma, I'm probably going to be riding a push broom for the next six months. I'm sure there'll be no end to the dust. If I stop washing pants, I'll be naked inside a week." Emily couldn't help but smile. Her mother was like a groupie at a rock concert and her energy was contagious. "What are you going to say when I tell you he held my hands? Will I ever be allowed to wash them again?"

Her mother stopped bouncing, her mouth agape. "He...he touched you?"

"And talked to me."

Trixie hit Emily on the arm. "Get out!"

"No, that's what he said to the other guy."

Chapter Two

Maximo stood, hair still damp from the shower, contemplating the raw piece of Italian marble secured to his working platform. Marble chips crunched beneath his heels. There was no question, his original plan for the piece was ruined. That incompetent Todd, whatever his name, had failed to follow simple instructions for the piece's rough-out and now the figure's heavenly reach was six inches too short. The proportion was hideous.

A twenty thousand dollar block of Carrerra marble was at stake. Not to mention the commission from the client. There had to be some way to save the stone. He'd been staring at it all day trying to see a new figure in its pristine white mass, but his anger at the damaged piece kept getting in the way. He'd finally gone upstairs to his apartment to shower and gain some sanity, some perspective.

But as sometimes happened—who was he kidding, this always happened—his mind refused to shut off. He'd obsess until he figured it out. There would be no escaping it.

The studio was vacant. Dante had been the last to leave and he'd left hours ago. Max's boots echoed in the cavernous space as he walked around scrutinizing the current works in process. His works, whether or not his hands finished the project. It was still the name

Vega that signed the lower edge. Was it any wonder he needed to be so exacting? It was his name.

This was his work, and his world, and his studio. It was quiet without the chaos that reverberated within these tall walls every day. He preferred it this way. Empty. No one to deal with. No awed fans whispering "Vega" as he walked by, grabbing at his sleeve. No one to try and impress. No one to judge.

The business of art was a lonely one. That was one thing most young artists didn't realize. They began with a whimsical idea of creation, sharing their dreams, leaving bits of themselves for time immemorial. What they learned early on, however, was the darker side of art. It was a landscape of hard truths and fierce criticism, constant critiques and cut-throat competition. A never-ending race to produce more and more and stay relevant in an ever-changing industry.

Max rewrapped a clay bust in heavy plastic to keep it damp and workable. The clay dried white on his thumb where he'd smoothed a shoulder and swept a jaw line.

Maybe a nice glass of vino. No, no wine, not tonight. Maximo Vega was off duty. Max wanted a beer. Two or three if he ever expected to sleep.

He headed to the refrigerator that held water for the models, everyone's food items, and Dante's stash of imported ale. He cracked one open and took a long pull. The cold liquid eased his dusty throat.

Leaving the office, Max noticed the large portfolio leaning against the wall. Wasn't that the case he looked at earlier? The new intern's? He opened it across Dante's desk. Yes, it was her work. She must have forgotten it. What was her name? Several of her sketches were initialed E.L.B. Had Dante mentioned her name? Max couldn't remember. What he did remember was the shape of her face and the spiky paleness of her disheveled hair. The color of her eyes escaped him, but he recalled they were wide and nervous. He recognized the look. He saw it often, especially with interns. They were fresh and eager and had heard and believed all the Maximo Vega hype. Hell, there were days even he believed it.

He could thank Daryl Greenburg for that. Greenburg was the reporter from the *New England Journal* who took a rumor of truth and created a mountain of a story that threw Maximo's work into the spotlight. Ironically, he'd given Max the ideal landscape to escape into—the perfect camouflage to hide behind—and allowed him the space, time, and lucrative commissions to bring his work to the next level.

Max finished a beer and opened another. He flipped through a few more drawings and photographs of finished sculpting projects of E.L.B. She was good. Really good. She had a great eye for balance and composition. Several of her pieces displayed an edginess he admired, yet her grasp of classic statuary pose was pretty good as well. *E.L.B. What is her name?* He rummaged through the wire basket holding Dante's work for the week. A file labeled Stoddard Internship Program sat near the top of the pile.

Emily Baskins. What did the L stand for? She was in her second year of graduate school, with exceptional grades. Held the Director's Scholarship, as well as the Huntington Grant. Impressive.

The main door squeaked open. He looked at the

clock. It was after 11. He was the only one to keep late hours. If it was that idiot Todd coming back…

A pretty face, framed in pale hair, peeked around the doorframe.

"Good evening, Ms. Baskins."

"Maximo! Mr. Vega." She paled to the color of alabaster. "I-I didn't mean to disturb you. I forgot—"

"Your portfolio." His hand swept over the pages open before him. "I took the liberty of another look."

"Oh. I would have waited until morning, but I need to turn a few of those sketches over to my professor first thing."

Maximo started to close the wide flap. She looked different. Her hair was softer. More tousled. She ran her fingers through the fine, pale strands. The color reminded him of corn silk.

She'd changed into a pair of hugging jeans and a tank top. He hadn't noticed before how slight she was. Given her resumé, she was in her mid-twenties, but she looked much younger. There was little curve to her. Slim hips, a hint of ribs and small breasts lay beneath the knit of her top. She reminded him of a sprite, of a picture he once saw of a woodland fairy wearing the blossom of a flower as a cap. Tinker Bell.

Green. Her eyes were green. Pale. In the gray scale of greens. They were wide and clear as if he could peer into her soul. They screamed innocence. He realized he was staring and looked away, closing her portfolio.

He zipped the case and handed it to her. "You do good work."

"Thank you. That's nice of you to say."

"I'm not nice. I tell the truth."

"Coming from you, it's high praise."

Max started to argue that his was just another opinion in a world of constant opinion, but he suddenly felt old and cynical and didn't want to tarnish the freshness of her. Curious, he ran a knuckle over the rough stubble on his chin. Perhaps she was what he needed. New. Unsullied.

"Follow me, please."

Her eyes widened. "Okay."

He took her portfolio and leaned it back against the wall and led her through the studio to his work area. Perhaps she could look at the ruined stone with her new, lovely green eyes and see something he was missing.

Max swept the scene with his hand. "My vision is gone." He handed her his original sketches for the piece. "You see?" He pointed to the rise of the figure's arms in their reach toward Heaven. "The stone is cut too short."

"*Implorare*." She read the sketches.

"*Sì*. It means beseech, pray."

"Pleading," she whispered.

"*Sì*."

"She's beautiful. So full of emotion. So impassioned."

He threw his hand up. "She's ruined."

"Perhaps not."

Emily laid the sketches down. Her fingers left pale trails through her hair as she tipped her head, considering the stone. She circled the marble, touching the white sides, looking at the sketch then back at the stone.

"What if you reversed time two seconds?" Emily lifted her arms in the pose from the sketch and looked over her shoulder at him. "Just before she reaches up for help. When she first feels the full weight of her anguish in her chest and her heart breaks." She pulled one hand to lay a tight fist to the center of her chest. "Still with her gaze skyward, but she's just beginning her plea." Bending the elbow of her other arm, Emily pulled the reaching hand down. Her weight shifted to her front foot.

The slender column of her neck and the gentle sweep of her back had Max grabbing for a sketch pad. "Don't move."

"Oh!" she gasped, turning to look at him with wide eyes.

"No. Don't move." His eyes locked with hers. Yes, they were a perfect sage green. Maximo grasped her chin and returned the angle of her face to tip skyward. She smelled like summer, warm and faintly floral, and before he could stop himself, he traced the smooth line of her jaw with the pad of his thumb. He was close enough to see the wild pulse beating just below her ear. He had a crazy urge to lay a kiss there. "*Rilassarsi. Relax.*"

"I only thought, perhaps…I mean, I have *no* business telling you what you should do. I shouldn't presume. Dante…Mr. Rizzoli told me never to—"

"Don't speak." Max was quick to sketch her, the pose, the angles of her body from the front, back and both sides. She'd found the perfect solution. This was good. It was very good. Here was his inspiration. As he roughed out the drawings, his mind could already see the figure in the marble. The milky curve of a thigh, the crush of a breast beneath a fist. He could see it all.

Max lifted his gaze to the sprite of a woman before

him. He could see *her*. Her thigh. Her fist. The creamy tilt of her breast.

"May I move?"

"Yes." The word broke. She was his muse. He cleared the catch in his throat. "*Sì*, you may move."

Lisa A. Olech

Chapter Three

Emily sat in the kitchen surrounded by her mother's over-the-top collection of roosters. Chocolate chip smiley "celebration" pancakes sat before her on their rooster placemat. Whipped cream eyebrows, hair and mustache together with a strawberry nose completed the breakfast that celebrated every happy event in her childhood. She couldn't touch Mr. Happy Cakes, however. Her stomach was twisted into a nervous knot.

"Did I hear you go out last night?"

"Yes. I forgot something." There was no way she was telling Trixie she'd gone back to Vega Studio. The woman wanted to save the dust from her pants. If she told her he'd touched her face, traced the line of her jaw with his thumb, and asked her opinion on a major piece of art, Trixie would flip out.

Em ran the back of her fingers across her jaw, remembering the gentle roughness of his touch as he angled her face to sketch her. Maximo Vega sketched her. *Her!*

Trixie was busy raking the fringe of a fire engine red throw rug. Literally. She kept a child's play rake in the closet just for the task. "Guess what I saw on the Bargain Shoppers Club last night?"

She scanned the room. *Please don't let it be another rooster.* "I don't know. What?"

"They're having a deal on language lessons. The same ones those folks at the State Department use to learn all their languages. We should learn Italian. You'd be able to talk to Vega in his native tongue. I bet he'd be impressed."

"I'd much rather impress him with my sculpting skills. Besides, he speaks English." *Rilassarsi. Relax...* Emily remembered his breath brushing against her cheek. Heard the way his tongue danced over the words as he whispered to her. It was a physical caress just to hear him speak. Her breath caught in her chest. "Sorry, Mr. Happy Cakes, he's got you beat by a mile." She ate the strawberry nose.

An envelope stood between ceramic-feathered salt and pepper shakers in the center of the table. She pushed her plate aside and picked up the pale pink card. It was addressed to her in a flowery script. Jeremy's wedding invitation.

"When did this get here?"

"Oh, that came yesterday. With all the excitement, I guess I forgot."

"You're such a lousy liar."

"I didn't want it to ruin your fabulous day."

"Ma, come on. Jeremy and I are still friends. I'm happy for him."

"Even though it should be you marrying him?"

"Don't start this again, please." Mr. Happy Cakes' expression was suddenly mocking. Em threw her napkin over the plate.

"I'm just saying—"

"Jeremy and I are *friends*."

Trixie stopped her raking. "Then why did he ask you to marry him first?"

19

"Wow, so much for 'just saying'." She stared at the elaborate curlicues making up her name. Jeremy must hate all this pouf. This had Cynthia's hand all over it. Word around town was this wedding was going to be beyond anything Stoddard had ever seen. Cynthia Weatherby, the bride-to-be, was the only daughter of the Senator and the latest Mrs. Weatherby. She gave a whole new meaning to the word spoiled.

Emily should hate her, but the honest truth was, she didn't. Cynthia was sweet and kind. She and Jeremy were crazy about each other. It was obvious they were a perfect match. It was everything she'd hoped for him. Yes, she loved him. And yes, he'd asked her first, but she didn't regret how things worked out. Except for the look on his face when she said, "No."

"You two were so cute together."

"We were kids, Ma."

"You were in love."

Em frowned. "Not enough."

"What does that mean?"

"It means…" She rubbed the ache forming between her eyebrows. "It means we weren't you and Dad."

The rooster on the wall crowed eight. *Saved by the cock.* Em stood and grabbed her bag. Her mother was giving her that horrible pity look she hated almost as much as the rooster clock.

"Think of it this way, if I hadn't said no, you wouldn't have the bride and her twelve bridesmaids booked for hair, mani, pedis, and spray tans."

"Don't forget the real mink false eyelashes." Trixie batted her eyes.

"How could I?"

"None of that even compares to what's waiting for

you today, sweetie. Remember that."

"This isn't a competition, Ma."

"I know. I just want you to be happy."

Cock-a-doodle doo, Cock-a-doodle doo.

"Phone's crowing." Emily kissed her mother's cheek. "I am happy."

Cock-a-doodle doo, Cock-a-doodle-doo.

"You better get that. It's probably the shop."

"I'm working late tonight. Stop by after you're finished and tell me all about your day."

Cock-a-do—"Hello, Bridget. Of course I knew it was you. Who else calls me at home?" Trixie covered the mouthpiece. "Have an amazing day, sweetie."

Emily was a bundle of nervous energy. Last night's events only added to the fact that Mr. Happy Cake's nose was sitting like a ten pound sack of concrete. She swung by the school on her way to the Vega studio to hand in her latest sketch work and turn over her internship paperwork to Madeline Sullivan, the Director of the Stoddard School.

She peeked into Madeline's office. It took a minute to find her in the kaleidoscope of chaos Madeline called her headquarters. Art of every description filled each corner of the room and covered the walls from ceiling to floor. Maddie was rummaging through a stack of wood block prints behind her overloaded desk. Her ample behind bedecked in a bright floral print was perfectly camouflaged.

"Excuse me, Maddie?" Emily tapped a knuckle on the doorframe.

Madeline gave a small screech as she spun about, knocking a driftwood totem and setting the mobile overhead flailing. She righted the totem with one hand.

Lisa A. Olech

The other she slapped over her heart. "Jeez, Baskins, you scared the hell out of me!"

"This office scares the hell out of me."

Madeline pushed her fluff of salt-and-pepper hair back from her face. "Things in my office don't sneak up on me when my back is turned."

Emily raised an eyebrow.

Maddie flipped a hand. "Fine, maybe they do. Did you need something?"

Lifting an envelope, Emily held it by the corner and dangled it before Madeline like she was teasing a cat with a catnip mouse. She followed the cleared pathway leading to Maddie's desk. "Thought you might like this."

Madeline snatched the envelope from Em's fingers and flopped into her wide desk chair in one fluid motion. Pushing her readers onto her nose, she gave a small gasp. "You got it."

"I got it."

She was quick to pull out the paperwork. "Nice job, Em. Paid gigs are pretty rare. That's why I recommended you over at Vega's."

"I appreciate that." Since coming home, Emily had become an expert at scraping for every penny to pay her own way and help Trixie out. "Every little bit helps."

"You'll do well over there. They gave me a tour last year. The facility and studio space are quite impressive. You couldn't have asked for more hands-on. Have they assigned you yet?"

"Not yet, but I'm sure I'll be scraping worktables or cleaning toilets to start."

"Doesn't matter. This is a huge opportunity."

"I know. Here comes the part where you tell me

not to blow it."

Madeline peered over the top of her glasses. "I wasn't going to say that, but since you did, yes, don't blow this." She double-checked the paperwork. "Now, don't be disappointed if you never see Maximo Vega. I've had interns who've spent the whole summer and never seen him. I hear he's becoming more and more of a recluse. I've only seen him once, but he's definitely a man and a half." Maddie sighed. "Did I ever tell you I had a *thing* for sculptors? They have amazingly talented hands—if you know what I mean. Like trumpet players make the best kissers.

I dated a sculptor once. Edwardo," she breathed his name. "Not great in the looks department, but he had these magic fingers *Holy cow*." Two bright red spots flushed Madeline's cheeks. Her upper lip started to sweat. "Just thinking about him gives me a hot flash."

"Easy there, Maddie. You're going to burst into flames."

Madeline tugged at her neckline and dug a small battery-powered fan out of her desk drawer. The sudden gust of air when she switched it on sent her hair billowing like smoke from a chimney. "So, when do you start over there?"

"This morning. I'm due there by nine."

"Well, get a move on, girl. Have fun and—"

Emily held up a hand. "I know, don't blow it."

The entire drive over to Vega Studio, Em worried maybe she'd already blown it. Would Mr. Rizzoli rescind his offer for breaking the rules? She hadn't even started and already she was in trouble. Vega had talked to her first and he'd asked her into his sacred space.

Still, she'd had the audacity to suggest a design change—to Maximo Vega—*oh, God!*

Madeline was right. Too much was riding on this. If she botched this, she'd lose her internship and probably her grant as well. She'd never be able to afford tuition on her own. Not now. She'd have to leave school. And, like Dante warned, her career would be in serious jeopardy.

She lowered the visor and checked her appearance in the mirror. "Keep your head down and do the job. Pretend last night never happened. If you see Vega, don't make eye contact. Even if his dark, espresso eyes make your knees sweat. Don't think about how he smells like warm spice. Forget that little rasp in his voice when he whispers in your ear with that delicious accent. And whatever you do, don't look at his hands, dammit. Worship him from afar!"

Dante Rizzoli was waiting for her outside his office. "Good Morning, Ms. Baskins."

"Good Morning, Mr. Rizzoli."

"I think we need to have a little chat." He held open the door to his office.

Chapter Four

Emily swallowed the lump in her throat as she passed Dante and entered his office. "Mr. Rizzoli, I can explain."

"Can you?" Dante held up a sheet of paper. "It's not every day I get a note from Vega regarding a lowly intern." He narrowed his eyes at her. "He wants you in plaster."

"Physically?" Em's head was spinning. Was this like cement shoes? Was she headed to the bottom of Highland Lake?

"Evidently he sees great potential in you. Most interns don't start in the plaster room."

"Oh, plaster *room*."

"You'll be working on pre-polish. One of the steps in the molding process."

"For his bronzes." Em nodded.

"Correct. If you handle that well, we'll move you into final polish and molding."

Her head jerked back. *Did he just say final polish?* "That's amazing."

"It is, isn't it?" He gave her another appraising look. "Any idea why you're getting preferential treatment? The plaster room is a third or fourth year pay-level assignment. I would have started you in clean-up or, at the least, prep."

Play dumb, play dumb. "I haven't a clue." She

shrugged. "But I'm thrilled. The extra pay aside, I never dreamed I'd get anywhere near a final piece."

"Well, I know never to argue with Vega. His studio. His rules. If he wants you in plaster, then that's where you'll be. I guess you can't get into too much trouble there. Come. Follow me. I'll show you where you'll be working."

Dante led Emily through the busy studio. He pointed out a large work area encompassing the entire back corner. "While you're here, you're free to work on your own pieces during off hours. You pay supply costs, of course, but the space and use of the tools is free. Plus, every two weeks I put in a large supply order for the studio. There's a request box outside my office. I can get anything you need at cost—within reason. The restrooms are over there. Model dressing rooms, there. Lockers, over there. I'll get you set up with one by the end of the day."

A high strip of paned windows ringed the building, pulling in an abundance of natural light. Large metal industrial lamps hung from tall ceilings and lit each work area.

Artists of all descriptions sketched, carved and molded. Wet clay scented the air.

For an active studio, it was surprisingly quiet. Many wore headphones and talk was little louder than a whisper. The soft rhythmic thump, thump, thump of a mallet to a chisel carried no echo in the cavernous space.

Em couldn't help but look toward the curtain area comprising Vega's private space. No loud Italian cursing today. There was no sign he was even there, although if the energy in the room was any indication, he was. Sequestered behind his pleated walls, his presence was palpable. *Rilassarsi. Relax...* Yes, he was there. She could feel him.

"Are you okay?"

Emily stumbled, startled. Dante had been talking, and she'd missed it. "Yes, I'm fine."

"Yesterday you were talking like a wind-up doll in overdrive. And today, nothing." He squinted at her. "I don't know which one worries me more."

"I'm fine. Really. Just taking it all in." She gave him a one-shoulder shrug.

Dante stood for another beat, appraising her. "Shall we continue?"

They'd reached what Emily believed to be the far end of the studio. Huge sliding doors stood before them. "You'll be working back here." He indicated a smaller door on one side. "We use the sliders to move large pieces in and out. Otherwise, you come and go through here.

When the door opened, Em felt like she'd stepped onto a different planet. Loud music thumped a heavy bass beat through the entire department. Compared to the quiet of the other, the room was deafening. The temperature was a good ten degrees warmer, too. Dust hung in the sunlight pouring through the floor-to-ceiling windows. Two enormous fans sat high in opposite walls, their blades a blur. They rumbled like jet planes. Three industrial mixers churned while those manning the process shouted at one another to be heard over the din.

Dante gave a shrill whistle and waved at someone across the room. A large woman barked at the man standing next to her before heading in their direction.

She pulled off her dust mask and tugged out earplugs. The woman was a linebacker with breasts—big breasts.

"Crystal, this is the intern I told you about. Emily Baskins." He held out his clipboard. "Emily, this is Crystal LeMar. She's in charge back here. You'll be reporting directly to her. She'll be the one keeping track of your internship hours."

"You mean babysitting," the woman sneered as she snatched the clipboard from Dante and flipped through the pages.

Emily held out her hand. "It's a pleasure—"

Crystal LeMar's icy stare stopped her. She looked Emily over like she was buying a used cow. "She's not gonna be able to move no hundred pounds."

"Then she'll have help."

Crystal slapped the clipboard against a denim thigh. A cloud of dust ringed her hips. "I haven't got time to be holding her hand!"

"Vega wants her back here!" Dante swatted the air.

The woman's lips pinched off her next comment. She glared at Emily again and rolled her eyes. Lifting the clipboard, she studied the paperwork. "Pre-polish? There's no way she's assigned in there. Give me a break."

"I'm more than qualified to work pre-polish on a plaster cast. I've been building my own mother molds for the last five years."

"Not in Vega Studio you haven't. We don't work in Play-Doh here."

What did she just say? Emily raised her hand. "Now just a minute—"

Dante whistled a shrill halt before Emily could further explain her experience to *Ms. LeMar,* courtesy of a few choice words she was more than likely to understand. "This isn't up for debate. Crystal, you're the best Casting Manager we've had, but if it's beneath you to—"

"It's *fine,*" she sneered.

"Fine," Dante countered. "Is it fine with you, too, Ms. Baskins?"

"Of course."

"Good." Dante pinched the bridge of his nose. "If that's settled, I'll leave you two to get better acquainted." He scowled in Crystal's direction. "Don't kill her."

Crystal rolled her eyes. "Try not to."

Dante wasn't through the door before Crystal LeMar flipped him the bird. *Nice.* Ten weeks was going to feel like ten years with this woman.

"Follow me," she barked. "Try not to get yourself killed."

Emily let out a breath. She followed the broad back of Ms. LeMar, watching her shake her head and slap the clipboard against her thigh. "I hope to hell you ain't one of those wimpy types who cry every time she gets a booboo."

Em thought it best to ignore the jibe. She'd prove she was tougher than she looked.

Crystal stopped short and spun on her. "This is hard, grueling work back here, and if you think I'm gonna cater to one of Vegas' little chippies and disrupt *my* department, you've got another think coming."

"I'm not one of Vega's—whatever you called them."

"Whatever." Crystal flipped her hand.

The tension in Emily's neck cranked up another

notch. *She did not just show me the hand!* Her fingernails bit into her palms.

"You keep up and keep your mouth shut, or you're out. I don't care what Rizzoli says. I'm in charge back here. Got that, princess?"

Emily set her jaw and threatened to reduce her teeth to dust. "Got it."

A short time later, she was outfitted with the proper safety equipment and warned never to be in the area without it. She was given a fast tour around the casting department and left at her station with orders to get familiar with her tools.

She pulled a deep breath through her dust mask. Exhale steamed her face beneath the itchy cover and escaped to fog her goggles. Cleaning them, she took a minute to look around.

Huge plaster molds lined the walls, each numbered and labeled. Some had wide rubber belting. Three enormous mixers churned plaster into a creamy slip, which moved swiftly to the pouring stations. Aside from her work in creating plaster positives of a sculpture, the Vega Studio also used the classic technique of the lost wax method to cast some of the smaller pieces.

Her job was to inspect the plaster copies, or positives, before a mold was formed for the final bronze pour. It saved the original sculpture's value while allowing multiple copies to be made. Pre-polish dealt with any air bubbles in the plaster or other imperfections which would be transferred to the finished piece. She was in charge of finding those mars and repairing them. Some of the larger pieces used up to fifteen separate molds. Seams needed to be invisible.

The quality of those seams and repairs at this stage meant the difference between a professional bronze and that of an amateur. Em looked at her impressive array of tools.

"Baskins!" Crystal's bellow made her jump. "Put those goggles back on and get over here!" She pointed to a rough cast statue of a dancer. The lines of which were pure magic. It was not quite full size, but it was still impressive at three-quarter scale. "Move this into your bay."

"Move?" The piece must weigh two hundred pounds.

"Too much for you, your highness?" Crystal crossed her muscled arms across her ample chest and tipped her head, giving Emily a smug smirk.

"No. Not at all." She set her jaw, got behind the statue and gave it a hard shove. The dancer didn't move an inch.

Crystals smirk got bigger. As did Emily's determination. The piece was on a tall, wheeled base. All she had to do was get it rolling. She put her shoulder into it and pushed off with her legs as hard as she could. Nothing. Sweat broke out on her face as she tried a third time. LeMar's laughter stopped her.

"You might want to take the wheel brakes off, Hercules."

Panting, Emily narrowed her eyes but kept her mouth shut. She flipped the toe lock on each wheel, and gave it another push. That was more like it, but still the piece was heavy and ungainly and it required all her muscle to get it from one side of the room to the other.

Crystal checked her watch. "Bravo. That only took you twice as long as it should have. We're off to a fine start."

Emily relocked the wheels and stood regaining her breath, puffing her cheeks. The muscles in her legs burned, but she'd done it.

Crystal shook her head. "You won't last the day." She turned to walk away.

Emily straightened. "You can keep trying, but you won't break me."

Crystal spun back. "What's this? A backbone?"

"Hey, I get it. You don't want me here. I'm just as shocked as you. But you need to know small and blonde doesn't mean weak and dumb. I know my stuff, and I'm stronger than I look. I'd love to learn what you can teach me. That's why I'm an intern. We don't need to be best friends or anything, but you need to know I'll work my butt off for you."

"What butt?" Crystal shook her head. "I've got an eight-year-old son with more ass than you."

"Lucky him," muttered Emily. She wouldn't win any points with this woman. This was going to be one long, ugly internship. "Do you know what a pain it is to buy jeans in the boy's department?" She slapped at her hips.

Crystal snorted.

Was that a laugh?

"I wouldn't know." She hitched her pants. "I've had these since I was four."

"It's pretty bad when you flunk Hula Hoop in kindergarten."

"Ha," she barked and narrowed her eyes. "There may be hope for you after all." Crystal jerked her head toward the statue. "So get busy showing me what you can do. I'll be back to check."

Wow, that almost sounded like a crack in the ice.
Em blew out a breath and wiped the sweat at her
temples. It was a start. But hey, the day was young.

Emily picked up a sheet of fine sandpaper and
inspected the piece. She hadn't lied to Crystal earlier.
She *was* shocked. This was a third year assignment at
least. She'd never known of anyone walking into this
kind of internship first year. Did her work secure her
the position or could last night's encounter with Vega
have been responsible? Whatever the reason, she
needed to be at the top of her game. Part of her was
thrilled—if she could get past the urge to toss up Mr.
Happy's nose. Riding that push broom wouldn't have
been so bad.

Near the end of the day, Emily was covered head to
toe in plaster dust. Thank goodness for the goggles and
mask. Crystal stood behind her, watching how she
smoothed a seam joining a hand to a wrist. While they
had forged some kind of odd truce over her lack of ass,
Em still had a lot to prove.

The whirling of the mixers was near deafening as
she used a strip of polishing cloth to smooth the side of
a finger. Not too hard. Fingers were the most delicate.

The three mixers shut off all at once. "BASKINS!"

Startled, Emily stared in horror at the plaster pinkie
in her hand. *Oh, my God!*

Crystal's mouth dropped open.

Dante stood at the door with his hands on his hips.
Emily's eyes darted between the two. "I-I, um…" She
handed Crystal the broken finger. "This was loose."

Pulling at her dust mask, she rushed toward Dante.
Of the two, he was the least frightening. The odd
expression on his face, however, had her contemplating

turning back to face the wrath of Crystal. Looking over her shoulder Crystal was coming at her like a freight train. The tiny hairs on her neck stood on end.

"Y-yes, Dante?"

"Vega wants to see you."

Chapter Five

"Me? Vega want to see *me*?"

"Yes, you. Why do you suppose that is?" Dante folded his arms over his chest.

Crystal's angry bull breath fanned the back of Emily's neck.

"I have no idea, but I shouldn't keep him waiting, should I?"

She slid past Dante and shot through the door before he could answer. The noise of the casting room still buzzed in her ears. She was sure she resembled the little boy from *Charlie Brown* who moved in his own cloud of dirt. Pulling off her goggles and tearing the dust mask from around her neck, she brushed furiously at her clothing before skidding to a stop in front of Vega's curtain. Should she knock? How did a person knock on a curtain?

She slipped inside. The same feeling from last night hit her. This was sacred space somehow, and she was in the presence of greatness. Mr. "Greatness" was standing behind a workstation in the far corner. Before him a clay figure's gentle form was taking shape beneath his skilled hands. Clay stained him to his wrists. He wasn't wearing an apron, although several hung on pegs on the back wall. His soft gray shirt hugged the muscles of his arms. Long sleeves were pushed past his elbows. Faded jeans bore chalky smears of clay below each hip.

Emily recognized those smears. When she was busy with a piece, she never slowed down to wipe her hands on the rags scattered through her work space, not when the back of her pants was handy. She smiled that somehow they shared smudged pants. Beneath all the fame and fortune, he wiped his hands on his ass just like she did. Was that like discovering your favorite sports figure ate the same breakfast cereal as you?

The block of snowy marble still stood prominently in the center of the space. Today it bore new markings.

"Excuse me?" Emily whispered.

Vega turned. Dark eyes lifted and met hers. Even from across the room, his gaze felt like a caress.

"Come."

She passed the white stone sentry, needing to reach out as she did so to steady her shaky knees. "You wanted to see me?"

"*Si*. Yes. Please sit." He motioned to a tall stool nearby. Turning away from her, he washed his hands in a deep work sink. With his back to her, she finished the study of his jeans. Yes, the fit of that clay-smudged denim was quite impressive. Not to mention the play of his knit Henley across a broad spread of his shoulders. She chewed a thumbnail and tasted plaster.

Drying his hands, he faced her. "How is your first day?"

Should she tell him about the pinkie? "Um, fine."

"Good. You're happy with plaster?"

Crystal's angry face flashed through her mind. "Yes. Thank you. I was surprised to be assigned such an advanced position. It was your decision?"

"*Si*."

"Why?" The word blurted from her mouth.

He cocked an eyebrow.

"I mean, I'm grateful. Don't get me wrong. It's an incredible opportunity. I just…"

"You question my decision?" He crossed his arms and frowned.

"No, no. Yes." She ran a nervous hand through her hair. Dust fell. She tried to wave it away. "I'm curious. It's a bad habit of mine."

"I put you there because you helped me. Your work tells me you can do the job." He placed his hands on his hips. "And I want something in return."

Beating around the bush didn't seem to be one of Vega's talents.

"Something from me?"

"*Si*." He moved back to the clay he was working on when she arrived and spun the stand around. The face of the figure made her suck in a breath. It was her. The body was unfinished, but there was no mistaking the face. He gathered several sheets and held them for her to see. They were all of her from different angles. How had he produced them in such exacting detail from the few minutes she spent here last night? They were incredible. She'd only achieved the same level of realism by working for hours with multiple photographs.

"Why? How? What?"

"Again, you question me."

"I don't understand."

"I need you to model for me. The piece, *Implorare,* it is you I see in the stone."

Nervous laughter spilled out of Emily. "Me?" She checked for hidden cameras. "This is a joke." She put a hand to her throat. "You can't be serious."

"Maximo Vega never jokes about his work." His dark eyes held hers. He certainly looked serious.

Oh, God, he's serious! "I-I-I—" What could she say? No? Was that even allowed? Who said no to Vega?

"When you posed last night, I envisioned the final work. I want you. My vision, it is of the exact moment of innocence lost. You are innocence." He motioned with his hand. "Your body, it shouts the word."

"I'm not innocent." She crossed her arms over her chest and curled her shoulders. Was he calling her a virgin? "I'm not. And I'm not a model."

"For me, you will be both. I need three or four sessions to prepare the *bozzetto*, the mock up. If you are nervous about the nudity, we'll schedule late evenings. No eyes but mine."

Wait. Nudity? Her eyebrows pushed toward her hairline. Her hand clasped her neck. The beat of her heart skipped beneath her fingertips.

"Once the bozzetto is finished, I may need you one more time. I pay my models top wage. I will make your beauty famous. If you are the subject of a Vega piece, you shall be immortalized in marble. You'll be my masterpiece."

Fame, beauty, and immortality? Who is he, the devil? A devil with an Italian accent. He could tell her he planned to rip out her fingernails and nail her to a wall and it would sound sexy. But model? For Maximo Vega? Nude? This was too much. Her head was swimming. She didn't know what to say.

"You will say yes, no?"

"No." She shook her head and choked on plaster

dust. "I need to think."

"Good, good. You think. Tomorrow you say yes. We start tomorrow night." Maximo went back to his clay work. The conversation was over.

Emily closed her gaping mouth. She recalled standing and walking out of Vega's sacred space, past a questioning Dante, and a fuming Crystal and into the parking lot. Her stunned brain didn't reconnect until her forehead hit the rim of the steering wheel.

As she sat wondering what the hell had just happened, her cell phone vibrated in her pocket. Caller ID flashed. Jeremy. There was a time when his name brought a flood of feelings that bounced and collided like bumper cars around her heart. It was almost a relief now that it didn't. Emily was happy they were friends. She needed a friend right now.

"Jeremy, you're a mind reader."

"Hey, Em. Why am I a mind reader?"

She couldn't tell him about Maximo's offer, could she? No, not until she'd wrapped her mind around it a bit more. "Um, I got your fancy invitation in the mail. I was thinking about you all duded up with twelve frilly bridesmaids. You must be *loving* this."

"Oh, man, you have no idea. I've been trying to convince Cyn to elope for the past two weeks. If we survive this, it'll be a miracle."

"Can I be a horrible ex-girlfriend and be a tiny little bit happy?" Emily tossed her goggles onto the passenger seat along with her mask. She pulled down the visor to check her appearance and was horrified. She looked like a ghoul. Other than the areas where the goggles and face mask covered, she wore a film of white plaster dust. Lovely.

"You can be my best friend and have coffee with me."

"Why, so I can listen to you whine about tux fittings?" She got out of the Jeep and shook her hair and beat on her clothes.

"Do you have any idea what a cummerbund is? 'Cause I sure as hell don't, but I'm wearing a pink one."

Emily laughed. Jeremy could always make her laugh, even on her worst days. "Fine, you crybaby, I'll have coffee with you. Java Jim's. Give me ten minutes." She juggled the phone from ear to ear swapping out her shirt for a clean tank top in one of those public clothes changing moves only girls can do. Like taking off your bra through your shirt sleeve. She finished and wiped her face on the inside of her tee before tossing it in the backseat. It was covered in so much plaster powder, Trixie would want to have it framed.

"Perfect, I'll even buy you a muffin."

"That's a given." Em bent at the waist and "did" her hair, ruffling the spiky mess a bit spikier and messier. Her cell phone clattered to the asphalt.

"What the hell are you doing?"

She picked up the phone. "Dusting."

Ten minutes later, Emily slid into the booth opposite Jeremy. A huge vat of steaming coffee sat waiting for her, along with a blueberry muffin as big as her head.

"Wow, you splurged for the King Kong Combo. Is it my birthday?" She ripped open three sugar packs and dumped them into the giant cup.

Jeremy smiled. He had the best smile. She

40

remembered all the months of kissing him with his braces, being careful not to cut his lips, or hers. The night he got those damn things off, they had made out down by Highland Lake for hours. Her lips had been sore for a week.

"No, we're celebrating, Miss Intern."

"Oh." She broke off a sugary edge of the muffin top and popped it into her mouth. "I hope I'm still there tomorrow."

"You just started today. What did you do?"

"Nothing," she mumbled around a mouthful and washed it down with coffee. "I kinda broke a sculpture."

"Already?"

"It wasn't my fault the finger was loose."

Jeremy threw back his head and roared with laughter.

"That's fine. Keep laughing, Cummerbund Boy."

"Oh man, Em, you never change. You fly around like an elf on speed. Do you even have a slow setting?"

"Nope."

Jeremy's phone buzzed on the tabletop before it started playing "Here Comes the Bride".

Emily grimaced. "Oh, that's frightening."

"I know. Cyn programmed it. I should answer this."

"Go ahead. Ask her where she hid your balls."

"Nice. Eat your muffin." He flipped open the phone. "Hi, hon. I'm at Java Jim's with Em. Nope, just got here. Don't worry about it. How about I pick up a nice bottle of wine and we relax tonight? No, the seating chart can wait until tomorrow. We need a night to just unwind. Okay?" Jeremy's eyes met Emily's.

"No, I haven't asked her yet, but I've bribed her with a giant muffin."

Emily stopped eating and looked at her muffin like it was poison. He was bribing her? She narrowed her eyes and pushed it across the table.

"Sure. I'll call you when I'm headed home. Love you. See you in a bit." He snapped the phone shut.

"What the hell are you up to?"

He pushed the muffin back. "I need a favor."

"What kind of a favor?"

"A big one."

"I may never eat another Blueberry Bongo again." She shoved the muffin back at him. "What do you want?"

"Just remember you're my best friend."

This couldn't be good. "Do you need a kidney?"

"No, but according to my soon to-be-wife, this is a matter of life or death."

"Now I'm scared."

Jeremy sipped at his coffee. "Bridesmaid Number Six had a waterskiing accident. She got jerked by the rope and fell on the edge of the dock. She broke her coccyx."

"Broke her what's yx?"

"Her coccyx. Her tailbone."

"She broke her ass?"

"Basically, yes."

Emily slapped her hand on the table and laughed. Covering her mouth, she dropped her chin. "That's horrible. I shouldn't laugh." She pressed her lips together. "Poor thing has…" A giggle escaped. "…her butt in a sling?" Em laughed until tears streaked her cheeks.

"Nice. Laugh at the girl's pain. She can't even sit down."

Emily held her side. She was getting a stitch. "I'm sorry. How terrible for her."

"She has to lug around one of those inflatable donuts."

"The poor thing." She bit her lip to keep from giggling again. Damn her ten-year-old funny bone. But come on, a bridesmaid with a broken ass? That was funny! "I can certainly see where Cynthia is upset." Another wave of hysterics was building. "Can't she get a pink satin donut in time for the wedding? Maybe if she stitched together two stuffed cummerbunds?"

"You're so funny. No. She obviously can't be in the wedding now."

"Of course not." Em wiped at her eyes.

"That's why Cynthia wants me to ask you to take her place."

"*Me*?" There was nothing funny about this. "You can't be serious." Oh, God, there was that look again. He was serious. What was with her today and serious men asking ridiculous things? "I can't be a bridesmaid in your wedding."

"Why not? You're coming to the wedding anyway. The dress is already paid for. Cyn will pay for all the alterations and the shoes."

"Cynthia barely knows me."

"What does it matter? I know you. There isn't anyone else that can fill in at this late date. If you don't, there'll be a giant hole and everything will be uneven according to the half-crazy woman I'm marrying who is this close to a nervous breakdown." He held his finger and thumb an inch apart. "Please. I'm begging. Cyn will be so grateful. I'll owe you big. A lifetime supply of coffee and blueberry muffins. All you can eat."

"You've ruined my favorite food."

"Please, Em. For your best friend?"

"I'd rather give you a kidney."

"But you'll do it?"

"Can I think about it?"

"No. I need you to say yes right now." He held up his fingers again. "Nervous breakdown, remember?"

She closed her eyes and held her forehead in the palm of her hand. "I hate you."

"You love me, and you know it."

Jeremy's phone buzzed again. "Here comes the bride, all dressed in white." He looked at her with pleading eyes.

Em dropped her head and rubbed across her eyebrows with the heel of her hand. "*Fine*."

He flipped open the phone. "She'll do it!"

Chapter Six

"She stays."

"She's a self-proclaimed klutz." Dante held the broken finger out to him. "Crystal is threatening to strike if she comes back. Let me move her into prep."

"She stays where she is."

"I don't understand." Dante threw up his hands. "I'm not proposing we get rid of her altogether. Let me just move her somewhere where she can't do any more damage."

"It was her first day. She'll be fine. Plaster we can fix. No *problema*."

Dante shook his head "We'll see how much of a *problema* she turns out to be." He consulted his ever-present clipboard. The man had his entire life organized down to the last inch.

Maximo was grateful. Without Dante there would be no Vega Studio. Time and order weren't concepts Max dealt with well. The work came first. Always. Ahead of anything and everything else. When the muse was strong, he could go days without food or sleep. Only the piece mattered.

He became obsessed. Or that was what his ex-wife, Judith, had cited on the divorce papers. It was a common complaint with most of the women he'd known. They started off telling him they could handle his odd hours and compulsive work habits, but in the end they all grew to resent coming in last on his priority list.

Judy had lasted longer than most, but the marriage ended shortly before the Art Journal article and the whole Vega mystique was born. He couldn't blame her. Had the positions been reversed, he would have left him long before she did. Now she was engaged to an accountant.

Dante flipped through his notes. "We have a new clay supplier sending us three hundred pounds. I'll get the guys to wedge it and check it for quality. Their man says he can get all we want, and anything over a thousand pounds, he'll give us a break on shipping costs."

"Good."

"I've hired a part-time tool master. He'll be in three days a week to keep everything sharp and in good working order. I'll talk to you if I think we need him more often." He tapped his pen on the page.

"I trust you."

"And don't forget, you've got Beverly Lavender from the Lavender Blue Agency scheduled to come tomorrow afternoon."

He had forgotten. "No. Can't you meet with her?"

"She has no interest in being *my* agent. You're the talent. Don't worry. I explained your hesitations to her, and she won't push any 'meet and greets' on you, but she's trying to bring both you and your work to celebrity level."

Max groaned.

"It's what you want, right?"

"Yes."

"Her client list has some pretty heavy hitters."

"She represents an elephant."

"That elephant's paintings sell for tens of thousands of dollars." He scribbled some notations on one of the sheets. "And if she's anything like her website photo, she's beautiful. Blonde. Leggy."

Max frowned at Dante. "You're married, no?"

"I am, but you're not. Take the woman to dinner. Go out on a date. It wouldn't kill you."

"I have work to do." Max stood to leave the office.

"You could do both." Dante tipped his head and shrugged a shoulder.

"No, I can't."

"Marble can be awful cold in the middle of the night."

Max called over his shoulder as Dante's door swept closed, "So can a woman."

Back at his worktable, Max looked over the sketches before him. When Beverly Lavender sent her first e-mail, she seemed to understand his need for privacy. It sounded like the perfect pairing. He did the work. She sold his sculptures to the highest bidder. He made the important career shift from filling commissions to doing his heart's work without bending his vision to what his client wanted.

Her track record was strong and, with his rising popularity, it was beneficial to both of them. The woman could sell, and although the elephant's paintings were hugely successful, she was trying to legitimize herself with the elite of the art world. That's where Maximo Vega came in. He was a traditionalist. His work was exacting at a time when artists were getting lazy, in his opinion. Throwing trash together and slapping an art tag on it wasn't ever what he wanted to do. He did the hard job and poured his heart and soul into each piece. It'd be nice if Ms. Lavender could show him a handsome payoff for all his sweat.

Blonde. Leggy. He shook his head as he lifted a sketch of Emily Baskins. Blonde, yes; leggy, no, but there was something about her that captured him. While it was her aura of innocence that first drew him, she was no child. Far from it, but there was an unspoiled quality to her. He found no hint of guile in those green eyes, as if life's cynicism hadn't reached her yet. Cynic was his middle name. Maybe he should stay away from her for just that reason.

No. he needed her. He had work to do, and she was it. She must agree to pose for him.

****

By the time Emily pushed through the belled door of Trixie's Pixies, her head was pounding. The bright lime green of the walls made her wince. The combination smell of hair bleach, nail polish, and industrial strength hairspray had her stomach twisting.

The shop consisted of four active chairs, a trio of wash sinks, two hooded dryers, a waxing station, a pedicure soak chair, a nail table, and a product corner full of shampoos, conditioners, tamers, curlers, strengtheners, stiffeners, gels, mousses, and sprays, oh my. It was high-maintenance heaven.

Trixie had three stylists working for her. Bridget was Trixie's best friend and helped manage the shop. She was the one who kept track of appointments and stocked the hair dye. Angel was a recent addition to the crew. She was a bit scary with her dark gothic look and tough as downhill skiing in the summertime. No one messed with Angel. Currently, she was under-shaving her client's deep purple hair. Angel had full sleeve tattoos and piercings in places no one mentioned in polite company, but she worked harder than anyone and could tie-dye dip a client one minute and produce a stunning bridal upsweep the next. Her clients loved her and many of them had followed her from her last salon.

Suzanne, the other member of the Trixie team, rushed to give Emily a hug. Em had known her since high school. They double dated to the prom. Em and Jeremy, and Suzanne and Tony. At least one couple had their happy ending. She and Tony married two weeks after graduation and were expecting their first baby around Christmas.

"Tell me, tell me!" She pulled Emily into her station.

"My head hurts."

"Forget your head. Tell me how gorgeous Maximo Vega is. If you tell me he's five three and has a gut, I'll hurt you, so if that's the truth, lie."

Emily dropped into the swivel chair. Suzanne spun her around and stood behind her. Ever since beauty school, most conversations with Suzanne happened in a mirror or over a couple of martinis. That was pre-pregnancy, of course. "What the hell do you have in your hair? Cement?"

"Plaster."

"Not good. Why must you torture your poor hair?"

"Forget my hair." Emily almost said, forget Maximo Vega, but she didn't. She couldn't. "No, he isn't five three." She needed to lift her chin to look into his deep brown eyes. "No gut." His Henley's fit tight in all the right places. Should she tell her about how he wiped his hands? No, she'd keep that for herself.

She was keeping his offer to herself as well. There was no way she wanted that kind of information getting back to her mother. This was one of those times when what her mother didn't know wouldn't hurt her. When and *if* she posed for Vega, after it was all over, maybe she'd tell her. If she had to. Like thirty minutes before *Boston Art Weekly* arrived with a full five-page spread on the newest Maximo Vega work that looked strangely like her daughter. Yes, then she'd tell her. Maybe.

Emily peeked over a shoulder at her mother. Trixie raised a gloved hand to wave. She had Joe Turner in her chair for his root touch-up. The creep had a standing appointment every six weeks to keep his hair looking sun-kissed. He even dyed his mustache. He believed it made him look younger. It made him look ridiculous. Em knew the real reason. He made no secret he had a thing for Trixie. The jerk asked her out a week after Em's dad died.

"That's all I get?" Suzanne's ultra-blue eyes captured hers in their reflection. "He's not short or fat? Come on, girl. You've got to give me more than that."

"How about I tell you I'm going to be in a wedding?"

An hour later, Emily stepped from the shower. It took two washings to get all the plaster dust out of her hair. She wrapped herself in a short oriental red silk kimono—a gift from Trixie on her last birthday. Jeremy called earlier and handed Cynthia the phone. She'd make him pay for that one. Add it to the growing list.

He was right about one thing, Cynthia was crazy. She rattled on for a good twenty minutes about how grateful she was and how Emily was saving her life and her perfect day. Then she hit her with could she wear a wig and platform shoes? And let's not forget the spray tan. It seemed all twelve of Cynthia's bridesmaids were tall, willowy, tanned brunettes chosen specifically to offset the gentle strawberry blonde of the bride. She knew it was a lot to ask, but poor Emily wouldn't want to stick out like…like a petite, bleached-out girl in an auburn-haired, bronzed forest! Em was paraphrasing.

"Please put Jeremy back on the phone." Emily counted between grinding teeth. *One Mississippi, two Mississippi, three…*

"Hey, Em."

"Hey, Em, yourself! Is she insane?"

"I told her you wouldn't buy it."

"Did you, for a second, think I'd say yes? Then you're both insane. Isn't it bad enough I'm in this stupid wedding?"

"You'll be fine just as you are." He emphasized the "just as you are." She assumed it was for Cynthia's benefit as well. "We're just thankful you've agreed to step in and help us out. The perfect part of our perfect day is going to be Cynthia and me becoming husband and wife, and it doesn't matter one bit about the rest. Right?"

"Nice speech, Romeo. Is she crying?"

"Yep."

"I'm still not wearing a wig and stilts."

"I'm not asking you to."

"Good answer."

"See, I do still have my balls."

Emily snorted. "Nice of her to let you use them now and then." She rubbed her forehead. "I'm sorry, that was bitchy. You know it's not too late to find someone tall and brunette to be bridesmaid number six.

Run an ad in the *Stoddard Shout*. Hold open auditions."

"Nope. You already said yes. It's all settled." Sniffling sounds could be heard in the background. "Cyn will call you tomorrow and let you know the time of your fitting."

"Is she okay?"

"She's just a little stressed."

Ain't we all. Em flopped back onto her bed. "Go unstress your fiancée."

"Are you okay?"

There it was. The softening of his voice. The sound always made her heart catch. He cared. He still cared. Beyond the breakup and their lives moving on, he was still her friend.

The events of the day tumbled down on her like bricks. She moved to the side of the bed and rested her forehead in her hand. "I'm fine." The silence on the other end of the phone told her he didn't believe her. He knew her too well. "Go hug Cynthia. Agree to live doves or something."

"I draw the line at a flock of albino pigeons crapping on me."

"You can cover your head with your cummerbund."

"So funny. You should do stand-up. Have a good night, Em."

She pressed the End button and stared at the phone. A good night? She'd be lucky if she slept at all. Throwing on a raggedy T-shirt and jeans, she flipped on the light in her makeshift studio. Compared to the Vega Studio, it was a closet. A tiny closet—with a window.

A plastic wrapped statue sat on her turntable in need of work. She opened a tub of conditioned clay and

52

added more to build up an area on the figure's hip and thigh. The cold moist feel of slick clay beneath her fingers soothed her.

Millions of thoughts raced through her mind and she attempted to sift through them, but it was too quiet. She didn't want to think about bridesmaid dresses or broken pinkies any more. Work had always been a good cure for her overactive mind. It was easy to get lost for a while and let her training and instincts take over. But lately it felt like such a struggle. Since she moved back home, everything about her work had ground to an agonizing crawl. Her professors at Stoddard School of Art had nothing but praise, but if they only knew the hours of working and reworking each piece took and how her work never quite hit the mark for her. Her muse was dead. Dad was dead. And she was back to working in a closet.

Tomorrow she'd move all her things over to the wonderful open space at Vega Studio. She couldn't wait to set up. Maybe it would be the inspiration she needed. Em threw a lump of clay at her statue. She needed *something* to inspire her and give her back her passion. Emily reached to switch on the CD player and stopped to wipe her hand across the back of her pants. Another pair of clay smudged jeans came to mind. Maximo.

He wanted her decision tomorrow. As much as she wanted to lose herself in her work, shutting off her mind and playing in the mud wouldn't help make a final decision about posing for him. She snatched a rag off the worktable to wipe her hands.

A knock at the window had her spinning around. Her heart sprinted in her chest. *Jeremy?*

"Hey, M&M, let me in." His voice was muffled through the glass.

She wrenched open the sash. "What are you doing here?"

"Making sure you're okay." He swept up the screen and swung a leg in. "When I didn't find you in your room, I knew you'd be back here."

Emily stepped aside as he crawled over the sill. "You're insane."

He groaned. "Did this window get smaller?"

"It's been years since you climbed the oak tree. Are you crazy? You could have used the front door."

"Then I'd have to wade through a Q & A with Trixie."

Her studio space was tight for one person. With two, they were practically on top of each other. "What do you want?"

"You said you were fine. You lied."

Emily rolled her eyes and squeezed past him to wrap her work back up in its protective sheeting. "So you snuck over here and climbed the oak like you were sixteen again to check up on me?"

"I didn't sneak."

She left the studio and led him back to her room. Trixie's television noise filtered up from downstairs. Jeremy flopped on the bed.

"Where did you tell Cynthia you were going?"

"She knows where I am. It was her idea for me to come over here."

"Are you marrying Mother Teresa? She's supposed to hate me. What kind of woman tells her soon-to-be husband to go visit his ex-girlfriend in the middle of the night?"

"The trusting kind." He propped his hands behind his head. "She's worried you're upset. I told her I didn't think you were, but something's going on with you. I sensed it at Java Jim's before the whole wedding thing ever came up. You gonna tell me, or do I have to start guessing?" The television got louder. "What the hell is she watching down there?"

"Shopping channel."

"Jeez."

Emily sat next to him with her back against the headboard. She hugged an orange pillow to her chest. "She can't afford to buy anything, but she watches it all the time. She's addicted." She gave him a sideward glance. "I can't believe you climbed my tree again. The last time you did this—" She stopped. It wasn't a good memory.

"The last time I did this was the night of your dad's funeral."

"I remember." She dropped her chin into the soft corner of the pillow. Tears pricked the backs of her eyes. Jeremy had climbed through her window and held her while she cried herself to sleep. He never said all those stupid things people said when they were trying to console you like *it's for the best*, or *time heals all wounds*. He hadn't said a word. He lay with her and wrapped his arms around her and let her cry.

"And the time before that was when you broke my heart."

"I remember that too." Her voice was small and quiet. He'd showed up in the middle of the night after they had a huge fight and begged her to marry him, stay in Stoddard, put up a white picket fence and have his babies. She'd said no. "So, why are you here?"

"You're still my best friend."

"I broke your heart."

"But you were the smart one. We weren't meant to be, no matter how much I tried to believe it. We never wanted the same things. You wanted bright lights and the big city. Fame. Fortune. I wanted lawnmowers and swing sets. You were absolutely right to say no. Remember how we used to lock horns over stuff. I thought you'd kill me the night I wanted to pick out names for our kids. As a couple, we were doomed. We're much better as friends."

"And now you have Cynthia."

"Yep."

"And she wants everything you want." It wasn't a question.

"Everything except the built-in swimming pool."

"Wow, you're maturing. That would have been a deal breaker." They sat side by side, both lost to their memories. The only sound came from the salesman downstairs, telling Trixie she only had three minutes left if she wanted the deal on kitchen knives. Emily broke the silence in the room. "I really am thrilled you're so happy. I'm not just saying it."

"I know you are. That's why I'm here. I want you to be happy too."

"I am."

"Bullshit."

"It's not bullshit. I am happy. Hey, I'm interning with one of the most gifted artists on the planet."

"Then why am I laying here. Something's up."

Emily pushed her chin deeper into the pillow. "I hate you."

"You love me. Try again."

"I hate that you can see through me."

"One of my many talents."

"It's annoying." It was also annoying he knew when to shut up. He knew she liked to avoid talking about the big things by picking little things to argue about. It was her best distracting tactic. It used to work. Not anymore. "Fine, I'll tell you under one condition."

Jeremy tipped his chin to look at her.

Em chewed her lip. "You can't tell my mother."

Chapter Seven

"Fine, I won't tell your mother." Jeremy's blue eyes showed his concern.

"And you can't freak out."

"That's two conditions." He grinned.

Emily threw the pillow at his head and got off the bed.

He pushed it to the side and sat up. "I won't freak. Tell me."

"I've been offered an opportunity of a lifetime." She tossed up a hand.

"Then why aren't you doing your happy dance?"

"It's complicated."

"How complicated?"

"You know the life and death thing? Well, it's similar, but without an actual body, although there is a body—mine. But I wouldn't be dead, unless Trixie found out, and then all bets are off."

"Whoa." He tipped his head to the side and stared. "Want to try that again? In English this time."

"Maximo Vega wants me to pose for him."

"Wow! That *is* huge."

"I know. He gave me the position I'm in because he wants me to do this. And I'm afraid if I say no…"

"He'll terminate your internship?"

She shrugged one shoulder. "He didn't say that, but…"

"So, don't say no."

"He wants me nude." She winced, awaiting the inevitable explosion.

Jeremy was on his feet like he'd been catapulted off the bed. "What kind of a pervert is this guy?"

"Shhhh!" She pointed at the floor. The knife guy was offering free shipping. "You agreed, no freaking," she hissed. "He's not a pervert. He's an artist. He's Maximo *freakin'* Vega!" She pushed her fingers through her hair. "I'd be a fool to pass this up. I'd be famous for goodness sake. And career-wise, I'd be set. We're talking the big time. Observing Vega at such a level is beyond anything I ever hoped for. I'm not a prude, and he's assured me no one else will see me. We'll be alone—"

"Whoa!"

"Again with the whoa?"

"This bastard wants you naked and alone."

"You're making it sound worse than it is."

"Em, you can't even go skinny-dipping at midnight without going into the water to take off your clothes."

"I was sixteen. I've matured." She crossed her arms over her chest.

"Have you?" He flipped a hand toward the poster of *Fame*. "Let's not forget you've had a mad crush on Vega for years."

"Now you sound jealous."

"Not jealous, worried as hell. This is like you walking naked into Johnny Depp's house to play Twister. I don't know if you're thinking rationally."

"Johnny Depp hasn't invited me."

"No, but Maximo Vega has."

"You're assuming he's interested in something

more than just his art."

"Hell, ya." He threw up both hands. "Doesn't this guy have some kind of reputation for sleeping with all his interns?"

"That's just a rumor."

"Are you sure?"

No. She wasn't sure of anything except the feeling if she didn't say yes, she'd regret it for the rest of her life. She picked at the dried clay around her thumbnail. The salesman downstairs was trying to sweeten the deal with eight free steak knives.

"If your internship wasn't in jeopardy, what would your answer be?"

Emily met his gaze. She did love him. She was glad they'd remained friends. She was thankful he climbed in her window tonight because, no matter what, Jeremy McCloud would never judge her.

"I'd tell him yes."

****

Next afternoon, Emily hit the studio at a dead run. She was late. The damn dress fitting ran two hours long. Almost as long as the pale pink "evening blush" satin bridesmaid gown fit for an Amazonian.

The seamstress kept shaking her head, telling her it would be easier to order a whole new dress, but there wasn't time. She must have repeated herself six times. "Where are your hips?" "You'll have to wear a higher heel." And Emily's personal favorite, "Perhaps a nice push-up bra. You are planning on wearing a bra, aren't you, dear?"

Pounding through the doorway, she rushed past Dante, dodged a short-wheeled cart of clay and skidded to a breathless stop mere inches away from colliding with Maximo—and a stunning blonde, who was, at that moment, glaring down at her from atop the sexiest shoes Em had ever seen. Were those Christian Louboutin pumps? Wow. She'd never seen a pair close up.

"Oh, jeez. I'm sorry."

"Ms. Baskins." Maximo's mouth tipped up on one side. "A bit slower. The plaster, she will wait."

"But Ms. LeMar, she will not." Had she not been watching his face, she would have missed the smile that skipped across his mouth, sparking a quick light in his eyes.

The woman beside him wormed a hand through the crook of his elbow and slid closer. Her perfectly manicured nails matched her purple, tissue silk blouse. Rising from her black silk pumps, a slim charcoal gray pencil skirt started mid-thigh and there was no question this woman had hips. Her matching suit jacket was draped over the arm not laying claim to Maximo. Long, blonde hair curled in perfect wide spirals fell over one shoulder. Emily spied classic level ten highlights with level eight lowlights. This woman lived in high-maintenance heaven. She was a gold card member at some salon.

"How nice of you to open your studio to high school students."

Emily cocked an eyebrow. So did Maximo. "Ms. Baskins is studying for her Masters. She's a talented intern here from the Stoddard School of Art."

"How nice for her." The grin on the woman's painted lips never reached the arctic chill of her eyes. "We need to go over the schedule I've worked up for you. Let's let Ms. Baskins scurry along."

Lisa A. Olech

Scurry along? Em bit back a response. Maximo had already defended her once. She held up a quick hand to keep him from needing to again. "It was lovely not bumping into you."

Who is that? She looked over her shoulder at the woman gushing over a piece of Maximo's work. Two steps later, Em's next "lovely" encounter was with the solid chest of an unimpressed Ms. LeMar. "Ooooof." The woman was a brick wall—with breasts.

Crystal plucked her off like lint. "You're twenty minutes late."

"Technically, I'm only ten."

"Technically, I don't give a damn. Get your goggles and mask. Today we'll learn the fine art of reattaching a broken finger. Won't that be fun, princess?"

Emily rubbed her forehead and sighed. *Loads of fun.*

****

Max witnessed Emily's collision with Crystal LeMar. He flinched. He hadn't had much one-on-one time with the head of his casting department. She was under Dante's domain, but she was about as intimidating as they came. Almost as intimidating as the woman with her arm currently glued to his.

Dante was right, Beverly Lavender was beautiful, by every Madison Avenue definition of beautiful, but she had an edge like broken glass and the warmth of an iceberg. An attack dog in thousand dollar shoes.

She had made no apologies for her drive and determination. She was hungry and Maximo's work was her next meal. Pushing into Dante's office, she released his arm and snatched her computer tablet from a purple leather briefcase.

Dante met Maximo's stare and gave him a nod of encouragement.

"With your permission, I'd like to ease you into the public's eye as soon as possible." She swept her finger across the screen. Max's stare turned into an angry glare.

Dante leapt to his feet. "We discussed Vega's reluctance—"

"Yes, yes, I know, but look at him. The man *has* to be seen. I have the perfect solution and it will give us just the exposure we want without compromising your need for privacy." She laid a hand on Maximo's arm. "I have two tickets to Friday night's opera opening. *La Boheme*. You love opera, and I have box seats. You won't have to talk to anyone. We'll arrive just before the curtain looking like this season's 'It' couple, and your photo will be splashed all over the society pages before the curtain falls for intermission. All will assume we are agent and client, but they'll secretly wonder if we're more." She squeezed his arm. "The odd lunch here, an intimate dinner there, and we can keep the rumor mill buzzing for weeks. Meanwhile, I'll contact all the major galleries on the East Coast and see which one wants a Maximo Vega exclusive showing. For a price, of course. We can offer to hold a premiere reception with the artist for a handful of adoring fans who'll pay huge amounts to be in the same room as you."

The words "adoring fans" tightened Max's gut. There was a reason he kept a low profile. If she got too carried away with her plans, she'd learn that secrets and rumor mills could bite you when you least expected it.

"You have nothing to worry about." She crossed her heart with the tip of one painted fingernail. "I'll do all the talking. You just have to show up looking handsome, and your work will sell itself."

She looked back and forth between him and Dante before reaching for Max's hands. Her fingers were icy. "I'm your agent now. You need to trust me. I'd never put you in a situation you're uncomfortable with." She squeezed his hands. "So, Friday night, is it a date?"

He looked past her to Dante. "A date? Was this your suggestion?"

Dante raised his hands in surrender. "Not me."

"Wonderful." She gushed.

He hadn't answered her.

"Do you already own a tuxedo, or do we need to buy you one?" She was a runaway train.

"He could rent one." Dante rushed to point out.

"No, he could not. I'll send a tailor over with samples in the morning, and I'll have the limo pick you up here Friday night at 7:20. We'll make the opera house just before the lights go down so we won't have time to speak to anyone."

She issued them a sharp nod. "Wonderful. It's settled then. Oh, look at the time. Walk me out, Maximo?" Packing her briefcase, she flipped a hand at Dante. "Mr. Rizzoli, my office will fax over copies of our contract as well as the artist's schedule. You'll have no questions."

She ensnared Max's arm again. "Ta-ta." They left a stunned Dante and her heels clicked across the floor to the door. "Now, don't you worry about anything." Pressing firm breasts against his arm, she smiled at him. Her eyes were an odd shade of blue. Periwinkle? She must wear colored contact lenses.

Beverly Lavender air kissed his cheek and left in a perfumed cloud.

Dante was standing in the doorway to his office. "Wow. That was something. The woman's a real tiger. That's the kind of agent you want."

Maximo set his jaw and crossed his arms over his chest. "Promise me you'll stop her before she eats me alive."

"It won't be as bad as you think. Her plan makes sense, and you'll get the exposure you need with the least amount of actual contact with the public."

"I just have to act like a trained monkey. I'll have the suit! Add a *giraffa* and we'll have the whole zoo."

****

Em finished sanding the delicate repair to the dancer's finger. She'd forgotten her earplugs and, between the noise in the casting room and Crystal's barking, she needed them. On her way back from her locker, she caught sight of Maximo and his mystery woman saying a cozy good-bye at the door. They looked like a photo-shopped couple clipped out of a magazine. Her blonde perfection. His dark sexiness. She would be the type of woman to drip off his arm.

The cut of Em's nails into her palm brought her up short. Was she jealous? That was crazy. It was just her rabid curiosity. That's what it was.

Who was this woman? "Hey, Crystal?"

"Now what'd you break?"

Em narrowed her eyes. "Nothing." She jerked her head toward the main studio. "The woman with Vega. Any clue who she is?"

Crystal snorted. "That's Vega's new fancy agent.

Did you get a load of her shoes? He gave her the royal tour and she had a fit that her precious pumps were getting dusty back here. Said her name was Lavender."

"Lavender what?"

"No, last name's Lavender. She's some hotshot out of Boston. I heard one of her clients was that African elephant at the San Diego Wildlife Reserve. You know, the one who paints?"

"The elephant paints?"

"Yep. His trainer sets up a canvas, hands the beast a brush full of paint, a few swipes—boom, twenty grand."

"You're kidding."

"I never kid about twenty grand."

"Why would Vega want to sign on with someone like her?"

"How the hell should I know? I'm thinking, if she can score thousands for some elephant crap, she can sell a Vega for huge bucks."

"It's never been about the money for Vega."

"Wake up, princess, it's always about the money." Crystal went back to work.

Em slipped in her earplugs. The sharp bite of noise dulled. Crystal was wrong. It wasn't about the money for Maximo. It was always about the work. Why hire a woman like that? Unless it was more than a business relationship. That had been an un-business-like good-bye at the door. Fine, maybe she was a little jealous. She was protective, that was all. Although she *did* have green eyes.

Her hands ran over the smooth lines of the sculpture. The dancer was on pointe and the muscle tone in the supporting leg was carved beautifully.

66

Maximo didn't need a fancy agent to market his work. The grace and beauty of his pieces did that.

She swept an inspecting hand along the curve of the dancer's back. In a few months would this be her? Maximo would want her answer soon. All signs were pointing to yes, but her pinball machine of emotions was making her a little crazy.

She wasn't a model. Modeling required skill and confidence and a strong sense of inhibition. Not that she was overly body-conscious. What was the direct opposite of that? Non-body-conscious? She didn't care about all those things. Clothes were just something to throw on. Hair and makeup were alien concepts—to Trixie's horror.

Emily couldn't understand some women's obsession with all of it. The lengths they went to have bigger breasts, fuller lips, flatter stomachs. Maybe it would have been different if she was fighting a weight issue in this culture of thin, but she'd seen just as many skinny girls obsessed with their bodies.

Maximo wanted her to pose for him, but it didn't mean he was attracted to her body type. He said she screamed innocence. Did that mean he didn't see her as a woman? Maybe he preferred Ms. Lavender's lush curves. *Ahhh! TILT!*

Jeremy was right, damn him. She wasn't thinking rationally when it came to Maximo. She could be seduced by the man asking her for a cup of coffee. Did she think she could stand there naked and not melt into a steaming puddle of hormones? Then what, jump him when his back was turned?

He did have a reputation for intimate relationships within his studio. Interns. Models. She'd be both. Emily looked at the serene face of the piece in front of her. "And who were *you*?"

Her eyes were getting greener by the minute.

It took Emily over an hour that afternoon to set up her own little bit of heaven in the Vega studio. She'd moved everything from her closet work space at home and pulled over her exhibit piece from school to work on along with some other smaller projects. The space and lighting here were perfect. The creative energy, phenomenal. The chance to think of something other than Maximo's offer for an hour or two, well, that was a true blessing. Too bad she couldn't stop watching the clock.

Chapter Eight

Emily stood in front of Maximo's magic curtain. How was she supposed to answer the man if she wasn't allowed to approach him? She kept hoping to bump into him again and made a point to casually walk past his area fifty or sixty times.

Dante was starting to giving her the hairy eyeball every time she wandered by him. Between this and the pinkie, she was on borrowed time as it was. He'd save himself half a bottle of aspirin by showing her the door.

Chewing a thumbnail, she studied the weave of the fabric. Should she slip a note under the pleats? That was ridiculous. The whole thing was giving her hives. She should just say no and face the consequences.

"Ms. Baskins?" The silk of Maximo's voice slipped over her name. Part of her body turned liquid.

She didn't turn around. "Yes?"

"You've come to give me my answer?"

"Yes." She held her breath. The heat of his body warmed her back.

"Bravo. Return here at eight. I wish for your hair to be softened, *si*? Like the first night I sketched you." He put a hand on her shoulder. "*Molto bene*, very good." he whispered as he passed her and slipped into his work space.

The air left her lungs in a rush. Wait, what just happened? Emily covered her eyes and groaned.

She'd just said yes to Maximo Vega. Twice.

****

It was 7:50 when Em pulled back into the empty parking lot of the Vega Studio. She'd told Trixie she had a late class starting this semester that was part of her internship. Technically, she hadn't lied. She debated calling Jeremy. For what? Moral support? *"Hey Jeremy, hon, I'm getting ready to get buck naked with the sexiest man I've ever seen. Okay, talk to you later, bye!"*

Emily pulled in a deep breath. Come on. Be professional. Forget you're naked. Forget it's Maximo Vega. *Ya, right!* She'd easier forget she had legs.

Grabbing the backpack, with her silk kimono robe shoved inside, she willed those legs to walk her into the studio.

Many of the lights had been shut off for the night, but Maximo's area glowed like daylight. Music played softly. Italian opera, but she had no clue as to which piece, or from which opera.

Her heart tap danced in her chest as she stripped out of her jeans and T-shirt and slipped on her thin robe in the model's dressing room. Bare feet on the polished concrete floor made her shiver as she moved into Maximo's area. The chill made her nipples tighten into ice picks and her teeth chatter. Em wrapped her arms across her chest and rounded her shoulders. The room was warm. Emily recognized two portable heaters used for a model's comfort. A dais was set and waiting. For her.

Maximo was angling a work light when he noticed her. "Come, come. I am ready for you."

Legs. You have legs. Please move. A tenor was

hitting a high note. The sound scraped against her spine.

Maximo raised a remote and the music lowered. "You are on time. Very good."

Emily could only nod. Her legs were working, but walking and talking seemed beyond her. Why was she doing this? Oh yeah, fame, fortune, success. That was crap and she knew it. This was all to be close to him. The Great Vega. She hated when Jeremy was right. She hugged her arms tighter and shivered again. It was one thing to be close to the man. It was quite another to be naked and close.

"You're cold?"

"No."

"Then your nerves are getting the best of you. Come. Stand here. We won't begin until you are ready. *Si*?"

"*Si*. Yes, thank you."

"There's no need to worry. You are safe here. I don't often use new models, but it is good for this piece. The shy reluctance will only add to the feel of innocence. You will do fine. I won't rush you."

Emily wanted to scream she wasn't innocent. She wanted to whip off her robe and strike a pose like she did this every day. To her, reluctance equaled cowardice, and that was something she just couldn't abide. She stepped onto the dais.

"I want your right side first. We'll set your blocking that way to start with."

She bobbed her head and turned to the left. Cold fingers clutched the ties of her robe. She closed her eyes. The rush of the heaters fluttered the hem of her robe against her thighs.

Soothing hands rubbed her arms and lifted to massage her shoulders. "You are an angel, *mio angelo*, to say yes to me. I wasn't certain you'd agree."

"You didn't give me much of a chance to say no." If he kept rubbing her shoulders, she'd say yes to pretty much anything.

"*Si*. I am selfish, no?"

"No."

The roughness of his hands caught at the smoothness of the silk. "You will see when it comes to my work. I think only of myself."

"Maybe at first, but then you share yourself with the world." The pressure of his fingers against the knotted muscles in her shoulders was a dance of pleasure and pain. She didn't want him to stop.

"Never me. I share the piece. I will share *you* with the world, but for this short time, you are only mine. My eyes alone. *Molto egoista*. Very selfish." Warm hands ran down her arms.

"May I ask you a question?"

"*Si*."

Emily looked over her shoulder. "Do you sleep with all your models?"

He stepped away and tipped his head, appraising her. "What answer do you wish to hear?"

"There are rumors."

"Rumors aren't necessarily true."

"Unless they are."

"I make no habit of sleeping with my models or my interns. Does that disappoint you?"

"No. I didn't want to think you were fickle."

"And what of you? You, too, are an artist. Do you sleep with all your models?"

"No." Emily thought about the models she'd used in the past. Jagger Jones popped into her mind. He modeled at Stoddard School last year. He was gorgeous. Now him, she might have made an exception, but he had to go and fall in love with another artist, Zee Lambert. They got married last September. The only other male models left were paunchy Phil and skinny Alvin. "No, I've never slept with any of my models."

"Good." Maximo pulled a covered cart of clay closer to his worktable. "The muse can be a curious thing. At times human, at times mystical. Elusive, yet consuming. She has been known to steal my heart."

"Mine too." Something about coming to Maximo as an artist, not simply a model, made her relax. Artist to artist they experienced some of the same feelings. She loosened the ties of her robe. Turning to the side once more, she pulled in another deep breath and tossed her robe clear of the dais.

"Ah, *perfecto*, at last." He whispered "*bella*" under his breath.

Maybe Trixie should get those language tapes. "What is *bella*?"

"*Sei bella*. It means you are beautiful."

"Th-thank you." She struggled to keep from covering herself. What the hell was she supposed to do with her hands?

"Do you remember the pose you made two nights past? Think like the artist again. Your body is your canvas. Remember the first drawings, the pleading? Show me the moment when all is lost and you are reaching to the heavens for guidance."

Emily placed a fist between her breasts and started her reach.

"Put your weight on the front leg. *Si, si.*" He was by her side with gentle hands, positioning her body exactly as he wanted it. "Tip the chin a bit more. This elbow down. Raise the fist higher." The back of his fingers brushed the tip of her breast as he moved her hand.

The jolt that ran through her made her gasp.

"*Si*, relax the jaw as if you're crying out." Moving behind her he placed his hands on her hips and turned them in a subtle adjustment. "Good. Ease the back. *Perfecto.*" Fingers raked through her hair, slipping it behind an ear. "Close your eyes. Good." He stepped back. "Ah, there she is, my vision. *Perfecto. Bella.*"

Her body hummed. Each nerve ending skipped along her skin where he'd touched her. She tried to control her breathing. If she dropped her fist, would he come adjust her again? *Dear God, please! Adjust me, adjust me!*

"*Si, si*, that is the perfect expression upon your face. Whatever you are thinking is perfecto. Can you hold the pose?" He grabbed for clay.

"Yes." The word came out in a desperate rush.

"Tell me when you need to break." The rich swell of the music swirled around them. She wished she knew the names of the songs. Maximo sang along under his breath while he worked. Emily could only watch him out of the corner of her eye. She didn't dare turn her head, but she was mesmerized by the way he laid in the clay and the ease with which he brought bone and muscle to life.

The heaters pulsed warm air around her, but she still trembled. She tried to move her mind past the fact she was standing there nude and toward the feeling of freedom many models speak of. Nope, it wasn't working for her. She was naked and as progressive as she'd like to believe she was, her every instinct was to duck and cover.

The steel door to the studio made its opening squeak and slammed shut. Emily let out a squeal, turned her back and covered all she could with her hands. She stared in horror over her shoulder, waiting for whoever it was to come through the curtain. She snatched her robe off the floor and draped her front.

"*Dannazione!* I told them all to leave me alone tonight!" He threw the clay in his hand onto the table. Maximo turned up the music and peered through the slit opening. Another door slammed before the main door opened and closed again. "It is Dante. He won't disturb us. He's leaving. I'll go lock the door behind him."

The breath she was holding released with a whoosh. Did Dante know her Jeep? Let's hope not. She didn't even think to hide her vehicle.

Maximo was back. "I'm sorry he startled you. Shall we continue?"

Emily fought her way into her robe. The battle in her mind was back. She was no exhibitionist, and she sure as hell was no model. "I don't know if I can do this."

"No, we were doing well. You can't stop now."

"I hate lying and sneaking around. It feels like I'm doing something wrong." She pulled the belt tight.

Maximo threw up a hand. "You are doing nothing wrong."

She gave a short laugh. "I know that, and you know that, but if Trixie finds out…"

He lowered the music again. "Who is this Trixie?"

"My mother." Emily rubbed the tense spot between her eyebrows.

"Ah, the mamma. She would not approve?"

"I don't know, and I really don't want to find out."

"Do I need to worry about the *padre*?"

"My father?" She shook her head. "No, he died a few years ago."

"I'm sorry. What about your boyfriend? Your lover? What does he think of you here with me? Will he barge in and fight me for your honor?"

"There is no boyfriend."

"No? This surprises me."

"I had a serious boyfriend in high school, but he's marrying someone else next Saturday. I had a few short lived things in Chicago. They didn't last long enough to be called relationships. I was always too busy with my work."

"I see." He stepped closer. "It is the same for me. My wife did not understand the passion for the work. She marries someone else, too." Maximo scanned her face. "What troubles you now? We were working well before Dante interrupted. Come let us get back to it."

"I thought I could…"

"You can. You did. You must." He stroked her cheek with the backs of his fingers. "You are lovelier than I imagined. You are my vision. I need you." The knuckle of one finger slipped down her neck into the vee of her robe. "You are doing nothing wrong." He lifted her hands and kissed their backs each in turn. "*Sei bella*." The tie of her robe slipped. Maximo released her hands and opened the edges of the silk, "*Sei bella*," and slipped it off one shoulder. He led her like a lost child back to the dais.

She couldn't argue that it was her mother's disapproval she feared most. Or any sense of impropriety. It was his ability to charm her simply by speaking her name that made her so hesitant. This man could talk her into skipping over hot coals. Her robe fell away, and he gently returned her to her pose. The warmth surging through her had nothing to do with the heaters. She was his to do with as he pleased. He could tie her in a knot and send her up a flag pole if he wanted. There'd be no further objection from her.

After twenty minutes he gave her a break so she could regain the feeling in her fingers. Another stretch of thirty minutes and Maximo announced they were done for tonight.

He helped her on with her robe and kissed her numb fingers. "You were *splendido*." After wrapping the piece to keep it from drying, he pulled a bottle of wine and two glasses from a cabinet. He handed her one.

"You could have offered me wine two hours ago. It would have made it easier."

"No. Work before *vino*."

Emily sat on a stool sipping the dry red wine. He cleaned his workspace. He was meticulous with his tools. She loved him. Okay, it was a crazy, mad rock-star crush. She didn't care. He was hotter than sidewalks in the Sahara and unbelievably gifted, and she was sitting here in nothing but a silk robe. She grinned into her wineglass. *How do you say "I want to have your babies" in Italian?*

"We work again tomorrow night?"

She raised her glass. "There's always tomorrow."

Chapter Nine

Maximo smoothed the clay over the angle of her hip bone into the slight flare of her thigh. Tonight he would capture the dip behind her knees and the muscled bow of her tempting ass. Using a scooping tool, he removed some material. He'd been too generous with the clay. Her behind was as petite as the rest of her but with a gentle sweep upward into the arc of her slender back. He couldn't wait to see her again. Touch those tender curves.

He loved the feel of her relaxing under the press of his hands kneading her shoulders. The tiny shiver she made when he kissed that shoulder. The gasp when he accidently brushed the sensitive tip of her tightened nipple. The faint floral scent of her skin lingered. What flower was it? The smell was familiar, yet he couldn't place it.

He turned the piece and worked on the sweet tilt of her peach-tipped breasts, the soft plane of her stomach framed by the tip of her ribcage. He'd seen all of her. He could work from memory alone, but he wanted to spend more time with the woman. Much more time.

She had surprised him last night. He had tricked her into saying yes and fully expected her to find a way to reject his proposal at the last minute, but she hadn't. She showed up in a whisper of a red silk robe and called his bluff.

It had taken a lot for her to pose last night. Her reaction to Dante's interruption told him that. Still, she didn't bail. He was glad. The girl had guts.

"Excuse me, Max?"

Max spun the piece to hide its face from Dante. "What is it?"

Dante jerked his head toward his office. "The tailor is here."

"Tailor?" He wiped his hands.

"For your tuxedo."

Max groaned, lifting his face to the ceiling. "Why do I feel it was a huge mistake to hire Ms. Lavender?" He was quick to wrap the figure and cover his clay. "I don't have time for fittings for a suit I do not need to wear to an event I don't wish to attend."

Dante just nodded. Max wasted no more time arguing. The sooner this fiasco was over the better. *Ms. Lavender would learn soon enough that there was a limit to what she could rope him into.*

"He's waiting in my office."

"Fine."

A heavyset man with a tape measure draping his neck was pulling samples of vests from a garment bag. "Mr. Bisby? This is Mr. Vega." Dante stood to one side. The office was a tight fit, but Max didn't care. This wouldn't take long.

"It's an honor to meet you, Mr. Vega."

Max shook his hand. "Mr. Bisby."

"Ms. Lavender gave me a quick idea of what you'll need, but I've brought along some samples I think will give you a nice selection of what we can do for you at Fancy Pants."

"Fancy Pants?" Max shot an angry glare at Dante

who coughed and picked up a clipboard and hid behind it.

"Ah, yes, we're the premier tuxedo provider for the area."

"I am certain you are, Mr. Bisby. We're both busy men. Let's not detain either one of us any longer than necessary. What is standard attire for an evening at the opera?"

"Well, a nice three-button, un-notched lapel is a fashionable choice. One-button, notched is a less formal option. Medium weight wool. Black, of course. I like a white tie with the tipped collar, but black is classic. Do you prefer a French cuff?" Mr. Bisby held up a tray of cufflinks.

Hide all you want, Dante. You're a dead man for roping me into this! Maximo unzipped a garment bag thrown over Dante's desk and pulled out the suit on top of the pile. "This one. Tipped collar. Black tie. No cufflinks. Are we done?"

Mr. Bisby turned an unhealthy pink. Sweat beaded on his balding brow. "But, don't you want to see—"

"No. Is there anything else?"

"I-I'll need to take a few measurements."

Ten minutes later, a flustered Mr. Bisby was escorted out along with armloads of unseen samples. Max heard him promising Dante the suit would be delivered by noon on Friday.

"Lucky for you they don't take inseams anymore." Dante grabbed a bottle of water from his refrigerator and tossed it to Maximo.

"No. Lucky for you." He took a long drink. The icy water made his teeth ache. He wiped his mouth with the back of his hand.

"You'll see, it will all be worth it. A beautiful woman on your arm, and a night listening to your favorite, *La Boheme*. I can think of worse ways to spend an evening."

Max could think of better. A nude Emily Baskins came to mind. A nice bottle of wine. *La Boheme* playing in the background. Candlelight.

"I stopped by last night, forgot my scheduling book. I would have poked my head in, but I heard your music. I hope I didn't disturb you."

The man must be a mind reader. "You did, but it was a small disturbance."

"There was an old Jeep in the parking lot. Are you working with someone new?"

Throwing the empty water bottle into the blue recycle bin by the door, Max folded his arms across his chest and leaned against the edge of the desk. "Yes. A new model for *Implorare*."

"I'll need their information so I'm able to pay them. They need to sign a W-9 form."

"I'm paying them myself. Off the books."

"But, that isn't how we do things."

"For this one, it is. She's modest."

"Are you at least going to tell me her name so I can add her to the schedule?"

Max pushed off the desk and crossed to the door. "No, and the door will be locked tonight, so don't forget anything."

Oh his way back to his workspace, he took a detour to see what was happening in the studio. Truth was, he wanted to see the object of his growing obsession. He found her. She was working on a unique piece of sculpture in the intern's area.

Encircling what looked to be a plain figured form of a shop mannequin, Emily had laid a swath of clay like a ribbon of features across a male's torso. It began with a sweep of a strong jaw and down his throat to cross his chest. The detail along the banding was exacting. The result would be stunning.

The ribbon wound around the figure's waist, swept across one hip to drape low and end on the figures thigh. Max had never seen anything quite like it. He'd never seen anything quite like her.

Emily was immersed in clay to her elbows. The mud stained her clothing and plastered her T-shirt across one peaked breast. She held a sculpting rib between her teeth like a Spanish dancer's rose. So engrossed in her work, she hadn't noticed she'd drawn a small crowd of admirers, including Dante who cranked an eyebrow and muttered, "Impressive," as he passed by.

She was more than impressive. She was breathtaking. Her passion for her work screamed in every move of her hands. Her talent, clear for all to see. It seduced him. He couldn't stop watching.

Emily took a step back and, tipping her head, appraised the piece. Muddied hands pressed into the small of her back and she arched against a stiffness there. Eyes closed, the slim line of her graceful throat was exposed. The fit of her shirt cupped the pert lift of her breasts. Max almost groaned at a sudden stiffness of his own.

****

Eight on the dot, Emily arrived back in his studio wearing her whisper of a robe and less nerves than the night before. She must have just showered, because her

82

hair was damp. Wet, it darkened to the color of honey. She raked her hands through and swept it behind her ears as he had last night. He relished the memory of it slipping past his fingers.

Lifting her arms raised the short hem of her robe and opened its top. The view teased his increasing desire. A gentle whiff of perfume followed her as she step onto the dais. What flower smelled so sweet? He had to know.

"Good evening, Ms. Baskins."

"Good evening. How do you want me?"

"*Pardone*?"

Beautiful green eyes met his in question, but there was no question in his mind. Oh, yes, he wanted her a dozen different ways—beneath him, on top...

"The pose. Which side?"

Images flipped through his mind like a slideshow and quickly ran from G-rated to XXX. He couldn't think. No, that was wrong. He was thinking, just with the wrong part of his body. Thank God for his apron. "*Si*, the pose."

She slipped off her robe. The ache in his jeans pulsed. "To the left?"

He had to turn his back to her. Dammit, he was a professional. *Get hold of yourself, man.* That only inspired another mental slideshow. He closed his eyes and stifled a groan. It had been far too long. His body was running on need and she was seducing him in more ways than one. The extra time he spent with her only added to his need to touch her, taste her mouth, and discover all her secrets.

Max made sure all was secure and hidden before facing her again. She stood with her robe clutched in front of her. Ah, not all the nerves were gone after all. God, she was beautiful. He loved the tender tilt of her breasts. The fragile sweep of her collarbones. The slight flare of her hips. Dammit all, it wasn't need feeding his body. This was definite *want*.

"I want you." His words tripped and fell flat on their face. He grabbed a tool off the table and waved it like an idiot. "The back."

"Oh, you want me from the back?"

Kill me. "*Si, si*, the back."

Emily turned away and tossed her robe aside. The view from the back was just as sweet. The slender back, the pale perfect curve of her ass. Her skin still held the mark of her panties low across her hips, but there were no such indications along the tops of her thighs. Dear God, she wore a thong. The air rushed out of his lungs like he'd been punched.

She peeked back over one shoulder, giving him yet another pose sure to haunt him in the middle of the night. "Are you okay?"

No. I'm trying to get some blood back into my brain! "*Pardone*. I'm distracted tonight. Too much in my…head."

"I know the feeling." She faced the back wall again. "My brain has been scattered lately. I'm not sure if I'm going or…or coming."

Her choice of words was physically killing him. "Well, then, we need to focus on the work." Good advice, focus on the work. She's work. She's work. She's *work.*

Emily assumed the pose from the night before. She was still putting a slight twist to her hips. It gave a sassy tip to her backside. He needed to adjust the angle.

He needed to touch her.

Wiping his hands, he moved behind her. "Turn your hips a bit." His tanned hands against the pale ivory of her skin struck him, as if his touch tainted her. The soft hint of perfume filled his senses. He ran a hand along her spine "Arch the back more."

She shivered even though the room was warm. Goose bumps rose on her arms.

"Are you cold, *la mia bella*?" He stepped closer fighting the urge to wrap her in his arms.

She only shook her head. Her breathing quickened. She trembled. "N-no. When you touch me," she sighed, "it feels…"

He ran two fingers along her shoulder, imagining laying a line of kisses along the same path. He whispered, "You don't like my touch?"

Emily gave the tiniest shake of her head. "No, it's not that." The space between their bodies hummed. "Just the opposite." As he palmed the blade of her shoulder, she released a small gasp. "It feels so… It makes me want—Ah! Cramp!"

Max jerked his hands away.

"Cramp!"

He was quick to rub the base of her back. "Your back is cramping?"

"No. Leg. Ow, ow, ow!"

He grabbed the back of her left thigh.

"No!" She spun, reaching for the calf of her right leg. "Wrong leg. Ow!"

She twisted, he dodged. An elbow connected with his shoulder. Pain shot down his arm. Her balance shifted off kilter. An arm flailed. He tried to catch her, but his body was turned the wrong way. He made a move to wrap an arm about her waist. She fell into him. Her forehead connected with his jaw just before they both ended up in a tangled heap on the hard dais.

"Ow!"

"Son of a—" He saw stars.

Emily clutched her calf. Maximo clutched her. All of her glorious naked self lay half on top of him, cradled in his arms.

Her eyes were wide when they locked with his. Her mouth formed a perfect O. "Oh. My God! I'm…I'm…Oh my God!"

She scrambled to get off him until the sharp ache in his shoulder caused him to wince. She froze. "Oh no, I hurt you! I broke Maximo Vega! What have I done?" She reached out to touch him with shaky fingers.

"It's nothing." His head cleared as he captured her hand and laid a kiss in its palm. "Are you hurt?" He soothed and kneaded the muscle of her calf. "Does the leg still pain you?"

Watching him, she shook her head. Neither of them moved. When she lifted her gaze to his, the air held its breath. Blood rushed in his ears. He was surrounded by her scent. When she worried her bottom lip, molten heat flooded him.

He pushed a hand into her hair and pulled her mouth to his, crushing her lips with his. She gasped when he swept his tongue into the sweetness of her. She whimpered, opened her mouth to his invasion and met his scorching kiss with one of her own. Her teeth nipped at his lips. Her tongue traced the edge before slipping in, teasing, tempting. Making his breath catch as she sighed against his mouth.

Her enthusiasm sent a fiery rush to his groin. He

tightened his hold and shifted to lay back across the dais with her beautiful body fully stretched out on top of him. He stroked her from hip to knee.

They shared another hot, deep, wet kiss that began with a slow intensity but flared into a fiery crush. She moved against him. Her body's response to his touches made him ache. She tugged at his apron and at the fabric of his shirt. Rolling them to one side, he removed both.

Emily lay on her back. Her breathing matched his. Her lips were swollen and blushed. Her fingertips played with the hair on his chest. Max cupped a hand over the peak of her breast. Each breath she took pressed the butter soft flesh into his palm. He thumbed the tightened tip of her nipple and made her whimper and arch.

Slipping her hand behind his neck, she pulled him down to kiss him again. Chest against chest, skin against skin. It was all a sweet torture. He must have her. Now.

She tugged at the waistband of his jeans. Impatient fingers pulled at the button. His zipper made a soft tap as each tooth released its hold. When she slipped her hand inside his boxers, a low pleasured rumble slipped from his throat. Her fingers reached lower. Max broke the kiss to watch her face. Their eyes held. Their chests rose and fell in shared arousal. Her hand encircled his erection.

Oh sweet God!

Closing her eyes, Emily sighed, "Vega…"

Vega…

The way she said it caused his mind to envision the passing faces of his fans as they reached out to grab at him. *Vega?* She wasn't making love to him, she was making love to Vega! The persona! Just like the rest, she wanted a piece of *the great artist.*

"*Vega....*"

No! He pulled away from her before his penis went soft in her hand.

Jumping to his feet, he turned his back to her. He fastened his pants and grabbed his shirt off the floor.

"Maximo?"

"You need to go."

"But? Wait. What just happened? I-I don't understand."

He couldn't look at her. He screwed his eyes tight. "Get dressed." He was being a prick and he couldn't even explain it to her. She needed to get out before he made an even bigger jack ass of himself. He braced his hands on the worktable and hung his head. "We're done for tonight. *Lasci prego.* Please leave."

Chapter Ten

Emily raced her Jeep out of the parking lot as if a horde of zombies was after her. She kept blinking to keep her vision clear as tears welled in her eyes. Looking into the passenger seat at her hastily packed bag, the red of her silk robe screamed at her. She pushed the button for the side window, ripped the robe from her backpack, and threw it out of the speeding car.

A sob caught in her chest. What was wrong with her? First she tried to kill him by falling on him then she practically attacked the man. Shoving her hand down his pants. What the hell? No wonder he pulled away. She'd ruined everything! What a flaming idiot!

Peering out the windshield, she didn't even know where she was, or where she was headed. She'd just jumped into her Jeep and drove off. How had she gotten on Huntley Street? Suzanne and Tony only lived a couple blocks from there. The clock on the dashboard read 8:39. She hoped it wasn't too late. She needed to talk to someone. Anyone.

Screeching the Jeep to a stop in front of 45 Melville Ave., she noted lights still burned in their front room. Em pushed the doorbell and stepped back, shaking both her hands as another wave of shock and humiliation washed over her.

The light over the door flicked on. Suzanne or Tony was probably looking through the peephole. She gave a feeble wave. The door jerked open and the light from inside spilled onto the porch.

"Em? Are you okay?"

"No. Is it too late? Can I come in?"

"No, I mean, of course. It's never too late for you. Come on in?"

Emily stood just inside the door, rubbing her hands together. Tony was on the couch, an afghan and a bowl of popcorn sat in his lap. A black and white movie flickered on the television. *An Affair to Remember*. It was Suzanne's favorite old Cary Grant movie.

"Oh, God, you're having a romantic evening, and I've barged in and ruined it." It must be a theme for her tonight.

"Don't be silly. We've watched this a hundred times. Tony, just pause it." Cary Grant's handsome face froze on the screen. Suzanne rubbed Emily's arm. "What's going on, sweetie? Is Trixie okay?"

"Yeah, Trixie's fine. Um," her voice dropped to a whisper. "Is there somewhere we could talk in private?"

"Sure, sure," Suzanne whispered back. To Tony she announced, "Honey, I'm going to show Em the baby's room." She grabbed Emily's hand. "Come on."

She pulled her down the hall and into the first doorway. Flipping on the light, Emily's chest constricted at the sight of a perfect little nursery done in butter yellow and white. A soft mural of the sky had been painted on the ceiling. A border of fuzzy ducklings followed one another around the top of the walls. The crib was set up waiting to be made. A small stack of polka dot sheets and gingham checked bumper pads were neatly stacked alongside.

"Oh, Suzanne…" Em sighed. "This is too cute."

She flipped a finger at a mobile of stuffed ducklings and sent one of them dancing. The music box attached started to play "Hush Little Baby."

"I just love the ceiling, don't you? Kay Winston from the Stoddard School did it. Do you know her? She's really talented, like you."

"I know Kay. Pretty long hair. Her murals are amazing. She's a sweetheart." Emily picked up a stuffed bear and hugged it to her chest. It smelled baby fresh and clean. She couldn't tell Suzanne she'd acted like a complete slut. Not in front of innocent ducklings and teddy bears! It had been a mistake to come here. She set the stuffed animal into the corner of the crib. "I'm sorry. I'm just being silly. You go back to your movie. I'll be fine."

"You're not fine. Tell me what's got you looking so spooked." Suzanne's eyebrows shot up. "Is this about Jeremy's wedding again? I still can't believe he asked you. Tony couldn't believe it either. I mean, come on, what was the man thinking? Oh, I know, you had your fitting." She grimaced. "The dress is horrible." Emily covered her eyes with her hand as Suzanne continued. "No. Worse. They paired you up with the ugly cousin?" She gasped. "You're still in love with Jeremy and don't know how to tell him."

"No." Emily squeezed her eyes tight as her head started to pound. She rubbed at her eyebrows "No, I'm not in love with Jeremy." *I'm in love with Maximo Vega.* She couldn't say the words. How was she ever going to explain what just happened in his studio? Simple. She wasn't. There wasn't anyone to explain this to. Not Suzanne, not Trixie.

"You guessed it." Emily threw her hand up. "The

dress is horrible. I'm going to look like a pink satin broomstick."

Ten minutes later she was back on the front stoop with Suzanne's assurance it couldn't be as bad as she imagined. She personally guaranteed Emily would look amazing for the wedding with or without mink eyelash extensions. Emily hated lying to her, but telling her she'd had Maximo Vega's penis in her hand wasn't happening. Not with little duckies staring down at her in judgment.

Emily pulled herself into the driver's seat and peered through the windshield. Tears she wouldn't cry stung her eyes. Melville Avenue was dead quiet. The whole town of Stoddard rolled up the sidewalks before nine p.m. She missed Chicago. The lights, the noise. The city was never quiet. How had everything gotten so messed up? She shouldn't be here. She held her forehead. She was losing her mind.

Pulling her phone out of her pocket, she started to dial Jeremy's number, but four digits in, she pushed the disconnect button and threw her phone into the passenger seat. She couldn't talk to him. Face it, she was alone. Besides, Jeremy had one crazy woman to deal with. He didn't need another one.

She drove around for the next two hours, burning time until she was certain Trixie would be asleep. No flashes of brilliance graced her as she drove. No answers to the questions screaming. No epiphanies as to why Maximo had his hands on her body and his lips on hers one minute and what happened to make him pull away from her the next. When she finally crawled between the sheets, her exhaustion should have been enough, but her mind continued to churn. There were no answers written on the bedroom ceiling either.

Next morning she grabbed a coffee and dashed out before Trixie could notice the dark smudges beneath her eyes. Em had one class before she was scheduled to work at the studio, and she was fully expecting to spend less than ten minutes there while Dante listed all the reasons why she was fired.

When she entered the studio that afternoon, Dante stood with his ever-present clipboard at his office door. "Ms. Baskins."

Here it comes. She stopped in front of him, sighed and pushed her hands into her pockets. "Mr. Rizzoli." She concentrated her gaze to the middle of his chest and steeled herself for the lowering of the ax.

"Did you want something, Ms. Baskins?"

She lifted her eyes.

He had one eyebrow cocked at her.

"Didn't you want to say something to me?"

"What did you want me to say? Nice shoes? Are we playing guessing games today?"

"No, no." She frowned. "You didn't want to talk to me?"

"About what?"

"Um, well, nothing, I suppose."

"Go to work, Ms. Baskins."

"Really?" She tipped her head. Had she heard him wrong?

Dante put his hands on his hips. "Are you waiting for an engraved invitation?"

"No, I'm going."

"Ms. Baskins, why is it every time I have an encounter with you another gray hair sprouts on my head?"

93

"I couldn't begin to guess, Mr. Rizzoli, but I'll give it some thought."

"Good. Now move along."

Emily rushed through the studio, eyes darting to catch anything amiss. Had she dreamed last night? No. She had a bruise on her hip from where she hit the floor. Naked. In Maximo's arms. Just before she shoved her tongue down his throat and her hand into his pants. He mustn't have said anything to Dante. She was confused more than ever. Her internship was still active. Was she still posing for him?

Grabbing her safety gear, she hit the noise and chaos of the casting room.

"Late again, Baskins?" Crystal was on her before the door closed.

"Mr. Rizzoli didn't want to speak to me." Emily shrugged and flashed the woman her biggest smile.

"What? Never mind." She frowned. "You look like something my cat threw up."

"Thank you." Emily shook her head. "I do my best." Nothing like kicking a girl when she was down.

"Well, do your best on the piece over there." She pointed toward a torso piece of a headless, armless male with huge shoulders, killer abs, and an impressive set of genitalia.

"Ah, the perfect man."

"I prefer them headless." Crystal quipped before she walked away.

I heard you bite their heads off after sex. Emily held her hands up like a praying mantis and grimaced at Crystal's back.

Crystal called over a shoulder, "No pinkies on this one."

"Great." Emily slumped onto a stool in her work area. It was just another day in Crystal's funhouse. Nothing had changed. As confused as she was, she couldn't help but be relieved. No matter what did or didn't happen with Maximo, she was still here. For now, that was enough.

"Hey, Baskins! You waitin' for an invitation?"

Emily jumped up and grabbed a tool. She shot a glance at Crystal's back then glanced in the direction of the side door. Maybe she was waiting for an invitation.

****

For the rest of the day, Emily worked on the thin seam running the length of the figure's right side. The play of the ribs was done brilliantly. The flow of pectoral muscles over the chest was flawless. As delicate as the dancer had been, this piece was all about strength and power.

It was Friday evening. Almost everyone cleaned up and cleared out by five sharp. The clock on the wall read 7:10. The casting room was quiet. The mixers stopped more than three hours ago. Emily had gotten lost in the work. It felt good. She'd caught her second wind and blocked out the commotion in her mind, pushing it aside, tucking it away. After her dad's death, she'd become an expert at burying her feelings away in little cubbies until she felt strong enough to pull each one out and deal with it…or not. Denial was a good thing.

The figure before her was coming along beautifully. Both side seams were gone. The few air bubbles along the top of the shoulders had been erased. She was working on the seam that ran up the inside of each thigh. Em figured another hour and she'd be done.

She cupped the figure's testicles. "Okay, Fred, turn your head and cough."

"Fred?"

Emily straightened slowly and removed her hand from the statue's privates and brushed her palm on her thigh before turning to face Crystal. Her cheeks burned.

"I'm sanding the man's balls, it's only polite to give him a name."

"You're an odd one, Baskins."

"I've been told that before." Emily pushed the goggles back on her head. "I thought you already left."

"Was on my way, but you gotta see what's going on out there."

Well, that raised her curiosity. It had to be something good for Crystal to come back. She'd been in a good mood all afternoon. Said she lived for her weekends, but she hadn't left with the rest and was still dedicated enough to put in some extra hours. "What's going on?"

"Just come look. You'll like it, I promise."

"Now I'm scared." She pulled off the dust mask and dropped the sanding block onto her worktable.

The main studio was quiet. Emily couldn't see what was so—

Crystal bumped her and jerked her chin toward the front of the studio, near Dante's office. "Now that is one hunk of man, right there."

Maximo Vega *was* the sexiest man on the planet. Put him in a tuxedo and, well… *Oh. My. God!* He was fitting a gold watch to his wrist and tugging at the cuffs of a crisp, white shirt. He buttoned the jacket. The elegant tux fit him like a dream. He unbuttoned the jacket, checked his watch and ran his fingers through his hair. Its dark waves shown from the lights overhead. He rubbed at his jaw. His five-o'clock shadow had an extra two hours of sexy. Where were the *GQ* photographers when you needed them? Maximo was gorgeous.

Crystal chuckled as she put a finger under Emily's chin and shut her gaping mouth. "Told ya you'd like it."

"Wow." The word rushed out on the breath she'd been holding.

"The man sure does clean up pretty."

Emily couldn't take her eyes off him. He tugged on his cuffs again. The tan of his hand set against the white of the cuff had her remembering those hands on her last night. Cupping her breasts, teasing her nipples. Beneath her T-shirt, they tingled and tightened. Maximo smoothed the front of his shirt and buttoned his jacket once more. Her mind flashed to the vision of her hands smoothing over his abdomen, reaching lower, just before—

The door to the studio slammed.

"Way to ruin it," grumbled Crystal.

A ray of setting sunlight through a sidelight hit the sequins of Beverly Lavender's deep purple gown and, for a brief moment, turned her into a tall, coiffed disco ball. Her hair had all the signs of a professional updo. Long, lazy spirals framed her face. Large amethyst and diamond teardrops dripped from her ears.

The slit of her skirt showed a length of shapely leg starting at her eyebrows and traveling eight or ten miles down to perfectly dyed, insanely high Louboutins.

"Wow, again," Emily groaned. "She's stunning."

"She's a cyborg. No real woman looks like that." Crystal snorted. "Crack her open like an egg, bet you'll find gears."

Emily crossed her arms over her chest. Ms. Lavender's dipping neckline offered a display of all her womanly charms. "She looks real to me."

"Well, fun's over. I'm outta here." Crystal thumped Emily's back. "Shut off the lights when you're done."

"Right, lights." Em's stomach dropped watching Beverly tip in to kiss Maximo's cheek, giggle and wipe her lipstick off his skin. She straightened his already perfect tie and ran her ringed hand down his lapels. Em was glad she was far enough away so she couldn't hear the gushing no doubt coming from her glossy lips. Watching was bad enough. Why was she torturing herself? She still had work to do. And yet, she couldn't turn away. It was like driving by a car accident. She didn't want to look, but she couldn't help it.

Beverly slipped her arm through his. They were leaving, but Maximo stopped them by the door and turned back as if he'd forgotten something. His face was set in a scowl, until his eyes met hers. Emily's first instinct was to run and hide. He'd caught her standing there like a starving orphan with her nose pressed against the bakery window. His pace slowed and he stopped. Their gazes held for an endless moment while the universe took a breath. In the next heartbeat, the purple people eater captured his arm again and tugged him away. He patted his jacket pocket and nodded. He hadn't forgotten anything after all. Turning back into the sunlight, the sparkling couple left in another sequined burst.

The door slammed against Emily's heart and she raced back to her corner in the casting room. All the emotions—love, hurt, anger, and frustration—tumbled out of her neatly cubbied mind and shattered at her feet. Seated before the sculpture, she thumped a fist on the smooth plaster chest. Longing made her open her hand and smooth it over the ridges of its stomach until she held "Fred's" penis. She shut her eyes and relived the scene of Beverly's kiss on Maximo's cheek with its pink lipstick smudge. Jealousy surged.

"Dammit!" Emily railed at the ceiling. Now, Monday morning she'd have to apologize *again* and try to convince Crystal "Fred's" penis had been loose.

Chapter Eleven

"You look incredible." The sound within the back of the stretch limousine was oddly deadened. Beverly crossed one leg over the other after handing him a glass of champagne from the bottle set in ice before him.

"A tuxedo does that." He drained half the flute in one swallow.

"I'm excited about tonight. I think you'll be pleased with how things work out. You'll see, by morning you'll be flooded with commissions."

"We shall see."

"You certainly are a man of few words." She sipped her drink and wiped the lipstick off the rim with her thumb.

"I don't do, how you say, the chitchat."

She laughed.

He hadn't tried to be funny. He put two fingers into the tightness of his collar and tugged. He hated ties. He hated suits. He hated champagne and he wasn't overly fond of limousines either. The last time he rode in one, he was nine and it was his grandfather's funeral. His Grandma Vega cried the entire ride.

"Not to worry. I'll do all your chitchatting for you. That's why you're paying me."

According to the percentage figures, chitchat was going to cost him plenty. He studied the woman before him. She was perfect in every aspect. Perhaps that was the problem, she was too perfect. There were no visible flaws. He should compliment something. Wasn't that the usual protocol? It would be if this was an actual date. But this was nothing more than a business meeting. Her perfume was giving him a headache.

He turned his attention to the passing scenery. If only he hadn't seen her. Emily. It was bad enough he'd been kicking himself all day for being a shit. It was inevitable he'd see her, though he'd avoided the studio area all day. After last night, he didn't know what to say to her. Standing there covered with plaster dust, she was still the loveliest woman he'd ever seen. Even more lovely than his purple-wrapped companion.

He was unsure what to do. He didn't want Emily to be another woman to want Maximo Vega. He wanted—no, needed her to want him—Max, just Max. The man, not the myth. To do that, she'd have to know the truth, and that was how he'd lose her for good.

He hurt her last night. Read it on her face. He couldn't continue to crush her feelings, but he couldn't bear the possibility of not seeing her again. Her kisses and the way she responded to his touch had ignited a fire deep within. No woman since Judith had had such an effect on him.

Beverly leaned toward him and placed a bejeweled hand on his knee. "You know, you don't have to look like I'm driving you to your execution. Relax. Enjoy yourself. I understand you love this opera."

"*Si*. I do enjoy *La Boheme*."

"I've never been. You'll have to explain it to me as it goes along."

"'Tis a simple story. A poor man, Rodolfo, falls in love with a girl, Mimi. Loses her to a wealthy man who can care for her better than he, but she is ill and the wealthy man abandons her. Rodolfo finds her again, but she is too ill and even his love for her cannot stop death."

"How sad."

"*Si*." Maximo finished his champagne and grimaced at the taste. "How sad indeed."

The limo pulled up in front of the opera house. Beverly seemed thrilled to see some photographers lurking by the entrance. "The driver will open the door, you'll get out first, and then offer me your hand. When I get out, we'll stop for a tiny moment while I straighten your tie. The perfect photo op. It would be a nice touch if you kissed my cheek." She looked about. "Where did I put my purse?"

Under his breath, Maximo mumbled. "It's next to my tin cup and little red monkey cap?"

"Here are the tickets."

The door to the limo opened. Showtime. The handful of reporters stood poised until someone recognized him. "Maximo Vega? Mr. Vega, over here!" "Look over here!"

The wine soured in his stomach as he helped Beverly from the car. She beamed at the cameras, fixed his tie and stood waiting an awkward half second too long for a kiss that wasn't coming. Max took her elbow and led her inside.

The lobby was near empty as the time was close to curtain, and Max never broke stride. Beverly had to double-step to keep up. An usher escorted them to a private box, high to the left of the stage. Maximo waited until she was seated before he unbuttoned his jacket and settled into the seat beside her.

Beverly fanned her face. Tendrils of pale hair danced about her flushed cheeks. "Had I known we were sprinting through this evening I would have worn more sensible shoes." She had a tinny laugh.

"You know I do not wish to speak with anyone."

She rested her hand on his sleeve. "I understand, but we could have taken it a bit slower, don't you think?"

He was saved from responding by the lowering of the theater's lights. He sighed, ready to enjoy the next few hours escaping into the beauty of the performance. And he would have if the beaded grape Popsicle sitting next to him had given him a moment's peace.

"You know, I've never been to an opera before." "Is he the hero?" "What are they saying?" "Who is that again?" "Oh, this is lovely. What's the name of this piece?" "The scenery looks a bit stark." "Do they have to sing everything?" She used her opera glasses to scan the crowd. "Oh, I think I see the governor and his wife. I sold her a piece for her private collection last fall. We really should be polite and say hello to them."

Thank goodness they were in a private box. Fewer witnesses when he killed her. At one point she pulled out her cell phone and began texting. The blue of the screen lit the entire box.

"You can't use your phone during a performance," he hissed.

"The sound is off." She shrugged a shoulder. "I promised a client."

"The light. Shut it off!" He snatched it away and shoved it into his breast pocket.

She crossed her legs and jiggled her foot. "How many acts is this?"

By the time intermission arrived, he was done and ready to leave, but to do so meant wading through a sea of people in the lobby and waiting on the sidewalk for the limo to return through Friday night traffic. No, he was trapped until the bitter end.

Beverly used intermission to point out the who's who in the audience, beg her phone from him to answer a call and visit the ladies' room. The lights were dimming when she returned.

"I would have brought you back a glass of wine, but the usher downstairs stopped me. Evidently you can only drink in the lobby. That's crazy. It's not like we're children and will spill on the carpet."

"This is an opera house, not a Cineplex. I beg you, please be silent for the last act."

"Of course, Maximo. I just thought it would be interesting to discuss it. I want to learn all the things you're passionate about."

"*Silenzio*," he hissed. "I'm passionate about silence!" Several people looked their way and shushed them.

"Fine," she whispered back. "I'll be so quiet you won't know I'm here."

If only that were possible. "*Grazie*."

"That means thank you, right? See, I'm learning."

The lights rose finally after three curtain calls and an explanation that there were no encores in opera. Max's head was pounding. All he wanted was to be rid of this woman and to get back to his apartment.

"Well, that was charming. Shall we go?"

"We wait." He leaned back and folded his arms over his chest.

"You said there are no encores."

"No, we wait for the crowd to thin."

"No need for that. I've arranged for us to leave through a private exit. The car will meet us out back." She snapped her purse shut.

"*Perfecto*." *Thank you, God!* "Let's go."

Stepping into a small, discreet alcove, another usher slid back a hidden panel in the wall to reveal a gated elevator. He handed the man a generous tip. The car creaked and crept the two floors to ground level and opened onto a short hallway and a door marked exit.

Thankfully, Ms. Lavender was silent. Up until this moment, he had serious doubts about her abilities. He prayed her silence would last during the drive back to Stoddard.

Maximo swung open the door for her and was blinded by a sudden assault of flash bulbs.

Dozens of photographers and reporters cried out to him. Yelling questions and shoving microphones into his face. This was his nightmare. His own personal hell.

Beverly was at his side. She didn't appear to be shocked or bothered by the intrusion. Did she know about this?

"Maximo! Did you enjoy the show?" a young reporter hollered and thrust his mic at them.

Beverly snatched it. "We had a lovely time. The performance was breathtaking."

More questions were hurled at them. She held up one hand. "We're not prepared to answer your questions this evening, ladies and gentlemen, but you're free to contact my office if you wish to set up a private interview."

Comments from the press corps swelled.

"But...but!" She held up one finger and regained

their attention. "I can share with you some amazing news. The great Maximo Vega will open this season's art tour with an exclusive ten-day showing at the end of this month."

An explosion of flashes captured the look of pure fury Maximo shot in her direction. She orchestrated this whole thing. *Private exit, my ass!* Tour? Ten-day showing? He never agreed to anything on that scale, and she knew it!

"My office will be sending out a full press release with all the details in the morning."

"Mr. Vega, would you like to say a few words?" "Will *FAME* be a feature at the show?" "How about a comment?"

"No comment." Grabbing Beverly's elbow, Maximo bulldozed his way through the crush of media and didn't stop until the driver shut the door to the limo, muting the rush of questions. "You're fired," he spit.

"Maximo, I'm sorry. I had no idea—"

"*Stronzate!* Bullshit! You arranged all this."

"Fine, I confess." She held up her hands in surrender. "You would never have said yes to a press conference, and I thought—"

"No, you didn't think." He ripped at his tie and unbuttoned the collar threatening to choke him. The limo inched its way through the crowd and turned onto the main street. "I'm not doing a tour or any ten-day show."

"It's all arranged."

"Then un-arrange it. No, better. I'll do it. You're fired."

"You can't fire me. We have a contract."

"I don't care about your contract. I cannot work

with a conniving, manipulative, *insopportabile,* insufferable—"

"You signed an ironclad, one-year exclusive with me. I'm afraid you have no choice." She smiled and poured herself a glass of wine. "If you fire me, I'll sue you for everything you're worth."

"Stop this car."

"Don't be foolish. We can discuss this rationally. Champagne?"

He grabbed for the phone to connect him to the driver. "Stop the car!"

"Maximo, don't be ridiculous."

He was out of the limo before the driver had a chance to open the door. Slamming the door he told the man, "Drive on."

"Should I call another car for you, sir?"

"No. Leave me."

"As you wish, Mr. Vega."

They had been close to the highway. Max started walking back toward the center of the city to find a taxi. It was close to midnight before he found a cab driver willing to drive him all the way to Stoddard, and only after he agreed to pay the man twice his usual fare.

Maximo paced Dante's office. Fury burned deep as he stood, reading over the fine print of his contract with Lavender Blue. Anger and frustration hit their peak. He was an idiot. Both Dante and he were duped by this woman, and there was no telling what she'd commit him to. It would only be a matter of time before it all blew up in his face.

He grabbed the phone to call Dante but dropped it back on the desk. It was one in the morning, and Dante was away for the weekend. It would have to wait until

Monday.

He whipped the contract across the room. There had to be a way out of this mess, but he was too infuriated to spot the tiniest of loopholes, and having spent an excruciating evening with Ms. Lavender, he was sure the document was just as she said, ironclad.

He pulled a beer from the refrigerator and made his way into his work space. He was too wound up. Staring at the wrapped figure of Emily, he couldn't help but feel here was another mess he could see no solution for. He unwrapped the piece. No, "mess" was not what this was. Emily was uncomplicated. Innocent wasn't the proper word either, but there was an air of simplicity to her that translated into a level of sincerity. She had none of the cold calculation of Beverly. Emily was warm and passionate and honest in her feelings, and he'd pushed her away. He really was an *idiota*.

Max tossed his jacket and tie aside, and rolled up the sleeves of his starched shirt. He needed to be close to her, if only through his work. Habit had him reaching to switch on his music. *"O Soave Fanciulla"* filled the space. Rodolfo sang to Mimi, 'Oh lovely girl...' Max snapped off the CD, wrenched it from the machine and threw it like a Frisbee into the trash. *La Boheme* was ruined for him now.

Opening the tub of clay, his concentration returned to the back of the piece. In his mind's eye, Emily peeked over her shoulder at him. Her perfume lingered. His thumb carved the dip of muscle hugging her spine as it swept into the arch of her lower back before flaring into her bottom. He wiped his hands on his pants. Holding the figure with both hands, he pressed his thumbs firmly into the clay to produce the two heat-inspiring dimples that decorated that delicious flare. He imagined kissing her there, feeling the soft warmth of her skin beneath his lips. Slipping his hands over her hips and between her thighs.

Max rubbed the back of his hand over his eyebrows at the realization that kiss would never happen. He'd be lucky if she agreed to finish the bozzetto. He wiped his hands on his thighs, ruining the fine pants of his tuxedo. He didn't care. He must speak to Emily. Even if he couldn't give her an explanation for his actions, he at least owed her an apology.

A feeling of apprehension settled over him. He'd ask her to pose again. The work needed her. Hell, he needed her. Needed her to forgive him for being the biggest ass on the planet. Forgive him enough to come back into the studio and help him finish the work. He needed to put his hands on her again and to try and soothe some of the pain he caused. How to do that he didn't know.

Chapter Twelve

Sunday morning, Emily drank her coffee and shared the newspaper with Trixie. It was another tradition they had stuck with since her father passed away. From the time she could read, her father handed her the funny pages from the front of his thick paper. It always made her feel grown-up reading alongside him.

"What time do you have to be at the country club?" Trixie sat at the kitchen table.

"Eleven."

"Don't let time get away from you. Have you decided what you're wearing?" So much for feeling grown-up.

Emily turned the page. "I'm thinking clothes."

"So funny. You can't wear a tank top and cut-offs to a bridal brunch at the club."

"I know, Ma." She fought the urge to roll her eyes.

Several seconds ticked by on the rooster clock. "Why don't you wear that pretty sundress?"

Emily frowned and lowered the paper. "Sundress? What sundress?"

"The one with the little green and blue flowers." Trixie made a U with her finger. "Scoop neck with cute ruffles on the straps."

"You mean the one I wore in high school? You must be joking."

Her mother lifted her coffee cup and propped both

elbows on the table. "I love that dress on you." She gave Emily a wistful smile.

"The last time I wore that dress, I was sixteen."

"I bet it still fits. I'm sure I saved it."

Em shook her head. She couldn't fight the eye roll anymore. "I bet you did. I'm still not wearing it. I borrowed a teal-colored wrap dress from Suzanne."

"Oh, that sounds lovely." Trixie sipped coffee. "How about we hop over to the shop? I can do your hair. A quick wash and set. A few curlers."

"I've got it, Ma." Emily pushed her mother the rest of the newspaper and went to pour another cup of coffee. Adding milk and sugar to her mug, she leaned against the counter's edge.

She was dreading this bridal shower. Why did she agree to this? After Maximo's rejection the other night, her nerves were still raw. Was that why Jeremy's wedding was starting to feel like another rejection? That was crazy. This had nothing to do with Jeremy and Cynthia and she knew it. This had everything to do with—

"Maximo Vega!"

Coffee sloshed over the rim of Em's cup. Trixie held up the society section. There, front page, in all his glory, Maximo and the grape, Ms. Lavender.

"Would you look at him? God, he's stunning in a tuxedo."

Emily couldn't argue with that. Stunning was the perfect word.

"Did you read this?" Trixie didn't wait for an answer. "Resident artist Maximo Vega surprised opera fans at last night's opening performance of *La Boheme*. Seen here accompanied by his agent, Beverly Lavender of Lavender Blue Art Agency. A source close to the artist revealed the reclusive Vega is planning to step out in grand fashion with his first major show in a decade at the exclusive Bruce Gallery located at Copley Place in Boston. Mr. Vega was reluctant to answer any questions, but details from the offices of Lavender Blue suggest we'll be seeing a lot more of the handsome artist and his amazing works."

A showing? Maximo didn't do showings.

Trixie studied the photograph. "Wow, what a beautiful woman. I love her dress. That slit doesn't leave much to the imagination, but she's got the legs for it." She jumped up and pulled a pair of scissors from the kitchen junk drawer and cut out the article, no doubt to add to her Vega fan scrapbook. "Now that's a handsome couple."

Em's coffee was eating a hole in her stomach. She dumped the rest of the mug into the kitchen sink. "They're not a couple. She's his agent."

"Sure look like a couple to me."

They sure did. Could that be why Maximo stopped the other night? Maybe it had nothing to do with her. Maybe he was trying to be faithful to Beverly Lavender and she had literally fallen into his lap—naked.

****

At the country club, Em tugged at her skirt after she scooted out of her Jeep. She handed her keys to the valet and patted the hood of her Jeep. "Be nice to her, she's a senior citizen."

"Yes, miss."

She entered the Kincaid Room of the Eagle Crest Country Club fashionably late in her borrowed dress and strappy flat sandals. The wrap of the deep teal linen dress allowed her the illusion of curves and much more leg than she was used to showing. She'd opted to keep her hair simple, no spiky mess today. Trixie insisted the straight comb back was classic and sophisticated. Silver hoop earrings were as fancy as she could manage, but the look worked.

Placing her gift among the tower of pink and white wrapped packages, Emily felt like a fool. For the third time in as many days, she second guessed her choice of sterling silver ice tongs for the lucky couple. It was the only thing on the registry list even close to affordable, and it was one of the few things left that hadn't already been purchased. What was Jeremy going to do with silver ice tongs? Knowing him, he'd use them to pull toast out of the toaster and end up electrocuting himself.

A waiter passed by with a tray of what looked like mimosas. Emily grabbed two. The room was packed. There had to be close to a hundred women sitting at a dozen round tables. Low vases overflowed with pale peony blooms and bright tulips. Cynthia and her ladies in waiting sat at a table at the head of the room. Along one side stretched a buffet of quiche and croissants, mini muffins, bowls of fresh fruit, pots of coffee and tea, frothy punch, and a tower of cupcakes frosted in perfect "evening blush" pink icing.

Hanging toward the back of the room, Emily hoped to blend into the wallpaper. She'd drink some fizzy orange juice, swipe a cupcake and sneak out the same way she snuck in.

"M&M!"

Damn. So much for sneaking out. "Jeremy, I didn't expect to see you here. Isn't this strictly a female-only event?"

"Not according to Cyn. I think I'm just here to help load up the haul. Did you get a look at all those presents?"

"I did. Can't wait to see what you think of mine. Just remember, unplug the toaster."

"You bought us a toaster?"

"No, someone beat me to that." She stopped another waiter. "Is there any way I can get the champagne without the OJ?" The waiter shook his head. *Damn.*

"You look great. Aren't you hungry? The food is incredible. Why aren't you sitting with the rest of Cyn's entourage?"

"I just got here."

"I think there's a seat up there for you." He jerked his head toward the bride-to-be.

"I'm great right here."

"Chicken."

"Says the man whose fiancée is wearing his balls on her charm bracelet."

"Come on. They don't bite, except for Cyn's grandmother, Winnie Weatherby. Watch your back. She likes to pinch asses." Jeremy took her elbow. "The other bridesmaids are looking forward to meeting you."

Emily started to argue she was perfectly happy hugging the wall.

"EMILY!" Cynthia spotted her.

Damn again! She leaned close to Jeremy. "If you truly value our friendship, you'll get me something stronger than a mimosa."

Jeremy laughed as Emily was swept into a sea of tall brunette beauties. Did he think she was joking?

Introductions flew. There was no way Em could

remember all the names so she made up her own: Buffy, Muffy, Skipper and Fluffy, Sweetums, Gidget, Mimsie, Poopsie, Flopsie, Mopsie, and Babs. They all wore three-inch heels and towered over her. They practically picked her up on their shoulders and dragged her into their fray. Mimsie just *had* to know where she got her dress. Skipper loved her earrings. Someone asked if her hair was her real color. It was Babs. Em couldn't have stuck out more had she been painted puce.

But Cynthia was sweet and gracious. She parted the sea of bridesmaids and set her at the head table with a plate of delicious-looking food and another mimosa. Well, at least Emily would get the daily dose of vitamin C.

Watching Jeremy and Cynthia unwrap their Everest of gifts, Em couldn't help the tiny pang of jealousy that plucked at her heart. They were over-the-moon happy. It was contagious to everyone around them. This wasn't a couple whose wedding guests were secretly placing bets on how long it would last. This was a pair so obviously in love, you could picture their great grandchildren playing in their yard—the one with the swimming pool.

By the time the last gift was opened and the tower of cupcakes toppled, Emily had lost track of just how many drinks had magically appeared in front of her. Thank goodness she wasn't part of the three-inch heel gang. She'd never have been able to walk across the room.

"Give me your keys." Jeremy slid into the seat beside her.

"I don't have keys. The cutie valet ha-has my

keys." She bumped shoulders with him. "I think he w-wants me. He called me miss."

"Oh, jeez, you're plastered." He moved her plate. It was still full of food she hadn't touched. "Didn't you eat anything?"

"I had a cupcake." She shook her finger at one of his two faces. "It's all your fault."

"Is it?"

"Yes. How come…" She paused. She hadn't meant to pause. What was she saying? Oh, yes, she remembered. She had to start over. "Yes. How come you made me love you when I can't love you anymore?"

"Okay, why don't we get you some coffee and a little fresh air?"

"Why? I don't understand." She lowered her voice, sharing a secret. "I love him too, but I can't love him either, you know?" She shook her head. Her brain sloshed in her skull. "I'm such an idiot. I shoved my hand down the man's pants!" Did she say that as loud as it sounded?

Several guest turned to stare.

She whispered again, "What was he supposed to do?"

"Who's pants? Em, I have no idea what you're talking about. Let me get you home."

"I can't go home. Trixie will know I'm naked."

"I guarantee you'll still be dressed when I get you there." He slipped an arm through her elbow and helped her stand. "You never could hold your liquor. How much did you drink?"

"Whoa, not so fast, cowboy." She leaned into him. "I need to say good-bye to your beautiful bride and thank her for a love-lovely time."

"I'll tell her."

"Will you?" Emily put her chin on his arm and looked into his pretty eyes. "You're so nice. She's nice too. I want to hate her, you know, because I can't love you anymore, but I can't, she's too damn..." She flipped her hand back and forth. What was another word for nice? She couldn't think of one. Wait, "good" was like nice. "She's too damn good! And pretty. And sweet. She's very sweet." How had they gotten outside?

Jeremy poured her into the passenger seat of his pickup and buckled her in. She rolled down the window and rested her head on the shoulder strap of her seat belt. "I think I drank too much orange juice." She closed her eyes and took great gulps of air.

"I think you're right." He pulled the truck onto the main road heading back into Stoddard.

"It was a nice shower."

"Having never been to one before, I'll take your word for it."

"It was. You got a ton of beautiful things. Great cupcakes." The air felt good rushing past her cheeks. Her head was starting to clear.

It was quiet in the truck as they rode past the golf course. Em closed her eyes. Jeremy's voice started her. "I'll tell Cynthia this was a bad idea."

"What? What's a bad idea? The cupcakes?"

He glanced in her direction. "No, you. We forced you into agreeing to be in the wedding, and it's obvious you're having a problem with it."

"No. Wait. What?"

Jeremy pulled the truck over to the side of the road and parked. "You never drink like this, Em. Are you going to sit there and tell me you're fine with this? And all that 'you love me but can't love me' stuff? What's that about?"

"Whoa." She sat up. "Hold on."

"I know you, Em. I swear I can read your mind. I understand you still love me. I still love you too, I always will, but I'm not *in* love with you. If you have those kinds of feelings for me, it would be cruel to make you be a part of the wedding. I thought you were over me."

All she could do was gape at him. "You know those moments when you're really really drunk and something happens to sober you up in one hell of a hurry. This is one of those times." She punched him. "Jack ass!"

"Ow!" He grabbed his arm. "Why'd you hit me?"

"'Cause you're being stupid."

"I'm trying to be nice."

"Don't!"

"Why are you yelling?"

"'Cause you're still being stupid."

"Aaaahh!" He slapped the steering wheel. "What the hell is going on with you? Tell me, 'cause I'm obviously too dumb to figure it out."

She glanced at him sideways and he glared at her.

"And I swear, if you say 'nothing,' I'm kicking your mimosa-ed ass out of this truck and you can walk home."

Emily unbuckled her seat belt. Putting her face in her hands, she doubled over. "Aaaahh!" She mumbled into her hands. "I can't talk to you about this."

"That's bullshit. We can talk about anything."

Images of Max filtered through her head. Running

her fingertips through the crisp, black hair on his chiseled chest. Feeling the rasp of his beard against her chin. The rush of warm breath against the side of her neck. The stunning picture he made in his tuxedo and the way he stared at her across the studio. Him leaving with Beverly, and her heart crumbling in her chest. Seeing their picture in this morning's newspaper bothered her more than she ever imagined.

"Not this." She lifted her head. "Please don't push it, okay? And please, get it out of your head I'm upset about being in this wedding because I still have 'those' kinds of feelings for you. I don't. I love you. I think you and Cynthia are going to be blissfully happy, and I'm thrilled about that. I sat there and watched you both today. What you two have is the real deal. Yes, I'm a tiny bit jealous, but not of her. Of what you have, you idiot. I'd give my right arm for a guy to look at me the way you look at her." She shot him a glare. "And if you say 'don't worry, you'll find someone too,' I'll kick my own mimosa-ed ass out of this damn truck and walk home."

She rubbed her forehead. "I'm sorry I drank too much. I was nervous about meeting everyone. I was way out of my element there. I don't exactly fit in with Cynthia's friends."

"You fit in fine."

Em shook her head. "They're all so tall and gorgeous." *Just like Beverly Lavender.*

"You're twice the woman they are, and I think you're beautiful."

"Dammit, Jeremy! Don't you dare make me cry. I can't be that drunken crying girl that's in every ladies' room every Saturday night in every bar I've ever been

119

in." She bit the inside of her lip and sighed. "Thank you for thinking I'm beautiful. I'm sorry I yelled at you."

"And punched me."

"I'm not sorry about that."

Chapter Thirteen

Monday morning Maximo was waiting for Dante to arrive. He'd spent the past two days combing over his contract with Lavender Blue Art Agency, feeling more and more trapped. His only distraction had been the hours spent in the studio.

Working on Emily's figure, however, he turned that anger and frustration on himself. As a result, the piece suffered. He had to step away from the work. Try as he might to hold onto the images of the pose in his mind, he couldn't erase the rest. His body still reacted to the memory of her in his arms. The heat. The passion. Even now the ache in his pants made him want to scream. But it was the look of hurt and disbelief on her face when he told her to leave that continued to haunt him.

Max was sitting behind Dante's desk reading through the impenetrable contract one more time, when Dante arrived.

He came up short at the sight of him. "Maximo."

"Get me out of this." Max held up the crushed contract in a fist.

"What the hell happened this weekend?" Dante raised a newspaper.

Max narrowed his eyes. "What's that?"

"You haven't seen it? You're all over the society page." Dante opened the paper and held it for him to see. "*You* held a press conference? And it says here you're booked into a show?"

"There will be no show. Find me a way out." Max threw the crushed pages.

"There's a termination clause. I read it."

"Oh, there's one. Page six. Says, *mutually agreed.* She won't agree. Told me she'd sue me for everything I'm worth if I tried. I can't work with her. I won't."

"What?" Dante sifted through the crush of pages and read. The frown on his face turned into a scowl. "I must have read this too fast. The wording is very misleading."

"Exactly."

"She won't get away with this. I have a lawyer who owes me a favor." Dante scanned another page. "Let me see if there's anything we can do."

A knock on the door interrupted them. Crystal LeMar poked her head in. "Sorry to bother you." She handed Dante a plaster penis. "Baskins has struck again."

****

"It was loose?" Emily chewed at her thumbnail.

"I highly doubt that." Dante rubbed a hand over his eyes.

Emily sat in his office. The detached penis lay on the desk. "I can fix it and would have if I had my drill. It was too big to glue. It needs pegged reinforcement. I mean, look at the size of it."

Dante groaned. "That's not the point, Ms. Baskins. The point is Crystal LeMar is extremely unhappy. Do you have any idea what that's like?"

"Sadly, I do."

"And for some reason I fail to comprehend,

Maximo is adamant about me not firing you. Here I sit, stuck in the middle, with a damn penis on my desk." He flicked at the white phallus with the end of his pen like it might bite him.

Emily reached over and grabbed the offending member. "I can fix it. Don't you worry. I'll handle Crystal. She loves me deep down. She just doesn't know it."

"Ms. Baskins…"

"I know this looks bad, but this is a piece of cake. You'll see. I'll have this little guy back where he belongs before lunch. Even his urologist will never know it was missing." She used the penis to emphasize her words.

"Don't point that thing at me, please."

"Oh, sorry." She slipped it under her arm.

"Fine, fine. Whatever. Just fix it." He flipped his hand sweeping her out of his office. "Oh, and stop by and speak to Vega on your way to casting."

"W-what? Why?"

"Maybe it's to name you intern of the month."

****

Emily stood at the opening to Maximo's space. She stared at the penis in her hand. *Isn't this why I left here last time?* She held her breath and stepped inside.

Maximo looked like the first time she met him with a dust cloth tied to his head, wearing his long leather apron. Stunning. He was busy sharpening the tip of a chisel. Em let out the breath she was holding.

His eyes met hers. "Emily."

The way his lips caressed her name made her want to weep. Her nerves caused her to fiddle with her hands. Maximo's gaze lowered. The corner of his mouth lifted.

Heat blazed into her cheeks as she realized she was fumbling with the plaster cock. Her ears got hot.

She whipped it behind her back and studied the dusty toes of his boots. "You wanted to speak to me?"

"*Si.*"

"Dante said you won't let him fire me."

"*Si.*"

"Why?"

"I need you."

Emily's eyes shot to his. Dust danced in a shaft of light that fell behind him. "I don't understand. I thought—"

"We are not finished." He twisted the chisel in his hand.

Emily imagined it tangling and twirling in her heart.

"The work, she is *incompiuto*, incomplete."

Em opened her mouth to speak, but she had no words. Maximo turned away from her to replace his tool in its proper space. The wall of his back barred her from any emotions she might have read on his face.

He picked up the next chisel in the row. "You will return tonight."

It wasn't a question. It wasn't an explanation. It wasn't an apology. He didn't turn back to her. Her fingers gripped the penis so hard her hand ached. She couldn't do this anymore. He couldn't issue orders and expect her to…to what? Act like nothing had happened between them? Return to baring her body and pretend she had thought of anything else but his lips on hers since he sent her away? No, she had more pride than that. No. This was cruel. She should tell him no. Demand an explanation.

The breadth of his shoulders looked like a stone wall. If she hurled the penis at him, it would shatter into dust. What could she do? Quit? Walk away from everything? Walk away from him?

No.

"Seven o'clock."

The words struck her like a cold fist. He *was* the devil. If he had a heart, it was lifeless, cold and hard like the plaster in her hands, and yet he had captured hers. Devil or not there was no escaping the rush of feelings she had whenever she was near him. She'd be back. At seven, sharp.

Entering the casting room, Crystal was on her as soon as she walked in. "Two. Baskins, that's two strikes. I've never seen an intern crash and burn quite so fast. You should be proud."

Emily maneuvered past the Great Wall of Crystal. "I can fix it." She set the penis to one side and slipped on the dust mask. Em grabbed her goggles. This wasn't like reattaching the pinkie, however. Given the size of the appendage in question, Emily would need to reinforce the repair with a peg, which meant drilling a pilot hole in each piece. She grabbed a power drill. "Don't worry, Fred won't feel a thing."

Crystal stood shaking her head studying the torso. "You must be loads of fun on a date. Maybe we should start a eunuch support group?"

Ignoring Crystal's jibes, she crouched in front of the statue and started to drill a loud, dusty hole in the figure's crotch. The drill bit screeched through the plaster. Off to the right, two men from the mixing team visibly winced and made protective grabs for their privates.

Crystal snorted behind her. "I'm almost gonna miss you when you're gone."

While the repair to Fred was setting, Emily escaped the barrage of penis jokes and new nicknames Crystal was delighting in trying out. "Cock-block" Baskins seemed to be a favorite among her and rest of the crew, or C.B. for short. It was going to be a special day.

She took out her frustration on twenty-five pounds of new clay that needed to be wedged and prepped in her space. Kneading the clay like bread dough, she was able to block out everything else. The aroma of moist clay filled her senses as it softened and warmed beneath her hands. Closing her eyes, the chore was almost hypnotic. As her hands worked each section of clay, her mind focused on another pair of hands.

All her life, Emily had noticed people's hands. She loved them. They told her so much about a person's life and work. Her first sculpture was of her father's hands. Of course, Maximo had amazing hands. Strong, rough and scarred from years of molding clay and carving stone, but when he touched her…ran his hands over her skin…cupped her breasts, they were warm and oh so gentle.

Setting a work base, Emily used the freshly wedged clay to create a small piece capturing the strength of Max's hands. His chisel and mallet carving a heart from a chest.

She worked straight through the rainy afternoon. At ten minutes to seven, showered and changed, she struggled with the ties of the only other robe she owned. Yes, she'd been unnerved the other night, but she'd kicked herself more than once for throwing away her red silk wrap.

The one she wore was supposed to resemble silk; however, the thin, white slippery material was cheap acrylic. Shangri-La Spa was printed in a swirly, hot pink logo over her left breast. It had been a free gift from a day spa near her school in Chicago. She and her roommates had splurged on a girl's day just before she left. It was much too big and the belt refused to stay tied. Em pulled it as tight as she could. Nerves made her stomach flop in her belly like a dying fish.

Slipping into Maximo's work space, she padded silently past him to the dais. She sensed the moment he caught notice of her, and her heart skidded in her chest. Heat washed over her skin as her emotions played ping-pong within her sense of reason. She was here to work—nothing more. Two more sessions and the bozzetto would be finished and all this would fade into a memory. A memory that would no doubt tease and haunt her for the rest of her life.

Neither of them spoke. The room held its breath. So did she.

Assuming they were picking up where they left off—before she'd become a naked pretzel in his arms—she tossed the robe aside and placed her back to him. Hand raised, fist to chest, weight on the front leg, she froze.

His shadow came up behind her and she flinched. He hadn't touched her. Not that it mattered. She could already feel his hands on her.

He blew out a breath. "Turn your hips more to the right. Not too far. Back. There. Good, good." His voice sounded low and graveled.

His music was off. Surely he heard her heart thudding against her ribs. The fist she held to her chest was so tightly clenched, her nails bit into her palm.

"Drop the shoulders," he clipped.

"Sorry."

"Don't be sorry. Relax."

Telling her to relax only made her tense up more. She tipped her head from side to side to loosen her neck and arched her back a bit to stretch. A tool dropped behind her.

It was too quiet. Where was his music? Should she say something? Discuss something benign, safe? Like politics, religion, world peace? "I saw your picture in the paper."

"*Si.*"

"Did you enjoy the opera?"

"No." His voice had a sharp edge.

"Oh." The word fell into the conversational abyss. The silence gaped. "Congratulations on your showing."

Another tool dropped, "*Grazie.*"

"Sounds like Ms. Lavender has plans to keep you busy."

"Don't speak."

"Sorry."

He huffed behind her. "Just be still. *Per favore.* Please."

She froze, but she still wasn't positioned right. She tried to loosen her shoulders. Maximo muttered something under his breath. It sounded like a curse. She cursed herself and stiffened again.

"You're hips are not straight. Arch the back more."

Her body ached with a tension that made every adjustment feel strained and unnatural.

After a few more agonizing minutes, Maximo growled, "Stop. Enough."

She straightened, crossed her arms over her chest, and jerked her head to peer over one shoulder.

"Your back looks made of wood. You're too rigid. What is wrong with you?" He threw a wad of clay back into the bin and pulled the covering back over the piece. "It's no good. It's over. Get dressed."

"But—"

"No! The mood is ruined." Passing her, he pitched his tools into the wash sink with a clatter. Then bent and picked up her robe from the floor and tossed it at her.

Nausea rolled over her. Tears pricked the backs of her eyes. She would not cry. She wouldn't give him the satisfaction.

The arm to her robe was inside out and she struggled in frustration and building humiliation to wrestle into the sleeve. If this was the price she needed to pay to be here, to be with him, the price was too high.

"I'm done. Find"—her arm punched through the end of the sleeve—"another model. Someone else. Not me."

The door of the studio slammed shut behind her. Well, now she'd done it. Bet there was no question of being fired at this point. Good-bye internship. Good-bye degree. Good-bye career. Dante was right. She hadn't lasted two weeks. That wasn't what was causing the pain in her chest, however. The bitter edge of Maximo's words cut her. He'd rejected her again. She didn't understand, but refused to keep throwing her emotions into a grinder.

Emily shivered. Cold realization joined the drenching rain that poured down upon her as she reached her Jeep. *Dammit!* Her clothes, but, more importantly, her car keys were still in her locker.

She thumped a fist on the hood and hung her head. Water dripped off the tips of her hair. There was no way she was going back in there. She was desperate enough to consider unsnapping the cloth roof and trying to remember what Elliot, that odd metal sculptor she'd known in Chicago, taught her about hot wiring a car.

Her soaked robe clung to her and the thin fabric had started to resemble cellophane. Through chattering teeth, she cursed herself again. Scrapping her last shred of dignity off the pavement, Em spun on her heel to head back inside.

Maximo. He stood a few feet away. His dark eyes captured hers beneath the watery lights illuminating the parking lot. "I'm sorry."

She swallowed the sudden lump in her throat.

He held his hands out from his sides and shook his head. "I'm a selfish *bastardo*." He stepped closer and ran his gaze down the length of her.

Emily didn't have to look to know her robe had turned transparent.

"Come back inside. You must be freezing."

Emily closed her eyes. She couldn't watch the rain plaster his shirt to the hard curves of his chest. She couldn't lose control of her emotions again. Water ran into the open neck of her robe.

"I can't do this." When her words met silence, she opened her eyes and met his gaze. "I don't know what you want from me. I don't know how to act when I'm with you. Part of me is so…so star struck by being in your presence, I end up acting like some goofy teenager with a crush. I'm so grateful to be here working on my art. Thankful for any opportunity to watch *you* work. To learn from you. But then…" She shook her head and dropped her gaze.

"Then?"

Emily raised her eyes to the bow of his mouth. "I kissed you and you kissed me back. Maybe it was nothing to you, but I was stupid enough to think it meant something. That you wanted me. If only for a moment. The way you touched me." She studied the middle of his broad chest. God help her, she couldn't meet his eyes. Here she was as bare and naked as she could possibly be, body and soul. If he rejected her now, at least she'd know why. Wasn't it better to know than play this endless guessing game?

She wiped the rain off her face. "I can't think of anything else but that night and how much I wanted to be with you. I replay it over and over in my mind, trying to figure out what happened, trying to understand why you pushed me away. If you're involved with someone else—"

"No." He'd stepped closer. His voice reached out to her through the rain. The single word touched her heart.

Emily made the mistake of looking into his eyes. The intensity she found there stopped time. The hush of the rain falling cocooned them. She clutched the front of her robe. "If there's no one else, then it must be you don't want me. Now I really feel like an idiot. I must have believed something that wasn't there."

Maximo closed the distance between them. He grabbed the tops of her arms and pulled her to him. His lips met hers in a crush. Emily whimpered as his tongue plunged hungrily into her mouth. Heated passion radiated off his body and she shivered as it engulfed her.

He pushed her back against the side of the Jeep. One strong leg slid between her knees as he pinned her to the vehicle. Cold rain water wicked through the thin fabric of her robe to chill her back, while the searing heat of his body pressed into her front.

Shoving his hand into her hair, he captured the back of her head and deepened his kiss. Em held tight to fistfuls of damp shirt along his sides, pulling him closer, crushing her chest to his. He broke the kiss to heat a pathway down the side of her neck. He murmured something along the delicate skin beneath her ear. It didn't sound Italian. She wished she knew what he said. Did he want her as much as she wanted him? All was forgotten in an instant when he sucked at the lobe of her ear.

Emily gasped, lifted her face to the kiss of the rain while Maximo licked and nipped his way to her shoulder. Impatient hands pushed the clinging fabric of her robe aside to knead her breast. When his fingers teased the firm tip of her nipple, she cried out and arched into the rush of pleasure that coursed through her.

"Oh, V—"

His mouth silenced hers with another fiery kiss. "Max," he whispered into her mouth. "I'm just Max."

"Max," she sighed. "Oh, Max, please don't stop."

He wrapped a strong arm around her and lifted her off her feet. Holding the back of her head, he moved toward the building while delivering a kiss that needed no translation.

Emily wound an arm around his neck and

murmured against his lips. "Where are you taking me?"

"To my bed."

Chapter Fourteen

They were both breathless by the time Max reached the second floor and carried her into his darkened bedroom. He'd peeled away the tissue of sodden fabric she called a robe and dropped it somewhere along the way. With her naked in his arms, the pressure in his pants made him groan. It had been close to a year since he'd been with anyone. If he didn't take her soon...

He laid Emily on the bed, kicked off his boots and stripped out of his clinging shirt and jeans. The only light spilled in from the lamp in the living room, but it was enough to help him find the condoms buried in the top dresser drawer. Ripping one from its foiled pouch, he unrolled it over the hard length of him.

Gentle hands soothed over the bunched muscles of his back. He hadn't heard Emily cross the room. She laid a kiss there and slipped her hands around to slowly caress his chest. Her fingers raked through the crisp hair. He still had his penis in his hand and gave it a squeeze, praying he wouldn't come too soon.

"*Bella...*" She sighed against his damp skin.

Oh dear God. He gave his rock-hard cock another squeeze. Max lifted and kissed her fingers.

He turned in her arms. "Men are not beautiful."

"You are." Her hands skimmed his stomach. "You're a work of art." When her fingers closed over

134

his penis, he held his breath.

"Easy," he teased, "I'd still like that attached when we're through." He grinned.

Her mouth dropped open in amused surprise and he took advantage of that parting to kiss her back into his bed. He pulled the thick comforter across their bodies and settled over her. The combination of their heat quickly warmed the space. The sweet smell of rain-washed skin and her faint flowered scent filled his senses.

A smile touched her lips. "Perhaps I shouldn't touch you. I am a klutz. I'm liable to break all sorts of things." Her smile faded. "Are you fragile, Maximo Vega?"

"Only the heart." He brushed her mouth with his. Their breath danced. "Will you break my heart, Emily Baskins?"

Their voices were muffled beneath the covers. She stroked his cheek and met his gaze in the dim light. "I'll try not to." Her thumb brushed his lower lip. "Will you break mine?"

"Yes." On this he couldn't lie. Even risking the passion building between them, he couldn't take her without some sliver of the truth. He couldn't give her anything more. He owed her nothing less.

Feather light fingertips grazed his lips. "I know," she whispered.

Her words reached in to squeeze at his heart. He'd been wrong. It wasn't an air of innocence that drew him to her like the clichéd moth to a flame, it was her honesty. There was no guile behind those clear sage eyes. No illusions of what this night would mean tomorrow. It was her. Wanting him. Here. Now.

Emily ran her hand into his hair and pulled him to her for a shattering kiss. One beautiful leg lifted to slide a silky thigh along his hip. She opened herself to him, welcoming him in, offering him everything.

He fought the urge to drive into her and satisfy his blinding need, but in that moment, he wanted nothing more than to love her as she should be loved.

Max lowered his head and ran his tongue over the tightened rosebud of her nipple. When he drew it between his lips and sucked, she sighed and ran her fingers into his hair, holding him to her. His hand grasped at her curves and drew her wet heat closer.

She arched. A small whimper escaped her throat. The hand holding his head moved to tug at his shoulder. Her knee pressed open. Her hips lifted.

Shifting to one side, Max skimmed her inner thigh with his fingertips until he reached the trimmed strip of soft hair between her legs. He teased that pale pathway before laying his palm against her sex. The heat and pulse there filled his palm. He watched her face. He didn't move, just held his hand still.

He loved the feel of her. Warm satiny skin caressed his fingers. For too long he'd created visions in cold stone and clay. He'd forgotten the heady pleasure of holding a flesh-and-blood woman in his arms. *This* flesh and blood woman. He wanted to savor every moment.

Emily opened her eyes to look at him in question. Her chest rose and fell in short pants. Her nails bit into his arm. Moaning, she closed her eyes and pressed into his hand, urging him, begging him. "Please…"

He bent a single finger, running it between the slick folds, making her cry out. She trembled beside him, still clutching his arm. Her other hand knotted the sheets. A second finger joined his first, stroking and teasing before sliding inside her. Her sheath throbbed. A low moan slipped from her as she rocked her hips upward.

The rush to his cock was almost too much to bear, but he wasn't finished with her yet. Her wetness bathed his fingers. She was more than ready, but he wanted to prolong her pleasure...and his. Her response only strengthened his resolve. He slowed the press and sweep of his touches and kissed her panting mouth.

"Oh, God. She ground her hips against his hand. When he dipped his head to tease her breasts with his tongue, she writhed and pulled him atop her. "Please, now!"

Cradled in the heat between her thighs, he ceased to think. Forgotten was the slow building fire. The flame had flashed into an inferno. Emily wrapped her legs around his waist and her nails clawed at his back. His heart was pounding out of his chest, as he drove into her tightness.

She gasped out his name and clung to him, matching his strength and rhythm as if they'd been lovers forever. He quickened their dance. Sweat broke out on his brow. The muscles in his arms tightened as he held himself from crushing her. He plunged into her faster and faster. Driving deeper with every thrust. Stronger. Harder.

Beneath him, Emily screamed as a powerful orgasm lifted her. The tremors within her rocketed his body into a world-shattering climax. Clinging to one another, they rode the waves of each other's pleasure higher as he ground his body into hers until the tremors began to still and they both fell back to earth.

Later, with their breathing returning to normal, he tucked Emily along his side. She curled around him, her body beginning where his ended. A languid hand teased the hair on his chest before making a slow sweep over his stomach to grasp his penis with her hand.

"Oh, thank God," she sighed. "It's still attached." She kissed his shoulder. "Yay." She smiled against his skin.

Max did something then that surprised and delighted him almost as much as the passionate woman in his arms. He laughed.

****

Silky sheets slipped over her skin. Emily loved the sensuous feel. The soft sound of distant music reached her ears, and she didn't have to roll over to know the bed was empty. What time was it? She stretched. A delicious ache thrummed between her thighs as she remembered their lovemaking. Maximo had been incredible. Three times, incredible. Emily hadn't believed it could get any better than their first time, but she had been wrong.

They hadn't yet caught their breath when she made the quip about his penis, and the next thing she'd known, he was slipping on another condom and pulling her on top. He lowered her onto his thick length and proceeded to send her into orbit again. He had magic fingers and what he could do with his tongue… Wetness pulsed from her core at the thought. Her whole body tingled with need.

She slipped from his bed. A thick, lush robe sat folded at the foot. Max's. It wrapped her in warm black terry cloth and surrounded her with his scent. Emily pushed the wide collar around her ears and drew his spiced smell deep into her lungs.

A small clock next to the bed read 4:12. The music was coming from somewhere below. Maximo must be working. She padded through the sleek living room decorated in black, grays and chrome. Clean lines and sharp edges. The floors were bare except for a thick area rug that resembled a dark, curly sheepskin.

Past a darkened kitchen, light came from a door left ajar. The music was louder. Opening the door, she was back in the studio's cavernous space. A set of stairs led to Max's private lair. She pulled his robe tighter and let the music carry her down the steps.

He was working on the bozzetto. Her breath caught in her throat at the beauty of him. He wore only faded jeans, which rode low on his hips. The muscles of his arms and back flexed as he worked. His feet were bare, dark stubble covered his jaw and his hair was a tousled mess. A dark curl fell across his forehead. Classical Italian music crested around her as she watched him pause to wipe his hands across his demined ass. *Oh. My.*

He turned as if he knew she was there and smiled. If she thought the image of Maximo Vega in a tuxedo was stunning, the sight of the man smiling was her undoing. Air left her lungs in a whoosh. She reached out and grabbed the edge of the workbench before her knees failed.

"Did I wake you?" He moved toward her.

She shook her head. Heat flooded her cheeks. Parts of her turned liquid.

With the tip of a clay-stained finger, he lifted her chin so he could kiss her. The music swirled around them as he slipped his tongue into her mouth. Emily laid a hand on his chest to steady herself. The dark hair tickled her palm.

Max didn't pull her to him. He didn't push her against the wall. He didn't even wrap his arms around her, yet the tenderness of his lips upon hers, the gentle sweep of his tongue against hers made her tremble with a need so fierce it forced a whimper from her throat.

He whispered against her lips. "I can't stop thinking of you."

"Welcome to my world." She smiled. "I think of you all the time. I've started humming Italian music in the shower." She closed her eyes and let the music weave its spell. "It's beautiful."

"It's Andrea Bocelli."

"He has an amazing voice." She played with the hair on his chest. "But, I bet he doesn't kiss like you."

Emily ran a hand up to the hand holding her chin. She wanted to guide it toward the tie of the robe and past the lush fabric to find a breast. She wanted him to take her in his arms and crush her chest to his. Feel his skin against hers. Feel his hands on her. Only a robe and a pair of jeans were between her and what she truly wanted.

"Last night was wonderful," she breathed.

"*Si*, it was perfect. I still taste you on my tongue. Smell the sweetness of your skin. It was just what the work needed."

Wait. Work? Did he say work?

He kissed the backs of her fingers and released his hold. "I can feel you now in the clay. The heat of your body. The play of your muscles. Your passion. I captured it and put it into the piece. You are my inspiration. *La mia ispirazione. La mia musa.*"

"Your muse?" Warring emotions skittered through her. After the night they'd spent in each other's arms, was he telling her she was nothing more than work to him?

He was smiling at her and then kissed her forehead and stepped back to his clay. "The work is good now." He turned the piece toward her. "*Si?*"

Her heart sat like a lump of his clay in her chest. "It's lovely." And she was a lovely idiot.

Maximo smoothed a hand over the figure's calf, into the slender narrowing of the ankle. His masterful hands created the bone of the joint in a few short manipulations. Had Emily not been so stunned by his dismissal, she would have marveled at his technique.

He paused to glance at her. "It's almost morning. Dante will arrive soon. You should go."

"Right. I need to get home."

"*Si*. But you'll come back. We finish tonight."

Emily pressed her lips together and nodded. Finish. Dear God, yes, let's finish this. The pull and tug of this insane emotional dance with him was tearing her to shreds.

The cold concrete of the studio floor radiated up through her feet and wrapped its chill around her chest as she walked to the model's lockers for her things. Behind her, the music grew louder. Maximo Vega's lyrical drawbridge had been raised.

Standing in the same place she'd stood the night before, she pulled her car keys from a pocket and stared at them. The rain had stopped leaving everything to sparkle in the first light of morning. The sun was streaking pinks and golds across a freshly scrubbed sky.

Would she ever be able to start her damn car without remembering last night? She really was an idiot. What had she expected? That one amazing night of sex with her and Maximo Vega would fall under her spell and love her forever?

Maybe this was what he did. Had he lied to her about sleeping with his interns and models? Perhaps this was how he treated them all. What made her think she was any different? Oh, God, Crystal LeMar might be right. Was she just one of his "chippies"?

Em slipped into the driver's seat of the Jeep. She closed her eyes as she inserted the key in the ignition and turned. An ache wrung out her heart. Putting it in gear, the Jeep splashed through last night's puddles on the way out of the parking lot. Another car pulled sharply in front of her. It startled her and had her slamming on the brakes. *Come on, Em, pay attention before you get in an accident.* She waved the other car on. It wasn't until it passed her that realization hit. *Dante.*

Chapter Fifteen

He was a real shit. Last night he only wanted to apologize for the way he treated her, but standing there in the rain with Emily in her see-through robe, hearing her want him in spite of everything, in spite of him, he'd lost his all-important control. What was he thinking? That was the problem—he wasn't thinking. He'd lost his mind.

Her response to his kisses and the little whimper of surrender she made when he touched her had evaporated his resolve. The way she held him, giving him as much pleasure as he tried to give her. No, he'd never regret taking her to his bed. Max's bed. What he regretted with all his heart was his urgent need to distance her once again from Maximo Vega before she saw him for the lying bastard he was, before he hurt her any more.

Max stared at the clay statuette. It was brilliant. *Maximo* had done it again. He'd captured all her honest passion in the figure. The pleading. The desperate desire. It was all there. It was his best work, and it took all his self-control not to hurl the piece across the room. Would the fame and fortune after the world saw this piece be worth the price of his heart? Was it worth *her* heart?

He needed one more night to finish the work and make sure Emily was safely outside his circle of deceit.

He'd protect her from caring too much. He'd put an end to it all tonight, no matter the ache that decision brought to his heart. Better to lose her now than watch her come to hate him.

The studio door slammed. Probably Dante. Max ignored it and kept working. The music turned off suddenly.

"I'm working." Max didn't turn around.

"And I'll let you get back to it as soon as you explain to me what the hell you think you're doing!" Dante's voice reached an octave it rarely saw. "Tell me that wasn't Emily Baskins I just saw pulling out of here in the same Jeep I noticed here last week. Tell me she isn't the new model you were so secretive about."

Max said nothing but turned and revealed the face of the bozzetto.

"Son of a bitch!" Dante looked from the statue to Max. His hand swept his view of Max's lack of clothing. "You slept with her!"

Max wouldn't deny it, but he wasn't about to discuss it with him. "That's none of your damn business."

"Like hell it isn't! I know she's a gifted artist, but the girl's a walking disaster area." He paused a second, then added, "Does she know?"

"Of course she doesn't know. I've got it all under control," Max lied.

"Doesn't look like it from where I'm standing. You have too much riding on this, Max. Let me get rid of her before she screws everything up." Dante rubbed the spot between his eyebrows. "She should have been gone last week."

"I told you, it's under control. I'm dealing with it."

"Emily Baskins?" Dante shook his head. "I don't get it. Why now? Why her? You've had hoards of women who'd do anything to get into your bed, and nothing. But 'Penis Buster' Baskins? I've had a perpetual headache since the day she arrived."

"Enough. You won't talk about her like that. She's better than both of us combined."

Dante was examining the bozzetto. Shaking his head, he gestured to the piece. "You may be hopeless when picking woman, but you're still the consummate artist. She's incredible. You've outdone yourself on this one. It's exquisite." He cocked an eyebrow at Max. "Maybe you should sleep with more of your models."

"One thing has nothing to do with the other."

"If you say so." Beyond the curtain, the door slammed again, followed by the voices of other studio workers arriving for the day.

They exchanged a quick glance.

"You'll say nothing." Max pointed a dirty finger at Dante.

"Don't I keep all your secrets?" Dante lowered his voice to a whisper.

"I mean to her."

"You don't have to worry about me." Dante raised a hand.

"Good." Max dropped a burnishing tool into his wash sink. A tiny sense of relief settled some of the tension in his shoulders. He could trust Dante. The man was as loyal as a St. Bernard and had just as much to lose as he did.

Max dried his hands and pushed his fingers through his hair. "So, what did you find out about my contract with Beverly Lavender?"

"You're not going to like it. My lawyer friend says unless a tornado drops a house on her or she agrees to the dissolution, she has you locked in for the next twelve months, solid. She has complete authority to book appearances, press conferences and events on your behalf with or without your consent, as long as she can state the booking was done to improve your standing in the art community and enhance your career."

"Doesn't mean I have to show up."

"She's going to be tough to ignore. She called six times yesterday. I don't know how far I'd risk pushing her." Dante shrugged. "She's aggressive. Could be good for your career."

"Not if she digs too deep. She could ruin everything. This could turn into an absolute nightmare. If it's true I'm locked into this deal, it's going to be a long year of trying to keep her contained."

"I'll do what I can from this end, but sounds like from what the attorney says you'd better play nice or she'll sue your ass quicker than it takes her nail polish to dry."

"When have I ever played nice? Maybe she'll decide I'm too much to handle."

****

By three that afternoon, Beverly Lavender had increased her messages to an even dozen. She might have him in a bullet-proof contract, but she didn't own him. He'd get back to her when and if he chose.

Maximo was leaving Dante's office with her latest messages balled in his fist. Before he could file them in the nearest trash bin, the door to the studio slammed open and the woman marched in his direction.

Damn! He headed in the opposite direction.

"Maximo!"

"I'm busy." He continued to show her his back as he moved toward his private area.

"We need to talk." Her heels clicked on the cement floor like a bulldog chasing a mailman down a sidewalk.

"Make an appointment."

Her hand clutched at his arm and tugged him to a stop. She was quick to move in front of him to block his escape. "Stop." She put a palm on his chest. "I know you're upset."

He plucked her hand off and crossed his arms.

Beverly lifted both hands in surrender. "Things got off to a bad start. I take full responsibility for that. But you have to understand, I did it for your own good."

He released a string of carefully chosen Italian expletives. "My own good?"

"Yes." She mirrored his stance. "You hired me—"

"Now, I fire you!" He pushed past her.

She called to his back. "You can't fire me, and you know it."

He wasn't listening.

"Just give me a chance. I'm great at what I do. I can make us both millionaires."

He spun around at her. "By turning me into one of the *animali dello zoo*!" He threw up his hands. "Do I look the *elefante*?"

"I don't speak Italian." She pursed her lips.

"Elephant, elephant! I'm not a trained animal you can shove a brush up my trunk and force me to work!" His raised voice echoed. Work around the studio stopped as workers stared toward the heated exchange.

Beverly gasped and planted her hands on her hips. "We *never* force Babu to work! He loves to paint. And I'll have you know, thanks to me, he pulled in six figures last year for the wildlife reserve in San Diego."

They glared at one another. Beverly gave a little huff and put her hands into some meditation pose, palms up with her thumb and index finger touching. She drew in a deep breath and let it out slowly. "Om…" She continued in a quieter tone, "Listen to me. It doesn't have to be this hard. Let me help you."

"I don't want your help."

Her calm was short-lived. She jammed her hands onto her hips again. "No," she snapped, "what you don't want, is me as an enemy. We have a solid contract, and I won't be bullied into submission, not even by the great Maximo Vega. I'm good at what I do. I can get you and your work the attention it deserves. You signed the papers. You've already given me the authority. If you'd only cooperate with me."

"You know nothing about me or my work." He shook his head and turned away.

"So you're not the least bit interested in the fact I secured you an exclusive premier showing at the Bruce?"

That stopped him. The Bruce Gallery in Boston was a prestigious one. The owner and director, Daniel Bruce ruled the art scene in the northeast. He had six other galleries scattered all over the country, with strong connections overseas and a wealthy worldwide clientele.

"Three weeks, Boston, four weeks, New York, three weeks, San Francisco. First-class travel accommodations, full transportation, promotion, and exclusive invitation-only black-tie opening in each city, the works."

He turned back. "I don't believe you."

Her perfectly shaped eyebrows reached for her hairline. "Why do you think I've been calling you every hour on the hour? Daniel Bruce loves you. Says he's been trying to get you into his galleries for the last two years. He's willing to give us anything we ask for. Whatever we want. You want plaid orchids from Istanbul at every opening, you've got them. Anything you could ever want or need."

She lifted her ridiculous purple briefcase and patted its side. "I have the initial paperwork outlining his proposal right here for your approval."

Behind Beverly, Max caught sight of Emily coming into the studio. Her pale hair was the spiky mess he remembered from her first day. A backpack hung from one shoulder. The baseball jersey, jeans and heavy boots screamed college intern, but he knew better. He saw beyond it all to the passionate woman beneath. The soft swell of blushed lips he had spent the night kissing. The faint smudges beneath her eyes that told him she hadn't gone home to sleep. The falter in her step when her eyes met his. He noticed all that, too.

Emily held his gaze for one slow-motion stride before looking to the floor and hurrying past them. When he glanced back at a now-silent Beverly, her eyes were drilling smoking holes into Emily's back. "What was that?"

"What was what?"

She turned her glare on him. "Don't be obtuse. I caught the way you stared at her. What exactly was that?"

"*That* was none of your business."

"Wrong. *You* are my business." She narrowed her eyes and pursed her lips. "Now I remember. She's the student. The intern from Stoddard. What's going on with you and her?"

"*Arresto*. Drop it."

Beverly's eyes bore into his before shifting back to Emily and back to him. "Fine. I'll drop it, on one condition. You give me twenty minutes to go over this paperwork with you and you stop fighting me."

"I don't respond to ultimatums."

"I'm not giving you an ultimatum. I'm giving you a brilliant future. Twenty minutes. I'm not beyond begging."

"Then you'll leave me in peace?"

"For today."

Chapter Sixteen

Emily was beyond exhausted. She'd gone home and managed to get past Trixie without raising any alarms. The shop opened early on Tuesdays and Em didn't have any classes at the school, so Trixie always let her sleep in.

Sleeping in would have been a fine idea, but it only proved to be a torture test. Lying in bed, Em tossed and turned. Every time she closed her eyes, images of her night with Maximo flickered past like some X-rated flip book. Her body ached in all the right places, but so did her heart. *His muse?* Was that all last night meant to him? She should be flattered. Right? The great Maximo Vega needed her to create one of his masterpieces? Would the art history books one day link her name with his? Would her lovemaking be credited with inspiring the master sculptor? And after he'd cast her aside, would she end up in an insane asylum like Rodin's mistress and muse, Camille Claude? Didn't the woman die stark raving mad in the floods of Paris surrounded by cats?

At least as Emily ran the four-minute mile wrestling with the covers in her bed, she came to a conclusion. She was foolish to not have trusted her initial instincts. Last night, while being the most amazing sex she'd ever had, it was also the biggest mistake she'd ever made. She had to end it. Tonight.

She'd just explain to Maximo that…that…What? That he was the most amazing lover, but she was over him? Thanks for the best night of my life, but I've decided to join a convent?

By the time she arrived at the studio, she'd decided it didn't matter how she said it or what words she used. She couldn't let things continue. Then she saw him talking to Beverly Lavender. Emily tripped and fell heart-first into the deep well of his eyes. From halfway across the room, the caress of his gaze reached her.

He flustered her so much, she raced through the studio and forgot the door to the locker room was a "pull" not a "push." She damn near broke her arm when she hit it at full stride. *Son of a biscuit!* No. Stop. She was stronger than this. Where was her self-respect? She would *not* fall for him. Not anymore. It had to end before he shredded her heart into party confetti. She'd be fine just as long as she didn't look at him.

Emily rubbed her elbow as she slipped into her work space. Crystal was nowhere to be seen. At least that was a blessing. However, standing in her space was her latest assignment. A simple bust of a beautiful woman. Attached was a note. "No fingers or peckers on this one, Baskins. Try to keep her head on!"

"Very funny."

Emily's phone vibrated in the rear pocket of her jeans. Caller ID told her it was the bridal shop. No doubt they were calling to schedule her final fitting. The wedding was in four days. Her ugly pink shoes must have come back from being dyed. She let the call go over to voice mail. It was too loud in the casting room to talk and, to be honest, if Emily had to think about the wedding right now, this poor bust's head might not stay on her shoulders. Pulling out her sanding block and mask, she began to work.

Miracle of miracles, by the end of her shift, not only had Emily not "loosened" any parts of the bust, but her resolve had held fast as well. Losing herself in the work often had the power to calm her. Shutting out the din of the casting room and concentrating on the job cleared her mind and eased some of her anxiety.

But later, as she worked on her exhibit piece, she struggled to get the features of the figure's hip just right, her stress peaked again. Max, deadlines, and this damn wedding. How much could one person take? One at a time, she could deal with them, but when they started stacking up like snow in February, she felt overwhelmed.

When seven arrived, Em was changed and ready. She was ready to let Max down easy by ending it as gracefully as she could. *Maximo, while last night was very special to me, I think we should end this physical attraction we seem to be developing for one another and remember we need to behave in a more professional manner. I care about you but don't feel this attraction will serve either of us in the long term.* Simple, kind, yet straight to the point.

The studio was quiet when she slipped into Maximo's area. No music played. Only a handful of lights burned. The space was cleaned. The dais cleared. His tools were hung and everything was neat. He wasn't there.

What was there, was the bozzetto. Finished. It stood drying in the middle of a spotless worktable. The piece was done. He hadn't needed the last session after all. Tears pricked the backs of her eyes as she looked over the statue. The anguish on the beautifully formed face mirrored the sudden ache in her heart. He'd captured her to perfection. The sweep of her body showcased his mastery. In clay, the work was magnificent. In stone, it would be breathtaking.

Emily swiped at an angry tear. She looked up the stairs to Maximo's closed apartment door. Well, this was what she wanted, wasn't it? He'd done her a favor. She hadn't needed to practice her carefully chosen words to end it. He had without uttering a single syllable. So why wasn't she relieved? Why wasn't she dancing for joy?

Because she loved him. Realization punched the air from her lungs. Dear God, she was *in* love with him. From the first moment he held her hands and asked if she was cold. She couldn't deny it. Even as the reality of his empty studio threw her heart under a speeding bus, she couldn't lie to herself any more. He'd told her he'd break her heart. At least he didn't lie.

She dropped onto a stool and tucked her chin into the neck of her robe. His robe. The smell of him stung her. *Oh God.* She shut her eyes against the sting.

"Emily?"

Gasping, she sat up. Maximo was coming toward her with a bottle of wine and two glasses. She turned away to wipe the wetness from her cheeks.

"I wanted to get word to you that you didn't need to pose tonight, but I've been fighting a lavender witch for the past hour. The woman drives me *completamente pazzo*. Crazy. Tonight was to be for relaxing." He lifted the bottle. "We celebrate the work, *si*? She is done."

She stood and tightened the ties of the robe. "I'll go change."

"Nonsense. It's fine." He held his arms wide. He wore a pair of black denim jeans and a blue button-down shirt with its cuffs rolled back off his forearms. It fit him like a dream. "We're dressing casual."

"It'll only take a minute. I feel foolish in your bathrobe." She couldn't meet his eyes. If she could just get past him and take a moment to pull herself together.

Maximo put the wine down and caught her as she tried to get by. "Are you crying?"

"No."

He tipped her chin and she had no choice but to look at him. "You are. Tell me why."

She pulled away from him and struggled to come up with a believable answer. She flipped a hand toward the bozzetto before crossing her arms over her chest. "It's the piece. It…it is so…brilliant. It makes me weep to imagine its beauty in marble."

He gave her a hard stare.

"Pour the wine. I need to toast your incredible talent."

As he pulled the cork, the studio phone rang in Dante's office. The muscle in Max's jaw jumped. "Let us drink to anything other than my talent."

Emily took the glass he offered. "Okay. Maybe we should drink to making mistakes?"

"Mistakes?" He frowned.

"Yes. About last night." She studied the center of his chest. The third button down on his pale blue shirt to be exact. It was a good button. "I mean, it was wonderful and…beyond amazing, but I can't help feeling like it was a mistake. I wasn't thinking straight, and I've been under a lot of stress lately, and we…I think we both got carried away with the passion of the work, and it didn't have anything to do with you and me."

"It *was* a mistake."

Emily kept rambling, "If I'm going to continue to work here, I can't…" She met his gaze. "Did you just say it *was* a mistake?"

Maximo emptied his wineglass in a single swallow and poured himself another. "*Si.* I agree with you."

Emily followed his lead and drank. The rich fruity wine warmed a path into her belly. "Wow. Great. I'm happy you feel the same way."

"We were caught up in the moment."

"Yes. Exactly." She took another sip of her wine. "I can't tell you how relieved I am."

"No, it is I who am relieved. It wasn't my intention to hurt you." He motioned to the bozzetto. "Sometimes the inspiration is too great. The passion and the emotion, too *grande*. It spills over."

Emily finished her glass and Maximo was quick to refill it. As he turned away, she raised her glass and muttered to herself, "Here's to spillage."

"*Pardone?*"

"Nothing." She raised her glass once more. "Great wine."

The office phone rang again. Maximo slammed the bottle down and a flood of Italian burst forth.

Emily caught at least one curse word in the rush. "Do you need to answer that?"

"No! I'm tempted to throw the damn phone into the parking lot. I've already spoken to her four times since she left here today. Enough is enough."

"The lavender witch?"

"The woman, she is relentless." He rubbed at the

back of his neck and took another strong drink of his wine.

Emily found the remote and filled the space with his music. The phone's ring could barely be heard. "Forget her."

"I wish I could." He sat on the stool and tipped his head from one side to the other.

"Don't let her ruin your celebration. It's a night to relax, remember?" She set her empty glass on the worktable and moved behind him. "Here, I can help." She smoothed her hands over the muscles of his shoulders. The tension rippled beneath her fingertips. "I'm an expert at neck massages. I used to give them to my father all the time. That was another lifetime ago, but I still remember how."

He sighed and tipped his head forward. "That feels good."

"Try to let it go." Emily kneaded at the bunched knots in his muscles. She hated feeling his stress. "Drop your shoulders. Try to relax."

"Mmmmmm…"

The wine on an empty stomach was doing more than softening the edges. Emily pulled a deep breath to clear her head. *God, he smelled good.* Too good.

She swept her thumbs along the thick muscles between his shoulder blades trying to forget the way they felt beneath her hands last night. "Wouldn't it be great if we could forget?" Damn, she said that out loud.

"Forget?"

Again Emily scrambled to explain herself. "I mean, just for a little while. You know, forget you're Maximo Vega. I'll forget I'm bridesmaid number six. Forget it all. No pressure, agents, deadlines. No expectations. No needing to be anything for anyone. Prove anything. Be anything. We could just be us."

"If only it could be that easy."

Em finished her massage, smoothed the fabric of his shirt over his shoulders and stepped away from him. Every cell in her body wanted to strip the shirt off him and feel his bare skin, lay with him again. But the one thing she *had* to remember was that loving Maximo would only get her hurt. She needed to leave before her common sense was the only thing she did forget. "The wine is starting to make me poetic, and I'm a lousy poet. I should go."

Maximo stood and caught her arm. "Wait. Please, don't go." The music swelled around them. His dark eyes captured hers before his gaze lowered to her mouth. "Forgetting who we are for a time," His hand stroked her arm, "may make it simpler to put aside the pressure and the stress of our lives, but there are things I never want to forget." He slipped his hand behind her neck and drew her in for a tender kiss. Emily tasted the wine on his tongue as it slipped between her lips and his mouth slanted over hers, deepening the kiss. A whimper whispered from her throat. She sighed against his kisses.

He pulled away and cupped her face in his palm. "Emily, I need to be honest with you. I've tried to tell you—"

Emily placed her fingertips on his lips and shook her head. "Please don't. I know your feelings. You've already said it quite well. Last night was a huge mistake. We're a mistake. I should listen."

But she couldn't listen. His gentle kisses had shattered her fragile resolve. She didn't want to hear him dismiss what was happening between them. She wouldn't deny it to herself again. She wanted him, if only for one more night. She was beyond caring about what was right or wrong. She needed him. Needed to feel the brush of his hands on her skin. Lose herself in his touch.

"I'm the one who needs to be honest. I lied to you just now. Last night...how I felt when I was in your arms. How could that have been a mistake? I've spent the entire day trying to convince myself it was. Trying to make myself believe I don't care what happens. I lied to both of us. I do care." Trembling, she stood before him and took the biggest risk she'd ever taken. She untied his robe. "How can my wanting you like this *ever* be a mistake?" She let the robe slide to the floor.

Chapter Seventeen

"Emily…" Her named slipped from his lips.

She reached to stroke his face and ran her fingertips along his mouth. "When you look at me, even the way you speak my name, makes me feel like the sexiest woman alive. I can relax and be bold and get lost in every moment." She shrugged and shook her head. "I'm not the girl who left this town years ago. I grew up, but no one sees the real me, except you. You see the artist. You see the woman. I see her in *your* eyes." She looked at the bozzetto. "I am that woman."

"They must be blind and stupid not to see how amazing you are." His hand held her face as he kissed her. "As stupid as an artist who would try to convince you that you are nothing more than his muse." The gentle kiss was quick to flare into an inferno. His strong hands swept over her, grasping and pulling her tight against him. He lifted her off her feet and moved toward the stairs.

Emily quivered with a burning need to feel his skin next to hers. When they came to the stairs, he set her down. She stood a step taller than he and relished the new height. Her clumsy fingers worked at the buttons of his shirt as he kissed her up each stair. Pulling its hem from his pants, she ran her hands inside his open shirt, over his chest and into his waistband. The metal button beneath her fingers slipped from its hole.

Max grasped at her hips and swept his hands up her back. He was at the perfect height to have his fill of her breasts. Her fingers caught in his hair as he drew each tightened nipple into his mouth. Her heart pounded. Adrenaline and pure heat pulsed through her. He blazed a trail lower over her stomach to tease her navel with his tongue before moving even lower.

His roughhewn hand caressed her from shoulder to hip as he moved to press a kiss against her aching sex. She hung on to fistfuls of his shirt for balance. As his tongue swept over her hot flesh, her knees threatened to give way.

"Oh, God." She clutched at his hair, his shoulder, feeling a desperate desire to have him take her right there on the stairs.

Strong fingers raked up the inside of her thigh, pressing her knee wider.

"Max…"

When he slipped two of those fingers into her, fireworks exploded through her limbs.

"Max!" She grabbed for the handrail to keep from tumbling down the steps.

Growling, Max scooped her into his arms, rushed them up the remaining stairs and pushed through the doorway into the apartment. Pinning her against the wall, his deep kisses left her breathless. Everywhere he touched added to the flames that threatened to consume her.

Emily wrestled the shirt from him and slid an impatient hand back into his jeans. When her fingers closed around his hard length, a heavy gasp released from him.

She insisted between hungry kisses. "We're not a

Lisa A. Olech

mistake. Never say it again."

Dark eyes bore into hers. His chest heaved beneath her hands. Emily trembled at the sudden intensity of him, at the relentless pull to wrap herself around him and not let go, and at the explosion of love she had for him at that very moment.

He crushed her mouth with his. His body strained against hers. "I promise. Never again."

****

For Emily, the next two days felt like she'd been wrapped in a cotton-candy cloud of rainbow-sprinkled bliss. Tuesday night's passion had continued well into Wednesday. She and Max had made love in his studio, on the island in the kitchen and on the curly living room rug. There had been no more talk of mistakes and truths. Given the fact they couldn't keep their hands off one another, there hadn't been much talking at all. His kisses left her breathless. She began to wonder if Max was secretly a trumpet player.

Wednesday evening arrived, and Emily was working on her exhibit piece. It was late. Everyone had left for the day. She removed the original form behind the ribboned image and was finishing edges and adding the final details to make the piece shine.

Crystal LeMar stopped by and watched Em work for a few minutes on her way out. "You know, I hate to admit this, but you're not half bad."

Emily did a quick double-take to see if she was joking. She wasn't. "Wow, that almost sounded like half a compliment."

"It was, C.B. Don't let it go to your head."

After Crystal left, the studio around Emily got quiet, except for the calming lilt of Max's music

162

filtering over from his area. She hadn't seen him since she left his bed early that morning, but she felt surrounded by him all day.

He'd told her he wanted to work on another piece and if the music was any indication, he'd been hard at it all day. Somehow the two of them working so intently on their own projects, honoring each other's space and work, filled her with immense joy. She couldn't wait to finish and see what he'd done today.

With a damp sponge, she smoothed an edge of the wide clay ribbon and worked on the section that crossed over the hip of the figure. She had overworked the area and still wasn't happy with the illusion of muscle there. Adding more clay, she tried again, stepped back and frowned. It still didn't look right. She planted one muddied hand on her hip and tipped her head.

It was then she caught sight of him out of the corner of her eye. Max stood watching her. He was in low-slung jeans and a sigh-inspiring black T-shirt, covered in clay with a day's growth of beard. He looked sexier than should be allowed by law.

"Hi." Emily held up her filthy hands and pulled at the hem of her mucked top. "We make quite the pair."

"Can you take a quick break? I want to show you something." Max held out his hand.

Emily glanced back at her piece. "I might as well. I'm not making much progress here."

"I won't take you away for long, and then maybe I can help."

"I'd love that." Emily slipped her dirty hand in his.

Max led her back to his space and she was blown away by what she saw. He'd created another piece with her likeness. Smaller than the bozzetto, this one was of her reclining. Her knees raised with her toes pointed. Her upper half was propped on her elbows with her head tipped back. The line of her throat rose into the peak of her breasts and spilled into the belly of the pose. The deep arching curve of her back swept into the rounded dip of her hips capturing a flowing sensuality that was visually stunning.

"This is how you see me?" She breathed.

"Yes." He cupped her cheek with a clay-smeared hand and kissed her before moving to the piece. He turned the base on its turntable, showing her each side. "She's drying, so some of the detail is muted, but I'm happy with it. Do you like her?"

"Of course I like her. Every time I think your work can't get any better, you show me how wrong I am. It's amazing. I love it."

"Good." He kissed the top of her shoulder and gave her a quick squeeze. "Come. You have work to finish. Then I will bring you upstairs and find us some food."

"You might have to eat without me. I have to finish this exhibit piece tonight, and I can't get this one section the way I want."

"Show me. I will try to help."

Back on her side of the studio, she turned the piece so he could see the area giving her a difficult time. "Here. Over the hip, where the muscle drops into the lower abdomen in that classic V-shape."

"The iliac furrow."

"Yes, that's it. Because of the visual break, I'm not getting the right angle or shape." Emily pulled some photographs off the worktable. "I've studied my reference photos, but I'm still not getting it."

"It's also called the Adonis belt." Max pulled his

shirt over his head and pointed to the area on his body. "Here."

Emily sucked in a breath. "Yes, that would be exactly what we're talking about."

"Photographs are good for some things, but they don't replace real flesh and bone." He stood next to her sculpture. "Now, I model for you."

Having him next to the piece was helpful, but him being so close, in only his jeans, was making it difficult to think. Her hands trembled as she gathered her tools and reworked the angle of the muscle. She added more clay along the furrow she was creating and blended it with wet fingers.

"Give me your hand." His dark eyes held hers. When she hesitated, he shook his head. "Come. Give it to me." He didn't wait but grasped her wrist and placed her hand, still slick with clay, along his hip.

Did the temperature in the room just rise twenty degrees? Emily gasped as he slid her hand over his hard body.

"Do you feel that?" He unfastened his jeans and lowered one side. "Close your eyes. Use your sense of touch. Can you feel the play of the muscle beneath the skin?"

Sense of touch? What should she do with her other senses currently on overload? She could smell his skin, the earthiness of wet clay. Her heart pounded, blood rushed in her ears, and his music filled the room. Her tongue traced her lip. She still tasted his kiss. Even with her eyes closed, she pictured him in complete detail. She opened her eyes and smiled. "Are you trying to help me or seduce me?"

He slid her hand lower. Her fingertips grazed the

length of his erection. "Which do you think?" Max grabbed her other wrist and tugged her against him. Her hands smeared his chest with clay before winding around the back of his neck. "All day creating my new sculpture, I've had my hands on your body, smoothing your skin, caressing your curves." His lips brushed hers. "Now I want your hands on me."

She shook her head. "How is this helping me?"

"You will see. Art is passion. *Your* passion. Seduction. Don't be afraid to infuse it into the work. Make love to the piece. Give it a soul."

Max led her back to the clay and encouraged her to paint him with slip. "Feel the heat of my skin coming through the clay? You must feel the same heat from your piece. Forget the angles, forget the photographs. Close your eyes. Feel it with your hands."

Emily moved back to her statue. Max stood behind her and lifted the shirt from her body. Slick hands ran cool, fluid clay up the overheated skin of her back and circled her waist. The sensation was erotic. Closing her eyes, she let him guide her hands to the figure's hip. Remembering the feel of Max, she smoothed and caressed the clay into the play of the muscles.

Behind her, he breathed into her ear, "Yes, that's it. Are you feeling me?"

"Oh, God, yes." Her fingertips tingled as she stroked the clay like a lover.

"That's right. Yes. Just like that." He kissed the top of her head. Slippery fingers teased the underside of her breast. "Perfect. Open your eyes." He pulled her back against the wall of his chest and kissed her neck. "You did it."

Emily gasped. The figure *was* perfect. It looked

brilliant. She sharpened the ragged edge of the ribbon and spun in his arms. Emily crushed her mouth to his. Relief and gratitude added to her desire. Her passion for him was spinning out of control. Wet, creamy clay from his chest stained hers. The sensation of his slick skin against hers pushed her need over the edge. "I want you now!"

"Yes. Now."

Emily left his embrace only long enough to rid herself of her ruined jeans and help him find the extra condom he'd luckily picked up this morning from the living room floor and shoved into his pants pocket. While he rolled the thin latex sheath over his erection, Emily gathered up even more clay slip and coated the strong span of his shoulders. She gasp as he spun around and decorated her as well. Clay plastered his hair where she clutched a handful as his mouth crushed hers. Dirt covered the side of his throat where she lay a line of kisses. The taste of clay in her mouth didn't slow her building heat.

Fingered smears raked up her thigh as Max lifted her and urged her to wrap her lubricious legs around his waist. He entered her in one impatient thrust. Backing her against the wall, he drove into her deep and hard. Over and over, until she bit against his shoulder to stifle the scream of her powerful release. Emily hung on tight until his body shuddered around hers in a fierce climax of his own.

With a satisfied moan, he lowered them both to the floor and cradled her in his arms. The clay on their bodies whitened as it dried. When she was able to breathe at a normal pace again, Emily was horrified by the state of the studio. Clay was everywhere. All over the floor, on the wall, on them. Her project was unharmed. It was perfect, but the workspace was a disaster.

"We've made one hell of a mess."

He kissed her hair and tipped her chin to place another on her lips. "No," he smiled, "we just made magic."

Scooping her up in his arms, Max carried her upstairs to his shower where he cleaned them both. Afterward, they picnicked on the rug in the living room, eating whatever they could find in his sparse kitchen, drinking wine, and talking.

Aside from the fact their lovemaking had reached epic levels, beyond the fact she could think of nothing other than him, Emily was coming to love spending time here in his apartment. She relaxed here. She could breathe here. No frills or overstuffed bookcases. Not a rooster in sight. It was decorated much like the man who lived here. Sleek and uncluttered. Hard lines and sharp contrasts. The more she came to know him, the more he continued to surprise her.

While he insisted on taking care of their mess in the studio, Emily stumbled upon *Fame*. She gave a little gasp of surprise discovering Maximo's most famous statue tucked in a corner of the living room. It stood on a polished black pedestal behind a sprawling houseplant. It wasn't the full-sized piece, but rather the original mock-up of the woman bound and gagged and blindfolded. The figure evoked strong feelings in Emily each time she saw it, but somehow, seeing it here, being able to reach out and touch it, increased those feelings tenfold.

Max stood behind her. So engrossed in admiring

Fame, she hadn't heard him come back upstairs. He handed her a glass of wine.

"This has always been my favorite piece of yours. It's so powerful. So emotional. Part of me feels her screams."

"She can't scream. She's been silenced."

"Yes, but she must be screaming in her mind. The idea of being totally out of control of your destiny. Blind to what's to come. Helpless. Unable to escape. I can feel her panic." Emily reached out and touched the piece. "I want to tear at the ropes holding her."

"That is the irony. She wants the ropes. She tied them herself."

Emily slipped an arm about his waist and laid her head on his chest. "But she couldn't have known they would strip away her soul. That's why she's screaming."

Max tightened his hold on her and kissed the top of her head. "You are beautiful, talented and wise." He stroked her cheek with the edge of his thumb. "Will you stay?"

She could stay just like this forever. Wrapped in his arms, feeling the strong beat of his heart beneath her cheek. Part of her wanted to rush out and tell the world she was in love with him, yet she respected his need for privacy. She understood the binds of success, so she was content to stay cocooned in this moment with him. The rest of the world could fall away. "I'll have to go home sometime, but not tonight."

****

"Hey, stranger." Trixie came into the sunny kitchen just as the rooster crowed seven o'clock. Emily was finishing her breakfast.

"Hey, Ma."

"I feel like I haven't seen you since Sunday. You've been getting in later and later."

Emily brushed crumbs from her fingertips. "I've been busy at work." It wasn't a lie.

Trixie poured coffee and popped bread in the toaster. "It's not good to burn the candle at both ends. You have a hectic weekend coming up."

Em scribbled some notes. "I know. I've been sitting here thinking of all I have to do. I need to get over to the school and turn in my final term piece today. I have my last fitting this afternoon and I still need to find something to wear to the damn bridal breakfast. I want to stop at the studio later." She'd only left Max an hour ago, but she missed him already.

"Well, make sure you wear something you can strip out of easily."

Emily shot her mother a look. "To the studio?"

"No, silly, to the bridal breakfast. You're all due at the salon for hair and makeup afterward, and you don't want anything you'll have to pull over your head. Are you sure you don't want me to book you in for a spray tan? Most of the bridesmaids are coming in tonight."

"Positive. I always end up turning orange. Not the look I'm going for next to pink satin. Besides, I can't fit one more thing into my schedule." *Not if I want to spend time with Max before the weekend.* "In fact, I have to get to school." Emily grabbed her keys and pushed her notes into her backpack before swinging it on to her shoulder.

"Your father always used to say, 'No rest for the wicked.'"

If you only knew. "Bye, Ma."

Chapter Eighteen

Emily wheeled her piece into the professor's exhibition hall. Several artists had already set up their end-of-term works and the display held some interesting projects. Next week Stoddard would open their doors to the public for their summer exhibit to showcase all their talents.

Her figure was titled *Steel Ribbon,* and she was still amazed at how it turned out. Max was right. Now it screamed passion. She would never look at it again without remembering how that level of passion came to be. It gave a whole new meaning to mud wrestling.

Em had spent the last three hours burnishing the exterior of the clay to a rich gloss, without the use of a fired glaze. She was pleased with the softer effect. The negative open space between the swath of muscled detail created a unique play of light throughout the piece. She and Max had made magic. She'd given it a soul.

After the weeks of frustration in her studio at home, her work was back on track. It was all thanks to Maximo. His studio inspired her. He inspired her, and to have him appreciate her work was the icing on the cake…or the clay on the wall. Both were incredible.

"There you are," Maddie called from the doorway. "I thought I'd find you in here."

"And here I am." Em was dusting the heavy stone

anchoring her piece. "What do you think?"

"Wow." Madeline crossed her arms and tipped her head to one side. "I love this one a lot. You had me worried there for a while. Your work wasn't showing the same spark I'd seen in your earlier pieces. Nice to see you back in top form, especially in light of this morning's phone call."

Emily turned the sculpture half an inch to the left. *Perfect.* "I'm sorry. What did you say?"

"I received a call from an art agent who's interested in talking to you about possible representation. She's planning to stop by sometime today and was hoping to catch you."

"She? Does this agent have a name?" Emily had a sneaky suspicion she already knew.

Madeline read from a sticky note stuck to her sleeve. "She's the owner of Lavender Blue Art Agency, Beverly Lavender."

"Did I hear someone call my name?"

Both Madeline and Emily spun toward the door. Emily tried unsuccessfully to stifle a groan. Maddie shot her a horrified stare before welcoming their visitor.

"Ms. Lavender? I'm Madeline Sullivan. We spoke earlier." She pumped Beverly's hand with a bit too much enthusiasm.

Beverly took the first opportunity to snatch her hand away and pasted a bemused smile upon her painted lips. "A pleasure, Ms. Sullivan." She glanced about the room. "You've some impressive students here, Ms. Baskins included."

"We do, indeed. If you have some time, I'd love to show you around. We—"

Beverly stopped her with a hand and a quick shake

of her head. "I wish I could, but I'm terribly busy today. Perhaps we might schedule a tour for another time. In fact, I'm wondering if I might steal Ms. Baskins away. Is there somewhere private could talk?"

"Certainly." Maddie peeked over her shoulder at Emily. "You're finished here, right? Why don't you take Ms. Lavender into the lounge, where you'll both be more comfortable."

Crossing her arms and leaning a shoulder against the wall, Em shook her head. "I doubt Ms. Lavender will be staying long. I'm comfortable right here."

"Emily—" Maddie hissed.

Beverly's smile never wavered, yet Emily caught the brief frown before she returned to her honey-coated conversation with Madeline. "Ms. Baskins is right. I'm sure our chat won't take too long. Here is fine." She flashed Maddie a hundred-watt smile. "Would you excuse us?"

"Yes, of course." She shot Emily one final, *What the hell is wrong with you?* glare before she left.

Beverly watched her go.

Emily pushed off the wall and returned to dusting the base of her sculpture. "I'm guessing this has nothing to do with representing me."

"You know, Emily—may I call you Emily?" She stepped closer. "I've underestimated you. You're a lot smarter than I first gave you credit." Her hand swept the display. "And much more talented than I initially believed."

Em huffed a small laugh, examined the toe of her shoe, and took her time meeting Ms. Lavender's icy gaze. "This has nothing to do with my brains or my talent. Why don't you cut to the chase? This is about my relationship with Maximo."

The hundred-watt smile was back. "See, you are intelligent."

"May I ask how the hell you found out? I'm sure Max didn't tell you."

Beverly tipped her head. "Well, I had my suspicions, of course, but you've just confirmed it for me."

Emily's jaw tightened. "My relationship is my business."

"Not when it involves my client."

"Fine. You know." Emily planted her hands on her hips. "That makes no difference to the situation. What Maximo and I have is a private matter."

Beverly gave a small laugh. "There are no private matters with public figures."

She could see where Beverly Lavender drove Max crazy. Smugness oozed off her like a purple fog. She had a comeback for everything and a plastic smile that was starting to get on Emily's nerves.

"Listen, I don't want to get off on the wrong foot with you. If it's true, and you care for Maximo, then we're on the same team. I'm his agent. All I want is what's best for him."

"Let me guess. You don't believe I'm what's best for him."

"I didn't say that."

Emily tried to ignore the condescending tone. "No, you didn't have to. Just your being here says it all."

Beverly paused, tipped her head and steepled her fingertips in front of her chest. "Try to understand, Emily, Maximo is on the threshold of becoming one of the most important artists of this century. Are you really so selfish you would put your dreams of fame and glory ahead of his?"

"What are you talking about?"

"I appreciate where you're standing, I do. You're a young artist struggling to get ahead. He's successful and respected. It's the oldest career move in the book. Hell, you wouldn't be the first woman to try and sleep her way to the top."

Emily's jaw dropped with a gasp. She'd never been so close to wanting to slap someone off their high heels. "We're done now. You can leave."

"I'm giving you an easy out, here. I'll even help you. You agree to leave Maximo gracefully, and I'll see to it all your...*efforts* haven't been wasted." She air quoted the word. "I'll do everything in my power to further your career. I'm thinking perhaps a local artist's cooperative and maybe some small showings to begin with—"

"I said we're done." Emily didn't wait for her to move. She grabbed her bag. She was out of there.

Beverly sidestepped to block Emily's exit. "You're only going to hold him back, don't you see that? I thought you cared about him. You'll end up dragging him down and damaging his future, and he'll come to resent you for it. This relationship will only stand in his way. Is that what you want?"

"What I want is to get out of here." Emily pushed past her.

"Don't be foolish. I'm giving you a very generous offer."

Emily called over her shoulder. "Screw your offer."

"How can you be so blind? Do you honestly

believe you're special? That you're the only one? Get your head out of the clouds. He sleeps with them all, you silly girl."

Emily didn't break stride although she felt the punch of Beverly's words.

"Go ahead. Ask him. But don't be surprised if he denies it. It's what he does."

Emily was running by the time she hit the parking lot and jumped behind the wheel of her Jeep. *"Don't be surprised if he denies it."* She felt ill as she turned the key in the ignition. She headed toward Vega Studio, but halfway there, she pulled over to the side of the road. What was she thinking? She couldn't confront Maximo. He'd think she didn't trust him. Did she trust him? Yes, but...

The past week had been like living on a fault line. The ground kept shifting under her feet. Things had just started to be amazing these last few nights. Max was wonderful. There was no way she was going to let Beverly Lavender throw things over a cliff again.

She dug her phone out of her bag and punched in Jeremy's number.

"Yeah."

"Jeremy?"

"Hey, M&M, can't talk. What's up?"

Several men congratulated someone on a nice shot in the background. "Where are you?"

"I'm on the eighth hole getting my ass kicked."

"What?"

"I'm at the country club with Cynthia's father and two of her uncles. We're having some male bonding thing. After I get my ass dragged around for another ten holes, they tell me we're going to have a steam." He hissed into the phone. "Doesn't that mean we're all going to sit around naked?"

Em chewed on her thumbnail. "I have no idea." Jeremy wasn't going to be able to talk her down off her ledge. He was up to his butt in in-laws.

"Hey, gotta go. I have to find my ball. And no smart mouth from you." He spoke to someone with him. "No, mine ended up in the rough." He whispered into the phone. "I'll call you back later, okay? You all right?"

Emily closed her eyes and fought to keep from bursting into tears. "Yeah, everything's just ducky. Don't worry about it. I'll see you tomorrow at the rehearsal."

The Senior Center shuttle bus parked in front of Trixie's Pixies made Emily groan. It was the first Thursday of the month when the residents of the Happy Trails Home were there to get their hair done. Trixie offered a group discount and, as a result, the place was always packed.

The scent of permanent solution was thick in the air as she pushed through the doors. Every dryer was in use, and all the chairs were full. The waiting area overflowed with walkers and wheelchairs.

Suzanne was in the middle of giving Mrs. Cleaver a blue rinse while Angel teased the top of Ms. Folsom's bob.

"Mr. Dawson!" Bridget's voice rose. "Hands *over* the cape, you naughty boy!" As Em passed, Bridget hissed at him, "And if you grab my ass once more, I'll shave half your damn head, you little pervert! Now, behave yourself!"

Trixie was in her corner. The elderly gentleman in her chair looked like he might have expired somewhere between shampoo and the chair. His eyes were closed, but Trixie was still talking to him as she cut his snow white hair. As Emily moved closer, she realized Trixie had headphones on.

"*Mi scusi signore, potreste dirmi dove trovare il bagno più vicino?*" She tipped her head, nodded. "*Il mio portafoglio è stato rubato! Dove posso trovare un agente di polizia?*"

Emily waited until Trixie's scissors paused to tap her on the shoulder. "Ma, what the hell are you doing?"

"Oh, hey, sweetie." She pulled off the headphones. "I didn't expect to see you. Did you change your mind about the spray tan?"

"No, Ma, I wanted to talk…never mind. This place is crazy."

Trixie shrugged. "First Thursday."

"I realized when I saw the bus. What are you listening to?"

"Language tapes. I found some at the library. I'm learning Italian. Listen to this." She stopped cutting and pointed with her scissors. "*Il mio portafoglio è stato rubato! Dove posso trovare un agente di polizia?* That means, 'My wallet has been stolen. Where can I find a police officer?'"

"What kind of tapes did you get?" The man in Trixie's chair hadn't moved. "And…is your client dead?"

Trixie laughed. "Of course not." As soon as she said it, she got an odd expression on her face and rushed to put her hand mirror under the man's nose. The glass steamed and she gave a small smile. "He's just asleep. I'm multitasking." She pointed to her headphones. "Lesson three, common Italian phrases while traveling. I can already say please and thank you, hello and good-bye any time of the day, tell you my name, and count to one hundred, and I know all my colors. I was going to surprise you."

"You never cease to surprise me." The permanent solution was starting to make her nauseous. "I'm sorry I forgot what day it was. I'll get out of your way."

"You could come back later. The Happy Trails bus leaves at four and the bridesmaids don't start arriving until six thirty. We could have dinner together. We're ordering Chinese."

"I've got to work."

Trixie rubbed Em's arm. "Try to make it an early night. You're looking a little worn around the edges, sweetie."

"Thanks, Ma. Just what I needed to hear."

The warmth of the afternoon brought some blessed fresh air as she left the salon. Emily took a minute to unzip all the windows in the Jeep. Why had she even stopped here? Because she need to talk to someone and Jeremy was off chasing his balls and, well, sometimes you just wanted to talk to your mother. Emily rubbed her forehead. She obviously wasn't thinking clearly. What would she have said to her? "Oh, by the way, Ma, I'm having a torrid affair with Maximo Vega, and I'm afraid I'm ruining his life as well as my career. But I've fallen in love with him. Could you pass the moo shoo pork?"

It wasn't as if she could run to Max and tattle like a five-year-old and demand he proclaim his fidelity. Beverly Lavender was a certified bitch, but she was only looking out for his best interest. Maybe she had a point. The last thing Emily wanted was to stand in Maximo's way.

Why did everything have to be so damn complicated?

A huge black pickup with dark tinted windows and off-road tires tore into the parking lot. Joe Turner, Trixie's creepy client, climbed out of the cab and strutted into the salon like he owned the place. Did his mustache need a touch-up so soon? Maybe he was here to get his back waxed. Em shuddered.

As if on cue, her cell phone started to play the *Looney Tune* theme. It was the ring tone she'd picked for Cynthia. Realization dawned on her as she read the time on the phone. *Dammit!* She was late for her fitting!

Chapter Nineteen

Max swung into Dante's office to check on a piece of marble he'd ordered from the quarry. He wanted to carve the second piece he'd done of Emily in a soft pink marble.

The last few days and nights with her had been unbelievable. Never had a woman inspired him as much or satisfied him so completely. Each new facet of her only made him want to know more about her. He was a man obsessed.

She surprised him at every turn. One minute she was the frenzied sprite racing past at ninety miles an hour, the next she was the most passionate, generous lover he'd ever had. Shy and gentle one moment, bold and uninhibited the next. She also shared his enthusiasm for the work. He admired her dedication and fierce talent.

And she was funny! When was the last time a woman made him laugh? God help him, he was falling for her. Hard.

Dante looked up from the note he was scribbling when Max entered. "What the hell's wrong with you?"

"What do you mean?"

"You're walking around with a freaking smile on your face."

Was he smiling? Son of a bitch, he was. That thought made him smile even more. "There's something wrong with that?"

"If you're Maximo Vega there is."

Max didn't respond. He shook his head and pulled a clipboard containing shipping notices off the wall.

"I still think you're crazy to get involved with that one."

"I would explain it to you if it was any of your business, but it's not."

"Fine. I will admit she's showing some fine talent around the studio, but what's between you and her—" He held up his hands in surrender. "The less I know about you and Baskins, the better I like it."

Max flipped through the thin receipts. "Her name is Emily."

"Well here's something to wipe the smile off your face." He handed Max the note he'd been writing. "Your presence is requested—make that *urgently required*," Dante pointed to his note where the words were underlined, "at the Huffington Museum Saturday night, seven thirty. There's an opening of a new sculptural exhibit the Lavender Leech insists will be a profitable appearance for you. You get to wear your fancy-assed tux again."

"You mean the tux I used as a cleanup rag?" Max crushed the slip of paper and hit Dante's wire trash basket dead center.

Dante followed the path of his toss. "You enjoy playing with fire, don't you?"

"She's welcome to void my contract." Max found the notice he was searching for, noted the date, and replaced the board on its hook.

"Just don't screw up the Bruce Gallery deal before then."

"If Daniel Bruce is as hot for my work as she says, it won't matter. Trust me."

Dante scowled beneath his eyebrows. "Do I have a choice?"

"You've always had a choice."

Dante leaned back and let out a sigh. "I know. I guess I'm as crazy as you. I'll stick around just to watch you try and juggle two of the most exasperating females on the planet and not lose your head in the process."

Max pointed a finger at Dante. "Not losing my head may no longer be an option."

Dante sat up straight. "Don't tell me you're falling for Bask—um, Emily?"

"What if I was?"

"How long do you plan on lying to her? God knows, I'm not her number one fan, but she deserves the truth eventually."

Max ran a frustrated hand through his hair. Dante was right. "I'll tell her. Soon. I've tried. There just hasn't been the right moment, but she's coming over later. I'm making dinner and—"

"You're cooking?" Dante's eyebrows tried to mate with his hairline. "Wow, you have got it bad."

"As I was saying, I'll make her a nice Italian dinner, light some candles, pour the wine, and when the time is right…"

"Be careful she doesn't snap off one of your attachments."

Four hours later, the table was set. Everything was ready. Max had forgotten how much he liked to cook. His kitchen smelled like Grandma Vega's. She'd be proud he didn't burn the chicken *involtine*. He pulled the cork from a nice bottle of *Sangiovese* and let it breathe.

Emily arrived a few minutes later. "Sorry I'm late."

He reached out to her, wanting to pull her in for a kiss, but she skirted his reach. He frowned. Something was wrong. "You're right on time."

She put her hands on her hips and studied the floor. "I forgot there were elderly people and I was late for my dress fitting. The woman took forever. I don't know how she's going to finish. The wedding is the day after tomorrow. Right now, it looks like I'm playing dress up. She tells me she can work miracles."

He had no idea what she was talking about, but she was upset. Max moved in front of her and ran his hands down her arms to sooth her. She wouldn't meet his eyes until he tipped her chin. "What's wrong?"

She stepped away from his touch. "Nothing."

A thread of panic wound through him. "Why don't I believe you?"

Emily chewed at her lip. "I've just had a long day. Setting my final exhibit and the wedding is the day after tomorrow." She took a breath, gave him a weak smile, and peeked toward the kitchen. "What smells so delicious?"

"No changing the subject. Tell me about your long day."

She turned and noticed the table. "You made me dinner?"

Max slipped behind her and wrapped his arms around her waist. He didn't know what was wrong. Emily was a terrible liar. Perhaps he could get her to open up later, but his sudden need to hold her was overpowering. It might be a night for truths, but not now. Not yet. Max's only desire at that moment was to comfort her and make her happy. He kissed the side of her neck. Her faint floral scent tickled his nose. "I hope you're hungry."

"You made me dinner."

He ran the tip of his nose along the shell of her ear and whispered, "Yes."

Her head fell back against his shoulder and tipped, giving him access to her tender throat.

He held her tight against him and kissed his way down to her shoulder. "Do you like Italian?"

She gasped as he nibbled at her neck. "I love Italian."

His tongue traced her ear. "The food or the man?"

She gave a little whimper and moved against him. "Do I have to choose?"

"No." He laid a line of kisses along her jaw. "Tonight, you can have both if you wish."

Emily turned in his arms and wound hers around his neck. She sighed against him mouth, "Oh, I wish." Then she kissed him. "I wish."

Tugging on the belt loops of her jeans, he pulled her against his erection as he welcomed her tongue into his mouth. One hand fingered through her hair, holding the back of her head, as their kisses deepened. Backing up, he half-carried her to the couch until he sat with her straddling his lap. He growled against her mouth. "I want you. That is my wish."

She stroked his face between small kisses. "Is anything in danger of catching fire?"

"Not in the kitchen."

She smiled against his mouth and straightened. Crossing her arms, she grasped the hem of her top and lifted it off in one smooth motion. His cock pulsed in the tight confines of his pants. He loved that she wore no bra. He loved how her peach tipped nipples tightened with a single brush of his lips. He loved even more the way she held his head when he sucked them into his mouth.

She rocked her hips over his swollen cock until he wanted to rip the jeans from her body, but she beat him to it. Standing, she made a show out of slipping them off. Max tore the neck of his T-shirt, pulling it over his head. By the time she shimmied out of the whisper of white laced thong, he had the zipper of his jeans down. Before he could stand and finish stripping, she was between his legs, tugging on the waistband of his pants. Lifting his butt, he helped her slip them off his thighs and down. He fumbled to kick his feet free. He felt like an impatient teenager having sex for the first time in the back of his father's Buick.

He was breathing hard and wanted her back in his lap, but Emily surprised him by kneeling between his thighs and pushing his knees wider. *Oh sweet God!* "Em—"

Circling the shaft with her hand, she slipped the warmth of her mouth over the end of his cock. His head hit the back of the couch as a deep moan rumbled out of his chest. *Holy shit!* Quick licks of her tongue over the sensitive tip had him panting, clutching at her shoulder, pushing his fingers into the softness of her hair, but before he lost control, she rose and straddled him again.

Her breathing matched his. She wasted no time impaling herself upon him.

"Ah!" Max surged upward surrounded by the slickness of her sex.

Riding him hard, she leaned over and kissed his

panting mouth as he held tight to her waist and moved with her. He tasted his muskiness on her tongue. She was hot and tight, and he was racing toward an earth-shattering climax when he realized in their rush he hadn't put on a condom.

"Em…wait… I don't have a condom."

She stared at him with wide eyes. "I'm…sorry. I got carried away…It's safe, though. I…won't get pregnant."

"No?"

"I'm on the pill. But…we can…stop, if you want." Her fingers were digging in to his shoulders. Her body shuddered around him as she tried to cool her fever. She moved to get off him.

"No!" He wouldn't let her go. "Don't stop now." He pushed upward.

"Oh, thank God!" She rocked over him, faster now. Making tiny circles with her hips she released little gasps of pleasure.

Her walls quivering around him, bathing him with her juices was more than he could bear. His fingers bit into the tight round flesh of her ass and he thrust deep. Hot semen shot from his bursting cock. "Ahhh," he groaned low and guttural as he pumped into her.

Emily continued to ride him. Sweat glistened on her body. He licked it from her skin as he continued to stroke her breasts. His cum ran from her, soaking his lap, as he teased the sensitive flesh where they were joined. Watching her respond to him, losing herself in her passion, he wanted to give her the same pleasure she'd given him. His strokes got bolder. He wanted to kiss every inch of her. Taste her on his tongue. Feel her body climax around him.

Lisa A. Olech

Swirling his fingers first one way and then the other, he pressed harder against her sensitive flesh.

"Max!" The rocking of her hips quickened. Her knees tightened along his hips. Her back arched.

Sucking a taut nipple into his mouth, he nipped at it with his teeth. She tasted so sweet. His tongue teased while he increased the pressure on the play of his fingers.

Emily's body jerked as the first wave of her orgasm crested over her. The walls of her vagina squeezed and contracted around him. He held tight to her, delighting in the sounds of her pleasure as the tremors peaked within her body and settled into a long, satisfied tremble.

"Oh, Max…" She gazed at him. Her cheeks were flushed pink. Her hair was a tousled mess and damp at her temples. Her lips parted. She struggled to catch her breath. She was the most beautiful woman he'd ever laid eyes on. The immediate rush of love he felt for her in that moment took his breath away.

She wiped at the sweat on his face and leaned in to kiss him. "That was…" She kissed him again. "…the most amazing…" A serious expression crossed her face, "I'm sorry about the condom. I swear, I'm fine. You don't have anything to worry about."

"It was my fault. I started this."

"But I was the one to take it from zero to sixty in less than a heartbeat."

He brushed at her damp hair "You weren't alone."

"I know, but…" she chewed the edge of her lip.

Emily still straddled him, still held him within her.

He kissed the lip she chewed. "Your passion is nothing to apologize for. Just for the record, you don't need to worry, either."

She nodded. Something passed over her eyes, but she closed them and kissed him before he could figure out what. Em laid her head on his shoulder, and he pulled her tight to his chest, fitting them together like erotic puzzle pieces. Her gentle heat surrounded him. She was perfection in his arms.

She sighed and brushed his skin with her lips. "I could stay like this forever."

"Good. I don't want to let you go."

Emily lifted her head and sniffed, "If only your cooking didn't smell so yummy."

He smiled into her hair. "We have worked up an appetite."

"I think we worked up a fine appetite. I'm starving." She kissed his shoulder. "Could I shower before dinner?"

"Of course. I'll finish things in the kitchen." Neither of them moved, as if neither wanted to break the spell.

"I'll only be ten minutes." Still she didn't move.

Neither did he. "Mm hm…Take your time."

With a deep sigh, she slipped off of him and padded toward the bedroom. Max missed her heat the moment she left. The shower turned on, and he was tempted to join her. His body stirred at the thought of soaping her breasts and taking her pressed against the slick tiled walls, the warm water pulsing against their skin. He caught her scent on him as he tucked himself back into his jeans. Just her smell caused a rush of blood to his cock. He *was* a man obsessed.

The pasta was boiling, and the salads and bread were on the table when she joined him in the kitchen.

She poured them each a glass of wine and handed him one. She had on the blue shirt he wore the other night and smelled of his shampoo. Seeing her in nothing but his shirt was sexy as hell. Her hair was combed away from a scrubbed face. God, she was beautiful.

"And you cook too." She smiled into her glass.

"Only one meal." He drained the pasta, threw in a handful of cheese and plenty of fresh cracked pepper and filled two dishes. "It's my grandmother's recipe." *Caprese* salad. He raised two steaming plates of pasta. "Then *cacio e pepe*." He pulled a baking dish from the oven. "*Involtine di polo*. It's chicken with prosciutto and parmesan. And *aranci in salsa di marsala* for dessert."

"*Aranci in salsa di marsala...*" She repeated his pronunciation perfectly. "I have no idea what that is, but it sounds delicious. Of course, anything you say sounds wonderful."

"Oranges with honey and *marsala*. It's my favorite. Sweet and light. I like to eat it with my fingers." He lifted her hand and sucked the tip of her finger into his mouth. "Licking the honey from them. I'll show you later."

Her lips parted in a sigh. "Oh, I can't wait."

"Come, let's eat."

She took the plates of pasta from the counter and followed him to the table. "It looks so good. I can't believe you cooked for me."

"I enjoyed it. I don't cook like this. Not for one. I cooked with my Grandma Vega growing up. Every Sunday we went back to her house and she made the best food. I have a big family. We sat and talked and argued and laughed and argued some more. The more wine, the louder the arguments. Meals lasted for hours." Max held her chair. "Even after my parents passed away, we still ate dinner with Nonna every week."

"Do you miss them?"

"Some." He refilled their wineglasses.

"I come from a tiny family. I don't remember my grandparents. I have one uncle, my father's brother, but he lives in Ohio, and we lost touch after Dad died."

"But you have the protective mother. Trixie?"

"Overprotective, yes. She's not a cook though." Em took a bite of salad. She closed her eyes with pleasure. "Mmmm, delicious." She dabbed at the corners of her mouth with her napkin. "I didn't know you came from a large family. Brothers? Sisters?"

"*Si*, brothers. Three. I don't talk about them. It's private. They are all in the family business. I'm the black sheep who wanted something different. I still have my nonna, six aunts and uncles on my mother's side, five on my father's. More cousins than I can count."

"So many. They must be proud of all you've done."

He shrugged and cleared away some of the plates. "Tradition is important. The business is important. Family loyalty. Art is not so important."

"With your talent? Art has a rich history in your family, too. You're a descendant of—"

"Michelangelo." The name choked him.

"Yes. They don't see that as tradition?"

Here it was. Here was his chance to tell her. He took a healthy drink of wine. "You need to understand—"

"Oh, I do understand. Why are there people who

still believe art is superficial? That it is an unnecessary luxury. That artists are all destined to starve." Emily speared a bite of chicken and held it up. "Then a gift like yours comes along." She slipped her fork into her mouth and sighed. "Mmmm. Artists are life's flavor. The heart. The world would be cold and gray without them. You can't let your family stand in the way of your success." A frown marred her face as she stared at her plate. "Someone, just today, said you were on the threshold of becoming one of the most important artists of this century." She placed her fork on the table and wiped her mouth with her napkin. "Nothing should stand in your way, Maximo. Not anyone. Not your family. Not even me."

"You?"

Emily pushed away from the table and stood. "If I ever thought my being with you was hurting you—"

"Hurting me?"

"Yes." She took a step toward *Fame*. "Your work. Your future." She turned back to him. "I love being with you. I mean, at first you were so intimidating and this larger-than-life persona, but now, knowing you…these past few days have been magical. I feel like I've broken through into some secret garden no one else can see. If I damage that—you, your art, your career, held you back somehow—I couldn't live with myself."

Lavender. He stood and took Emily's hand. "Who put this in your head?" *I'll kill her with my bare hands.*

"No one." She placed a hand on his chest. "I've been thinking about us and—"

"I think about us too." He lifted her face to peer into her eyes. "I can't stop thinking about us. I think about you every moment. When I open my eyes in the morning. When I lay in my bed at night. I see you. Feel you. Smell your perfume on my sheets. I sketch you and sculpt you in my mind. Pull your image from the clay. Find you in the stone." He ran a thumb across her cheek. "Hurt me? My work?" He was more afraid of hurting her. "You? Never." His words hung up on one another, but he had to say them. He had to fess up. He prayed she would understand. "Emily, I—"

"If I ever do," she rushed on, "you'll tell me the truth, won't you?" Green eyes filled with worry peered up at him and snatched at his heart. "Promise me?"

"Yes, you have my promise. I'll tell you the truth."

Slipping her arms around his waist, she embraced him.

He held her tight to his chest and kissed her hair. *You have my promise.* "Is this what was bothering you earlier?"

"Yes, no. It's everything." She shrugged.

He ran his hands over her back, the smooth heat of her body coming through the crisp cotton of his shirt. "You delivered your exhibit piece, no?"

"Yes. It's all set up. It looks great."

"I'm anxious to see it displayed."

"The show isn't until next week, but I could arrange a private showing."

"I would like that." He tucked her hair behind her ear. "Tell me about this wedding."

Em groaned and buried her head into his chest. "I'm old friends with the groom, but the bride asked me, and I foolishly said yes."

"This is the boyfriend. The one from high school?"

She stared at him with wide eyes. "How did you remember that?"

"When you told me, I thought he must be an idiot to marry someone other than you."

"You and Trixie share the same mind."

"Even the mother thinks it's true?"

Emily pulled out of his embrace and started clearing the table. "It's not his fault. I broke things off. He wanted to settle down and make babies, but I had bigger plans. I don't begrudge him anything. He and Cynthia love one another. I'm happy for them, but it's one of those bittersweet things. I'd much rather go to the ceremony, wish them well, and leave. Now I'm part of a whole weekend of bridal activities. By myself. I know Jeremy and his parents, but Cynthia I've only just met, along with her posse of tall gorgeous bridesmaids, and me in a dress that…" She sighed. "I'd much rather spend the weekend with you."

"It's only a few days. We have tonight to be together." He reached for her.

"I wish I could stay all night, fall asleep in your arms, and not wake up until Monday."

He smiled at her. "Again with the wishes?"

Emily handed him back his shirt an hour later, dressed and headed home. They'd taken their dessert to bed and fed one another plump sections of orange, licking honeyed wine off their fingers and each other.

Max walked her to her car, kissed her good-bye, and watched her drive away. It had been another amazing night. Even though he still hadn't found the right moment to confide in her, their time together only strengthened his resolve and gave him hope their growing feelings would somehow be strong enough to withstand the blow.

He went back up to the kitchen and started to clean

up from dinner. The apartment already felt empty without her, and yet, she was everywhere he looked. He hated the thought of not seeing her all weekend. He'd grown so attached to seeing her face every day.

As he stepped out of his shower that night, an idea struck him. Wrapping a towel around his waist, he rummaged through the back of his closet and dug that ridiculous tuxedo out of its trash bag. Tomorrow, he'd take it to the cleaners.

Chapter Twenty

Emily hugged Suzanne and patted her friend's tummy before sliding into a booth at Java Jim's. She ordered the King Kong Combo.

Suzanne sat with a bran muffin and a large glass of milk. "I'll be happy when I can drink coffee again. And cosmos. And see my feet."

"Stop. You're not that big."

"Yet." She leaned toward Em and propped her elbows on the table. "So, are you ready for the big day tomorrow?"

Em huffed a laugh. "Not even close."

Suzanne stretched her back. "Thank goodness I have today off. The shop is going to be crazy in the morning."

Emily ripped open several sugar packets and dumped them into her vat of steaming coffee. "You're still doing me, right?"

"Absolutely."

"And you won't make me look like a hooker?"

Suzanne's jaw dropped. "Don't you trust me?"

"Of course I trust you, but don't you recall when you did my makeup the first time?" Em grimaced.

Suz threw up a hand. "I was eight."

"And I looked like an eight-year-old hooker."

Suzanne flipped a hand at Em. "Don't worry about it. I promise. You'll be gorgeous."

"I'll settle for average. Don't try to talk me into the mink eyelashes, either."

"Your eyelashes are fine. They're just blonde."

"AKA, invisible."

"I can fix all that." Suzanne broke off a corner of her muffin and popped it into her mouth. "Did you get the picture I sent of the hairstyle I want to try on you?"

"Yeah." Em shrugged. "It wasn't horrible."

"I told you."

Even talking about it made Emily a tad sick to her stomach. She dropped her face into her hands. "Why did I agree to this?"

"Because you're still in love with Jeremy."

Em's head shot up. "Wrong. I'm still in 'friends' with Jeremy."

"If you say so." Suzanne shrugged one shoulder and pursed her lips. "I saw you the way you were looking the other day. All moony like. I know that look. If you're not in love with Jeremy, then you're in love with someone."

"What? This pregnancy is messing with your brain." Emily tried to hide behind her giant coffee cup. "You're seeing things."

"I am not. How long have I known you?"

"Evidently, too long," Em grumbled and shot her friend a hard stare. Was she that transparent? If Suzanne was sharp enough to guess, then would she be having this conversation with Trixie next?

Suzanne lifted her eyebrows and gave a little gasp. "I *knew* it! Girl, you can't fool me. I know that look a mile away. Spill it."

"Fine, but I'm evoking the pact of the Blood Barbie Besties." The B.B.B. was formed when Em and

Suz were ten and they became "blood" sisters by pricking their fingers and swearing on their favorite Barbie dolls. It all started after Jimmy Easton kissed Suzanne behind the school and had the nerve to stick his tongue in her mouth. Suzanne had been horrified and made Emily swear on the pact to take the whole sordid story to her grave.

"Whoa! The B.B.B.? Who is it?"

Emily chewed at her lip, pushed her cup to one side and leaned as close to Suzanne as she could. "Do you swear?" She held out the sacred pinkie.

Suzanne linked her pinkie with Em's. "Yes, dammit. Who?"

"Maximo Vega."

"What!"

"Shhhhhh!" Em shot a glance around at the faces of the other startled customers. "Lower your voice," she hissed.

"Oh my God. You serious? Oh my God. Oh my God!"

"You can stop saying that." Emily proceeded to tell her the whole story about posing for him, what happened the night she came to her house, the night of the rainstorm, the mud, even about her run-in with Beverly Lavender yesterday. "I've been thinking maybe she's right and I should walk away, but things are so great between us, and after last night, I don't think I can. I don't know what to do."

Suzanne flopped back. Emily took a bite of her muffin, but it turned to dust in her mouth.

Suzanne leaned forward again and frowned. "Wait a minute. The night you stopped by the house was only like a week ago."

"Things moved a little fast."

Suzanne's eyebrows shot toward the ceiling. "A *little* fast?"

"Don't judge me. Tell me what to do."

"I'm not judging, I'm just trying to wrap my brain around all this. Wow. This is huge."

Em twirled her coffee mug around and around. "I know."

Suzanne lowered her voice. "Is the sex good?"

"After the clay story, you really need to ask?"

"Oh my God, it's amazing, isn't it?" She danced in her chair.

Emily sighed and nodded. "There needs to be a new word for how amazing it is."

Suz covered her mouth and screamed again. The older couple sitting at the next table left, giving them both a scowl as they passed their table. Suzanne waited until they were out of ear shot and whispered, "Does he know you love him?"

Em chewed her lip. "Not yet."

"When are you going to tell him?"

She twirled her cup some more. This wasn't helping. Could she turn the clock back and start over. Whoever said confession was good for the soul? This whole conversation was making her feel ill. "I won't see him again until Monday."

"So you'll tell him Monday?"

Em mumbled, "Unless I talk myself out of it by then."

"Wow. I still can't believe this." Suzanne shook her head. "Oh. My. God."

"Would you please stop saying that?"

"Do you think he feels the same way about you?"

Lisa A. Olech

"I don't know." Em rubbed her forehead.

"Well, you *have* to know. You can't run around dropping your panties every other minute if he doesn't feel the same way."

And there was Suzanne's perfect black and white logic. The only problem with it was all those lovely gray bits in between. Em knew the reality of things but didn't want to face it. It hurt just to say the words. "What if he doesn't?"

"Simple. Walk away."

"Simple? How is that remotely simple?" Emily rubbed her forehead as she considered the other alternative. At this point, she wasn't sure which outcome was better. "What if he does feel the same?"

"Make me your Matron of Honor."

Emily groaned. "I'm serious."

"So am I. Just promise me I'll be there when you break this news to Trixie. Front row tickets. Hey, I think it's great. Why shouldn't you be in love? And why couldn't it be with," she leaned in and whispered, "Maximo Vega?"

"What if Beverly Lavender is right and he's playing me, and who knows how many others? What if I'm not the only one he's having unprotected sex with?"

"Oh my God! You didn't tell me that! Are you nuts?"

Em shot another glance around the restaurant. "It just happened once."

"That's all it takes. You're still on the pill, right?"

"Of course."

Suzanne leaned closer again. "Do you think he's sleeping around?"

200

"No. I thought there might be a thing between him and Lavender, but she would have reacted a whole lot differently when she found out we were in a relationship."

"Okay, then, get through this wedding from hell." Suz held up one finger. "Go to him on Monday and be totally honest with him." Two fingers. "Tell him Lavender harassed you." Three fingers. "Tell him you're crazy about him." Four fingers. "And jump the man." Suzanne held up her hand.

"Sex isn't the problem. What if he doesn't love me?"

Suzanne shrugged and slipped her a sly smile. "Jump him anyway."

Emily spent the rest of the afternoon packing everything she needed for the weekend. She still had to swing by and pick up her dress and shoes from the bridal shop, stop off and buy some stockings, and get to the church by five for rehearsal. She left Trixie a note. She'd see her in the morning at Pixie's.

Cynthia had arranged for all twelve of her bridesmaids to stay over at the hotel. She said she needed their moral support.

From what Emily saw at the rehearsal, the girl was hanging on by a thread, and Jeremy wasn't fairing much better. The three-ring circus of a wedding was already taking its toll, and they hadn't entered the center ring yet.

Emily broke away from the pack to stand next to Jeremy. "Why couldn't you have made me your best man? I'd look great in a tux."

"Believe it or not, I did make that suggestion."

"Shot down by the mother of the bride, huh?"

Jeremy gave a short bark of laughter. "I still have the shrapnel scars."

Em stuck out her bottom lip. "Poor baby."

He slipped his arm around her shoulders. "I never got a chance to call you back yesterday. Are you okay?"

She dropped her head on his shoulder. "I will be. I'm praying my dress fits." She glanced around at the melee going on around them. "I suppose they frown on drinking in the church."

"Take it easy there, M&M. You're entering three days of open bar. Pace yourself."

She bumped him with her hip. "I'll behave. Don't worry about me. Is Cynthia's Grandma Winnie still trying to pinch your ass?" Em tweaked his side and remembered he was ticklish.

Jeremy jerked away. "Stop it! I don't know what you're complaining about. You haven't been dragged around for the last week. Golf, a stag luncheon, brandies, and cigars with Daddy and the senior Weatherby's. They even took me skeet shooting."

"How'd that go?"

He shrugged. "The skeets won."

Em laughed. "I'm sorry. Cheer up, by this time tomorrow you'll be *Mr.* Cynthia Weatherby."

"Very funny." Checking his watch, he sighed. "I thought this thing was supposed to start half an hour ago."

Em peeked over her shoulder toward the door. "I think we're waiting for the minister."

Jeremy rolled his eyes. "Great. Oh, I forgot to tell you—"

"Let me guess, the Reverend broke his what'sis

and you need me to fill in."

"No, smart ass. Cynthia's Uncle Lester is anxious to meet you."

It was her turn to roll her eyes. "Do I want to know why?"

"He wants to talk to you about your art. Lester's life partner, Phillip, is a huge Vega fan and somewhere along the way your name came up. They asked me about you, and I told them how great you are. They want to meet you."

Emily groaned.

"It's not as bad as all that. They're great guys. Huge art collectors. They were very impressed when I showed them your pictures."

She frowned. Jeremy didn't have any photographs of her work, did he? "What pictures?"

He flipped a hand over his shoulder. "The ones from the show you did. A while ago."

"From high school?"

"Yeah, that's the one." He nodded.

Em gasped. "You're kidding, right?"

A ruddy cheeked man clapped his hands to get everyone's attention. "Ladies and gentlemen, I'm sorry I'm late. We need to move this along if we could. Ladies, could you please go line up in the foyer? Gentlemen, I'm going to position you at the altar first and describe your ushering duties later. Jeremy, can you come with me?"

Emily leaned close to Jeremy's ear and growled, "Remind me to kill you later."

"You can't kill me. I'm the groom."

The rehearsal lasted more than an hour. How difficult was it to step, pause, step, pause? The flower girl had a meltdown because she couldn't wear her princess gown and glittery pink shoes *NOW*. The three-year old ring bearer flung the white, ribboned pillow like a Frisbee and threw himself face first onto the aisle. After he crawled into a pew to lie along the kneelers, the Reverend suggested the "real" rings be held by the best man. Just in case.

Three of the groomsmen had pre-gamed the rehearsal and were already way past drunk and obnoxious, and the mother of the bride might or might not have taken one too many Valium. Was it time to send in the clowns?

Dinner afterward was a lovely three-hour affair with speech after speech dedicated to the lovely couple. Emily didn't have to kill Jeremy, this wedding would do it for her.

Making her way back to the party after escaping into the ladies' room, two handsome older gentlemen stopped her as she passed the bar.

The first man was fit, tanned and silver haired. His eyes were blue blue blue. "You're Emily Baskins, am I right?"

"Yes, I am, and I'm guessing you're Cynthia's Uncle Lester."

"I am. Lester Grimm. I'm delighted to meet you. This is my partner, Phillip Bosworth. We've heard so much about you."

Phillip stood shorter than Lester, but had a similar build.

Emily shook their hands. "Yes, Jeremy mentioned he talked to you."

"We chewed the boy's ear off at dinner the other night. We heard you're an artist. We're such art snobs, but we love discovering fresh new talent. Jeremy's very complimentary of your work."

Phillip asked, "Do you really work at Vega Studio?"

"Yes, I'm interning there this summer."

"His work is intense. We *love* him." Phillip gushed like a fan.

Emily smiled at his enthusiasm. *I love him too.* "His work is very powerful."

Lester bobbed his head in agreement. "I understand he's quite demanding of his artists. If you're part of his studio, he must think highly of your work. We saw a few photos. They looked ancient, however. We'd love to see some of your newer work. Would that be possible?"

"I think I can arrange that."

Phillip raised an eyebrow at Lester and the two exchanged a quick smile. "We have a dear friend, Margo Abbot, who puts together a small show every season down in Cohasset to showcase upcoming artists. We'd be happy to pass your name along."

"That's very nice of you. I'd appreciate that. I might be able to show you some recent work right now. I don't travel with my professional portfolio, but I always have my sketchbook with me. I believe I have a few photos tucked in there. It's out in my car."

"Oh, how wonderful."

The three drunken groomsmen were heading in their direction. Emily had already heard enough about how one had thrown up in the bushes behind the church but was getting his second wind. "I'll run and get those. Be right back."

When she brought the half dozen prints back,

Lester and Phillip became even more animated. "We have to show these to Margo."

"I have copies. You can keep those if you'd like." Emily flipped one over. "My name and contact information is on the back."

Phillip grabbed Lester's arm. "Where's the closest fax machine?"

Lester laid them out on the nearest table. "Take a picture of them with your phone. We can text them to her."

"What a good idea. You're so techno savvy." Phillip hugged Emily. "I'm very excited. We'll let you know as soon as we hear from her."

Chapter Twenty-One

At eight the next morning, Trixie's Pixies was a beehive of activity. It was all hands on deck. Cynthia, her mother, Grandma Winnie, twelve bridesmaids and the flower girl were all in line for hair and makeup. Trixie had supplied pastries, juice, bottled water and several bottles of champagne to serve her clients. It was lovely. The shop looked great. Trixie had outdone herself.

Cynthia was frightfully pale in her glittery "Here Comes the Bride" sweats, but she was putting on a brave face. Suzanne did her hair first. A photographer was busy capturing every curl of every eyelash. The wedding of Senator Weatherby's only daughter was sure to be the lead story on tomorrow's society page.

Bridget was in charge of doing the bride's makeup. Trixie teased Grandma Winnie's hair, and Angel was on Bridesmaid Number Two when Emily dropped into Suzanne's chair.

"How you holding up?" Suzanne rubbed Em's shoulder.

"I'm fine."

"Does the dress fit?"

Emily shrugged. "I don't know. I haven't had time to try it on."

"What? What if it's horrible?"

"What difference does it make?" Em swept the

Lisa A. Olech

room with a hand. "Look around. Fit or not, I'm going to look like the poor adopted second cousin."

Suzanne stood behind the chair and fluffed Em's hair. "Nonsense. I'm going to make you gorgeous."

The bells over the door rang, and a delivery man armed with what appeared to be three dozen white, long-stemmed roses came into the shop. "I have a delivery for..." he checked his notes, "Miss Cynthia Weatherby?"

The photographer went wild. Her flash blinded the poor guy.

"Over here, over here!" bridesmaids chirped.

Cynthia raised her hand. The man handed her the beautifully wrapped bouquet tied with a wide silver ribbon before adding a small wrapped box to the delivery. "I'm to give this to you as well. Have a nice day, and congratulations."

She read the card on the flowers, but everyone knew who they were from. "Today you'll make me the happiest man on earth. J." The entire room of women breathed one collective swoon. Cynthia started to cry.

"Open the box!" "What's in the box?" "Oh, dear, isn't he the sweetest..." "Rip the paper!" "Show us!" "He's so romantic!" The group gasped as Cynthia cracked the lid of the small blue box, held up a stunning pair of diamond drop earrings, and proceeded to ruin her perfectly applied makeup.

"Shit." Suzanne swore behind Emily and squeezed her arm.

Emily grinned at her in the mirror. "I know. Bridget's going to have to clean her up and start all over."

"That's not what I mean, and you know it. This

208

must be *killing* you."

Em caught her mother watching her too, with a pitiful expression. "I'm *fine*. Stop it. Just do something with my hair and let me get out of here."

"I bet if Trixie knew about a certain someone, she wouldn't be feeling so miserable for you right now."

"B.B.B. You pinkie swore!"

Suzanne whispered, "I didn't say anything."

"Good. Don't."

She spun the chair around so Emily couldn't see her reflection in the mirror and grabbed a small barreled curling iron.

"What's that for?"

Suzanne gave her a snarky smile. "It's my magic wand. Sit back and relax. This won't hurt a bit."

All around Emily, hairdos were upped, cheeks were blushed, mink bits were glued to eyelids. Bridget had finished with the bride, and Cynthia was beautiful. Her makeup was flawless once more. Bridget had pinned tiny crystals into her hair. Cyn wore her new earrings and looked every bit the bride. Glowing. She was glowing.

Grandma Winnie walked past Suzanne's chair and patted Em's hand. "Very pretty."

Emily peeked back at Suzanne. "Winnie thinks I'm pretty? What are you doing up there? It's taking you forever. I don't have that much hair."

"Will you stop fussing at me and let me work." Suzanne doused her in hairspray. "I'm ready to work on your face next."

Em's makeup didn't take long at all. Suzanne promised no smoky eyes or contoured cheeks. A little eyeliner here and some mascara there. Putting a simple rose gloss on her lips, she handed Emily the tube. "Here, you'll need to reapply later."

"Thanks. Am I done?" Emily tried to look at the mirror.

Suzanne held Em's chin and looked over her face in a final appraisal. "Yes, you're done. Jeez, you'd think I was torturing you."

"You are."

Suzanne turned the chair.

"Nice." Emily leaned closer to the mirror. "Very nice. You're a miracle worker." Emily's hair swept back and up slightly on the sides. Somehow Suzanne had created a soft piece-y texture and half curls on the top with several pale tips brushing one cheek. The bridesmaid mandatory pink crystal heart hair clip graced the other side. What were truly astounding were Emily's eyes. "What did you do to my eyes?"

"You hate it." Suzanne sighed and placed her hands on her hips.

"No, I like it." Emily peered at her reflection. "Is that glitter?"

"Yes. Don't panic. The light plum eye shadow I used had a tiny hint of shimmer, but the color brings out the green in your eyes."

"It sure does. They look really green."

Suzanne held her hands palm up. "Hello? Behold the wonders of makeup."

Em puckered her mouth. "I like the lips too. This shade should complement the dress quite well."

"She likes it, she really likes it. I may faint."

Trixie came up behind her. "Nice job, Suz. Em, you're lovely." She looked around the room. "You're all lovely. I'm sorry I'm not going to see you walk down the aisle."

The photographer took that moment to snap a picture of Emily and blinded her with the flash. "Son of a—! There'll be pictures, Ma. Eight million pictures."

****

Emily had never observed the use of so many pushup bras, pantyhose and industrial strength undergarments in all her life. Thirteen women trying to get dressed in the same hotel suite resembled something akin to twenty raccoons fighting in a gym bag, but once they'd all figured out whose shoes were whose and zipped each other up, they all looked great.

Bracing herself, Emily stepped into her gown and slid it over her hips. The length seemed right. Maybe it wouldn't be so bad. One of the other girls came over to do her zipper. Em held her breath. *Here goes nothing.* The zipper went up. *Oh my God.* The dress fit. Holy cow, did it fit. Like a pink "evening blush" glove. It hugged her hips and nipped in at the waist. She had a shape. The top gave her a little lift and showed a hint of actual cleavage.

"Wow, Emily, you look so pretty."

Em spun around. Cynthia stood behind her. The maid of honor fussed with her veil.

Cynthia was a bride wearing the princess gown of every little girl's dreams. The beaded bodice and frothy skirt dusted with crystals was made for her. She looked like she'd stepped out of the pages of a fairy tale. "Oh, Cynthia...look at *you.*"

"Do you think he'll like it?" Cynthia plucked at her skirts.

"You'll knock him out."

Cynthia squeezed her hands and gave her a watery

smile. "I'm a nervous wreck."

"Don't be."

Cynthia's tears were contagious and three bridesmaids and her mother started sniffing behind her.

"Stop it. You have nothing to sniffle about. Didn't you hear, you're making him the happiest man on earth."

The bride gave her a hug. "Thank you for that. Thank you for being here. It means a lot to Jeremy to have you in the wedding, and it means even more to me."

Emily smoothed the front of her skirt. "Who knew 'evening blush' was my color?" She dabbed at the corner of Cynthia's eyes. "You're getting a really great guy."

"I know I am." She held her hand. "Will you do me one more favor?"

Emily fluffed the sides of her veil. "Sure, name it."

"Will you go check on him for me?" She handed Em an envelope. "Give him this?"

Emily looked at the swirly words "To Jeremy, my love" and nodded. "I'll see he gets it."

The men were dressing on the next floor up. When she knocked on the door, it was answered by one of the drunken three. He only wore boxers. "Whoa, what do we have here? Hey, guys, look at this. We've got a defector from the other team."

Emily put a hand in the middle of his chest and shoved. "Move aside, idiot. I'm here on a mission from the bride."

"Of course, your highness." He bowed as she passed.

The men's suite smelled like a cross between a

brewery and a gym sock. Garment bags with the rental shops tags were thrown over chair backs and the bed. None of the men seemed in too big a hurry to get dressed even though the limo was supposed to be taking them to the church in less than an hour.

Emily scanned the room. No Jeremy. "Where's the groom, guys?"

"Oh, he's in there." One of them pointed to a closed door. "I think he's practicing his vows or something."

"Or he's still puking," said another.

Oh jeez. Emily tapped on the door. "Jeremy? It's Em. Can I come in?"

"Come on in."

Emily slipped into the bedroom. Jeremy sat on the edge of the bed, fully dressed in the darkened room, breathing into a paper bag.

"Oh, sweetie, what are you doing?"

"What—does it look like I'm doing? I'm hyper— hyperventilating."

Oh jeez! Em opened the drapes and sat beside him rubbing his back. "It's going to be okay. Take nice, deep breaths."

"How's Cyn?" The brown paper sack crinkled in and out.

"Right at the moment, better than you." She kept rubbing his back. "Want to tell me what's going on?"

"I'm getting married in less than two hours." His voice was muffled.

"Hence, me in a pink dress."

Jeremy stopped freaking out for a second to look at her. He lowered the paper bag from his mouth. "Ems…You're beautiful."

"If you think I'm something, wait until you get a load of your soon-to-be wife."

He looked at her like she'd just promised him a puppy and a new bike. "Really?"

"She's going to knock your socks off."

The paper bag was back. He was shaking his head. "I'm never going to make it."

"Sure you are. Why are you so worked up?"

"I'm not good enough for her, Ems. I've spent this last week surrounded by the legacy that is Weatherby. These are wealthy, powerful people who expect me to keep Cynthia in that lifestyle. I'm a poor kid from New Hampshire. I'm doing okay for myself, but I can't compete with that."

"Who's asking you to—Cynthia?"

"No, of course not. Cyn's not like that."

Emily brought him a glass of water from the bathroom. "Then who's pressuring you?"

"No one's pressuring me, exactly, it's this unspoken thing." Jeremy waved a hand and took a drink.

"Sounds like it's you creating all this pressure."

"Cynthia is special, Ems. Maybe she deserves better."

Emily put her hand on his shoulder "There is no one better than you. There's only one thing she needs and you've already given it to her." She sat beside him again and nudged him with her shoulder.

"What's that?"

"Your whole heart."

Jeremy looked at her and heaved a deep sigh. "She does have my heart."

"And don't ask me why, because you can be a

royal pain in the ass, but she's crazy about you, too." Emily held up the envelope. "She wanted me to give this to you."

Jeremy took the envelope and stared at the message on the outside. He flipped it over and popped the flap. Emily laid a hand over his and stood. "If you're okay, I'll leave you to read that in private."

"I think I'm going to be fine now, thanks to you."

"I'm just in this for the lifetime supply of coffee and muffins. I'll be expecting the first payment the minute you get back from your honeymoon."

He pulled Emily into his arms and held her for a long moment. "You know, all this changes nothing. You're still my best friend."

"Lucky me." She kissed him then used her thumb to wipe the lipstick from his cheek.

Jeremy gave her that smile that would forever catch at her heart. "No, lucky me."

The ceremony was breathtaking and went off without a hitch. Even the tiny ring bearer behaved and to the delight of the assembled three hundred guests skipped down the aisle. The church overflowed with flowers and candles. A string quartet accompanied the bride and her father down the aisle. As predicted, the groom was blown away by the sight of her.

The vows were said, the "I do's" exchanged, and when Jeremy McCloud kissed his wife for the first time, the guests broke into applause and the bells in the steeple rang.

At the reception, Emily set her bouquet of full-blown peony blossoms in the silver vase waiting by her place setting. It was engraved with her initials, and each bridesmaid at the table received one. With this many attendants, the head table would have looked like a bubble gum train. Instead, the happy couple decided on a lovely sweetheart table for the two of them with their bridal party and their significant others filling the five round tables behind them.

Em glared at the empty seat next to hers. According to Bridesmaid Number Ten, the original Number Six had a fiancé, and the seating plan had been made before she broke her ass. Couldn't she find anyone for her "plus one"? *Guess, George Clooney didn't get his invitation.* She should have asked Max, not that he'd have come. God, she missed him.

What had Jeremy said about an open bar? Actually, there were three. One at both ends of the hall and one outside on the wide patio overlooking the ninth green. Emily opted for the one outside. The line was shorter. "Champagne cocktail, please." She dropped a few bills into the tip glass and carried her crystal flute to the far end of the patio.

After the heat of the hall, the gentle breeze felt good. A few more hours and this day would be over, not that she believed anyone would miss her if she slipped out early. Sipping her wine, she thought of Max. What was he doing tonight? It had been two days since they'd last been together. Parts of her ached for him. Instead of talking herself out of telling him how she felt—maybe it was being surrounded with pink love all day—she was more determined than ever to tell him she loved him. And more than a little worried he wouldn't share her feelings.

"Ms. Baskins!" Uncle Lester and Phillip startled her out of her thoughts. "You are a vision today."

Emily smiled at the men who looked as if they had

stepped out of a copy of *GQ* in their black tie. "Gentlemen, you're quite handsome yourselves. How are you enjoying the wedding?"

Lester leaned in and kissed her cheek. "Lovely ceremony, just lovely, and such a beautiful couple, but frankly we've been anxious to talk to you. We bring good news."

Phillip raised his cocktail to her. "We spoke to our friend Margo last night and texted the pictures of your work. She is extremely interested in talking to you about participating in the show. Isn't it fabulous?"

"That's great news." Em lifted her glass. "I can't thank you enough for contacting her."

"It's our pleasure," said Lester. "Like I said last night, we love discovering new talent and we have a good feeling about—"

Beside him, Phillip gasped.

"What's wrong with you?" Lester followed his line of sight. "It's can't be…"

Emily peeked back over her shoulder just as Phillip sighed, "Vega."

Chapter Twenty-Two

Emily pressed a hand to the sudden flutter of her stomach. Maximo was here? Maximo was here! Looking more handsome than any man had a right to be. Someday someone would bronze that tuxedo.

"Emily, you scamp," Phillip scolded, "Why didn't you tell us *he* was coming?"

She started to say she knew nothing about it, but watching Max walk toward her had made her speechless. His eyes bored into hers.

Uncle Lester rushed to extend his hand in greeting. "Mr. Vega, what an honor it is to meet you."

Max broke his gaze upon her to briefly acknowledge the man. Emily introduced them. "Maximo Vega, this is Mr. Grimm and Mr. Bosworth. They're great admirers of your work."

"*Grazie, buona sera.*" He shook the men's hands and returned his heated gaze back to her. "*Mi scusi*, gentlemen. I need to speak with Ms. Baskins, if I may." He didn't wait to hear their answer before he took hold of her elbow and began to lead her away.

Lester and Phillip fell over one another moving aside. "Certainly, certainly."

Emily gave the two gaping men a quick smile before Max pulled her toward a shadowed end of the patio. "What on earth are you doing here?"

"When I saw you just now, you stole my breath

away."

She was having trouble breathing herself. "That doesn't explain why you're here."

Maximo ran the back of his finger along her cheek. "I'm trying to tell you how stunning you look."

People had been telling Emily how nice she looked all day, but somehow hearing him say the words, she was finally able to believe it. Warmth flooded her cheeks. "Thank you."

He ran his gaze down the full length of her and back again. "So beautiful."

Inside the hall, the orchestra began to play. Emily laid a hand on his lapel. His dark eyes looked almost black in the shadows. He was watching her mouth. The spicy scent of his cologne wrapped her in its subtle seduction.

"I-I still don't know why you're here."

His gaze dropped lower as his fingers trailed down her arm. "I've come to dance with you." His eyes met hers again.

Each look, each touch sparked along her skin. "What?"

"I couldn't stand the idea of groomsman number six holding you in his arms, dancing the night away."

Em grinned. "Groomsman number six is only seventeen, and I believe he brought his own date to dance with."

"You see, it's a good thing I came. You can't play the wallflower looking as gorgeous as you do. Come." He raised her hand, kissed the backs of her fingers and started to lead her out of the shadows.

"Wait." She hesitated. "Are you sure you want to go in there? There must be a half-dozen society photographers capturing every second of this wedding. You hate photographers. They're sure to recognize you."

"Let them."

The dance floor filled the center of the room. Jeremy and Cynthia's table sat at one end. A dozen other couples were already dancing. As the song ended and another began, Max faced her, slipped one hand behind her back, and grasped hold of her right hand with the other.

The orchestra started playing "Unforgettable" and he drew her toward him. Her body pressed against his. She loved this song. The rest of the room melted away as he led her around the floor.

Emily finally found her voice. "He can dance, too," she teased.

"And *she* isn't as clumsy as she proclaims."

"I said I was a klutz. I never said I couldn't dance."

He put his cheek next to hers and her eyes fluttered shut. His breath tickled her neck and shoulder. "Where is he?"

"Who?"

"The idiot who let you get away."

"Oh, Jeremy? He's with his wife. You can't miss her. She's the one in the flowing white gown and veil."

Max raised his head. "Ah, yes. Found him. He's shorter than I imagined." He sounded immensely pleased by that small fact.

Emily was stunned. Could he be feeling insecure? *Maximo Vega jealous?* "Is that why you're here?"

Max put his cheek back against hers and drew in her right hand to hold it against his chest. "I told you why I'm here." He tightened his hold on her and whispered in her ear. "Would you rather I left?"

Parts of her body were turning liquid. "No," she said in a rush.

Max shifted so his leg rested gently between hers. His knee pressing against her thighs made her breath catch. He murmured against her hair. "Good, we haven't finished our dance."

"What happens after that?"

"We could dance some more, eat some cake, or…"

He'd captured her. She was lost to anything but him. She would go and do whatever he wanted. He could suggest they juggle rattlesnakes and she would happily agree. "Or?"

He dipped his head and kissed the top of her shoulder. "Or I could take you somewhere else. A private little restaurant? A walk by the lake? My place?"

"And then?" She sighed.

"Then I'd work on getting you out of this beautiful dress."

Emily missed a beat and stepped on his toe. A knowing warmth flooded her. "Do you think of nothing but work?"

His laughter tickled her ear. "Some say I work too hard." His hand moved lower and he pressed against her.

Emily felt his erection against her hip and gave a tiny gasp. "I've heard you're tireless."

"I can be," he whispered, "especially when the inspiration is flowing and the piece begins to sing beneath my hands."

The sexy rasp of his voice made her tremble. "I…I can't sing, only dance."

"Not true. I've heard you sing. My favorite note is the tiny little whimper you make when my fingers trail up the silky skin of your thigh and I tease that sweet spot." His tongue traced the edge of her ear.

A jolt of pleasure shot through her limbs. "Ah…"

"Yes, that's the one."

They continued to sway against one another. Emily's knees weakened at the images racing through her mind. His fingers unzipping her dress ever so slowly, sliding the satin over her skin. Thank goodness he had a tight hold on her.

"Max?"

"Mmmm?"

"We need to stop."

He pulled back and searched her face. "Why?"

She glanced around at the other dancers leaving the floor. "The song ended."

"I'd say it's only just begun." And he kissed her.

Flash bulbs exploded around them. People spoke his name as they passed and began to recognize him.

Emily shielded her eyes. "I think you've blown your cover, Mr. Vega."

"I think you're right." He tucked Emily against his side and led her off the dance floor. "We should say good-bye to the bride and groom before we leave. Unless you'd rather stay?" He indicated the towering five tiers of pink frosted wedding cake they passed. "We could wait for cake. It looks delicious."

Emily wiped her lip gloss from his mouth. "*You* look delicious."

He smiled at her and again the cameras caught the moment. Taking her hand they approached Jeremy and Cynthia.

"Maximo Vega?" Jeremy raised his eyebrows at Emily.

Emily made the introductions. "Max, this is my friend, Jeremy McCloud, and his bride, Cynthia."

"Mr. and Mrs. McCloud, *congratulazioni*! I didn't think I was able to accompany Emily this evening, but my plans changed. I hope you will forgive my late intrusion."

Cynthia glanced back and forth between Emily and Max with a bright smile. "Not at all, Mr. Vega. You're not an intrusion. We're delighted you could join us."

Max kissed Cynthia's cheeks. "I fear my presence may be a distraction, however. Your photographers have forgotten the beautiful bride is the most important person in the room tonight. This will not do. *Mi dispiace*. I'm sorry. I think it would be best if I leave."

"Oh no, you mustn't go. We'll speak to them." Cynthia gave a pleading look at Jeremy.

"Nonsense. It's your time to celebrate. You should be dancing. Enjoying your special night. I'll slip out unnoticed." He lifted Emily's hand and kissed it. "Would you mind if I stole Emily away with me?"

Jeremy looked like Max had just suggested they all go rob a bank. He shot Emily a sharp stare. "You're leaving with him?"

She shrugged. She didn't want to be rude. He had a point. This was his wedding and she'd promised. "If you need me to stay, I'll stay."

Cynthia placed her hand on Jeremy's sleeve. "Emily, you've been an absolute blessing to us *all* day. To both of us. I can't thank you enough. It's fine. You are officially off duty. Go. Enjoy yourself. Have fun."

Emily hugged her tight. "Thank you, Cynthia.

Have an amazing time in Greece. Watch out for this one. Ouzo makes him think he's Superman." She tipped her head toward Jeremy. He was still giving Max a cold glare.

"Don't forget my parents are hosting the after party tomorrow. You should both stop over." To Max she said, "There'll be tons of food and drinks and, I promise, no photographers."

Emily hugged Jeremy and asked in a quiet voice. "You don't mind, do you?"

"I just want to see you happy." He sounded sulky.

She straightened. "Look at me. Don't I look happy?" She flashed him her best smile.

He conceded. "You really do."

"See, you can stop worrying. You better call me the minute you get back from your honeymoon. I'll be in serious need of coffee by then."

Jeremy hugged her again. "I love you, Ems."

"I love you, too."

Max settled into the deep leather seat next to her as the driver closed the door. Two photographers had followed them out of the reception, but their flashes stopped as soon as the darkened windows of the car interrupted their shots.

"You hired a limo?" Her voice sounded hushed in the rich cocoon of black leather and polished burl wood.

"It came with the tuxedo." He pulled her toward him and kissed her. "Where do you want to go?"

Her first instinct was to tell him to take her home to his bed, but then her stomach rumbled and she remembered she'd never eaten her meal, or had cake for that matter. He owed her. "Skip's Burgers?"

He grinned as he picked up the phone to talk to the driver. "Yes, the lady would like to go to Skip's Burgers. Thank you." Max hung up the phone and pulled her onto his lap. As the limo slipped along the road leading out of the country club, he kissed her.

Emily wound her arms around his neck. "This is like a lovely dream. I still can't believe you came tonight."

"I missed you. The studio was empty without you. Everywhere I looked, I saw you, but you weren't there." He played with her hair. "I needed to see your face." He brushed her lips with his. "Also, you said you were uneasy about your friend's wedding. I was concerned for you."

She stroked his handsome cheek. "It wasn't as bad as I imagined. The ceremony was beautiful. The flowers were amazing, and there were a million candles. I was glad to see Jeremy marry Cynthia. I know they'll be together forever."

He watched her intently. "You love him." It wasn't a question.

There was that tone in his voice again. "Are you jealous?" Just the idea he might be gave Emily a bit of a thrill.

"Perhaps I am."

She smoothed her hand over his hair. "Don't be. Jeremy's more of a brother to me now. We grew up together. He's seen me through some rough times. I do love him. I think I always will, but not in a romantic way. That part was over for both of us a long time ago." Emily tried to read his face in the dim light of the car. "Were you worried?"

"Not about you." He took her hand from his cheek

and laid a kiss in its palm.

"You've nothing to be worried about."

A quick frown darkened his look. "There are things I want to say to you. Things hard for me to say, but I want to enjoy our night first."

Em nodded. "There are things I want to say to you too. Maybe if we say them together, the words won't be so difficult." A little rush ran through her at the thought of him telling her he loved her too. Since her conversation with Suzanne, she'd been practicing just how she'd tell him. This was going to be a night she would never forget.

The car pulled into the parking lot of Skip's and stopped. The phone next to Max beeped. He spoke into the receiver, "Yes?" Covering the mouth piece, he asked, "What would you like?"

"Besides you?" She raised a sassy eyebrow at him.

"Yes, besides me."

"Cheeseburger, no onion, fries...lots of fries, and a strawberry milkshake. Pink seems to be my color."

He grinned and repeated her order to the driver. "Double that and get something for yourself. Add everything to my bill." He hung up.

A short time later, the driver brought their food and they talked and ate. Emily told Max about the pillow-flinging ring bearer and thirteen women getting dressed in the same hotel room. She shared her good news regarding Lester and Phillip's friend Margo and talked about the upcoming show at the school. Max was excited to see everyone's reaction to her ribbon piece.

After, they took a drive over to Highland Lake. Holding hands, they walked along the water and kissed in the moonlight. It was a perfect night.

"What should we do now?" Max murmured as they walked back to the waiting limo.

"You do have work to do." Emily slipped her arm through his.

"I have?"

"Yes, you mentioned it earlier. When we were dancing? Something about working on getting me out of my dress?"

"Ah yes, I do remember. You could help me with this?"

She broke away and teased him over one shoulder. "I *am* qualified."

He tugged her back into his arms and kissed her. "It may require we keep at it until dawn. Are you up to the task?"

"It takes great dedication to work as hard as you do, but I'll try to keep up." The driver opened the door for them and Max held her hand as she entered. She paused and looked back at him. "If we get too tired, I could always sing to you."

Later, Max needed no help working the zipper of Emily's gown. He sang a song of his own when he saw her lace-topped stockings and tiny panties. Lying in his arms in the afterglow of their lovemaking, she brushed his skin with her lips and whispered against his chest, "*Ti amo.*"

He tensed beneath her. Part of her froze. Had she said it wrong? Was it too soon?

"What did you say?" He tipped her chin.

"*Ti amo.*" The room held its breath. In the dim light of the room, she couldn't read his expression. "Did I mess up the pronunciation?"

"No, you said it right. You love me?" He ran a

thumb over her lower lip.

"*Si. Ti amo.*" Her heart was pounding. "I do, more than I ever imagined I could. I know it's soon, but I can't keep it a secret any more. I wanted you to know how I feel. I love you."

In one move, he pinned her beneath him and began to kiss and stroke every inch of her. Before he was finished, he'd taught her an entirely new song.

Emily woke to an empty bed. After making love to her half the night—how did the man survive on so little sleep? Just another fact about Maximo Vega that amazed her. She blinked at the clock. It would be light soon. The apartment was quiet, but someone was talking downstairs. It was a too early for Dante, plus it was Sunday. She hoped nothing was wrong.

Rising, she couldn't find Max's robe, so she wrapped up in the top sheet from the bed. Tiptoeing to the top of the stairs, she stopped and listened. She didn't want to eavesdrop, but she was curious as well as concerned.

"She loves you. You lying bastard, she loves you!"

Who was that? The voice sounded familiar, but she couldn't place it. Were they talking about her?

She opened the door fully and peeked down into Max's work space. She could just see Max's shoulder. He was working with clay before a wired form, but she couldn't see anyone else. The brightness of the studio lights made her squint as she started down the steps. If someone was arguing with him over her, calling him a bastard, she'd set them straight.

Chapter Twenty-Three

"What the hell were you thinking?" Max berated himself. "You weren't thinking. You see her and the only thought in your head is taking her to bed." He threw a wad of clay at the aperture. "She loves you. You heard her, you lying bastard, she loves you! Go up those stairs, wake her up, and tell her the truth. You were going to tell her yesterday and the day before and the day before that. Do it now. The sun's coming up. It's another day, and you still haven't told her. Tell her you're a fake. Tell her—"

"Who are you talking to?"

"—you love her." Max spun around.

Emily stood at the bottom of the stairs. He'd been ranting at himself like a lunatic. How much had she heard?

Pure white panic raced through him. "How long have you been standing there?"

Emily pulled the sheet from his bed tighter around her. "I thought I heard... There's no one here?" She shook her head, blinking, and frowned. "Was that *you* talking?"

He didn't answer. He didn't move. His brain raced to come up with the words to explain. He'd practiced how he'd tell her, the exact words to say, but she'd caught him off guard. All those carefully chosen sentences shattered around him like glass. "I thought you were asleep."

She pointed at his mouth, put a hand over her eyes, and shook her head. "I think I'm still asleep. I'm dreaming. I swear your accent is gone. Say that again."

"You're awake. It's not a dream."

She crossed her arms over her chest and looked at him sideways. Confusion and disbelief twisted her features. "What are you doing? Why are you talking like that? Stop it!"

He stepped toward her. "Emily…"

She stared at him as if he was crazy. She shook her head and paled. "No! That's not how you say my name! Say it right!"

"I'm trying to tell you. That's why I came for you at the wedding last night. I couldn't wait any longer. I've been trying to tell you for days. But I can explain everything."

"Explain what? You're faking your accent? You're pretending to be Maximo Vega?"

"No, I *am* Maximo Vega. I'm just not the Maximo Vega you think I am. I'm Max."

"What are you saying?" She backed against the stairs and held her forehead "You're not who I think you are? You're not Italian?"

"My family is Italian. I'm just not *from* Italy."

She seemed to be trying to make sense of everything. She rubbed her forehead. "Your family is from Italy, though, right?" She tossed out her hand. "Michelangelo?"

"That's a lie. I'm not related to Michelangelo. My great-great-great-grandmother came from the same little town. It started as a joke."

"Wait, what? A joke? What the hell are you telling

me?" Confused panic etched her face. "If—if you're not from Italy, where are you from?"

There was no point in trying to back out of this now. He wished he could find some way to soften the blow, but the pin had been pulled. "Cleveland."

"Cleveland? As in Ohio?"

"Yes, Ohio. My parents started a dry cleaning business there. Two shops. My brothers run things now." He was talking as fast as he could. The incredulous look on her face was scaring the hell out of him. He had to make her understand.

"*That's* the family business you were talking about? Dry cleaning in Cleveland?" She started gulping air. She put a hand to her throat. "I think I'm going to be ill."

Max didn't know what to do. He held up his hands to calm her. "I know you're upset, but you have to listen. Please. I can explain everything." He reached out to touch her and she jerked back as if he'd burned her.

"No! Don't touch me. I-I don't know what sick, perverted game you're playing—"

"I'm not playing, Em—"

"Don't say my name!" She shoved past him and raced up the stairs.

He followed her, dodging the door she slammed in his face. He caught up with her in the bedroom. She was pulling her rumpled gown back on. He had to make her listen. "You need to understand. I got caught up in something. It got out of my control. Way out of control and it was easier—"

"Easier?" The word stopped her short. "Easier to what? Get women into your bed?"

"No!"

Lisa A. Olech

The color drained from her face. "All this time…Now I understand." Her voice got quiet. "All that business in the beginning of pushing me away. You were just laying the trap. Playing hard to get so I'd keep coming back."

"No, that's not true. If you'd just listen."

"Listen to what? To what a complete and utter fool I've been? To why everything—EVERYTHING—that has ever come out of your mouth has been a lie?"

"I never lied about how I feel about you." He pointed to the bed. "I *never* pretended when we were together. I never spoke Italian to you there. I was always Max." He opened his arms wide. "I never meant to hurt you. I'm sorry. Please, if you believe nothing else, believe me when I tell you I love—"

"STOP! No! You don't get to say those words. You haven't got the first clue about loving someone." She scrambled to gather her purse, shoes, and stockings and bolted for the door. She took the private stairs out.

"You can't leave. Wait!" If she walked out that door she'd never come back. He'd lose her forever.

She spun on him. Her body shook and her eyes filled with tears. His heart crumbled in his chest as a tear spilled over and ran down her cheek. She shook with the effort of holding it together. He'd destroyed her. He'd destroyed any feelings she had for him.

Emily held up a trembling hand. "D-don't follow me. I never want to see you again." Her voice cracked. "It's over."

"How will you get home?" If he could just keep her there a little longer. If he could calm her down, maybe she'd listen. "Your Jeep is still at the country club. Let me take you."

"No. Leave me alone."

Max's heart broke as she pulled a cell phone from her purse and walked away from him. For good.

For the next hour, he paced like a caged beast around the empty studio. He had to fix this somehow. If she would only see him. He could explain how in a moment of frustration he spoke to a reporter and feigned an Italian accent and sealed his fate. How a stupid columnist's ridiculous assumption had morphed into this lie and formed a tidal wave so huge it swept him along, despite all his efforts to rectify it.

He should have fought harder to set things right, but all of a sudden the lie had given him the perfect screen to hide behind. It was easier to pretend not to speak English well. If they couldn't speak to him, they left him alone to do his work. The work was the only thing he cared about. Until now.

He was lousy with all the rest—the promotion, the schmoozing, the selling little bits of his soul for a commission. Max hated doing it. *Maximo* couldn't. His art was a better voice than the few halting words that ever came out of his mouth. It added to his appeal. It created this aloof persona and disguised his dismal lack of social skills.

He had to find Emily and get her to listen. Pushing into Dante's office, Max rummaged through the file cabinet. Copies of her internship papers would give him her home address. They had to be here. He saw them just yesterday. *Found them!* He prayed she'd see him.

Grabbing his keys, he was heading out when Beverly Lavender burst through, flinging the studio door to the wall with a crash.

"You fucking son of a bitch!" She hurled a

newspaper at him.

As it hit the floor, Max caught a glimpse of a large photo of him and Emily kissing at the wedding. "I don't have time for this. Get out of my way!"

She shoved him backward. Her hair was pulled back in a scary tight twist at the back of her head. It was the first time he'd seen her when she wasn't decked out in some putrid shade of purple. She was a lot shorter without her heels. "I don't think so. Not this time. If you think I'm going to have my reputation ruined by you, you've got another think coming."

"For what, ditching some museum opening? I've got bigger problems than your precious ego. Don't shove me again." He pushed past her.

"This has nothing to do with you being an ass last night and bailing on me to go suck face with your little protégée. That only lit the fuse. No, I'm going to expose you for being a fraud and a liar! I know the whole truth about you, *Max Vega from Ohio*. I spoke to your ex-wife. She told me the whole sordid story. I'm going to destroy you!"

"What? You talked to Judith? Why? What right do you have talking to my ex-wife?"

"Right? Right! I have every right! When you didn't show last night, I came by. I was livid. You made me look like an inexperienced hack. There were promises made to important contacts. All you had to do is show up for ten minutes to satisfy the appointment, but no. You had to go play Fred Astaire with that little bitch, Baskins." She kicked at the newspaper. "I told her to stay away from you. I warned her."

"You what?" Max's hands curled into fists. "What did you say to her?"

"Like it matters. I don't give a rat's ass about her. I figure when she hears what I'm about to let loose on you, there isn't a chance in hell she'll stick around. Internship gone. Scholarship gone. Career gone. She'll regret the day she ever heard your name."

Max's back teeth were in danger of crumbling to dust.

"So after you made a complete fool out of me, I started to do a little bit of investigation work. Took a bit of digging, but when I'm properly motivated, I can be someone's worst nightmare. I found a little mention in a tiny little newspaper about your itty bitty life before you started lying to the entire world." She held up a copy of his and Judith's engagement announcement. "Smart girl took back her maiden name. The internet search to find her took me less than ten minutes and we had a long, heartfelt conversation over the phone this morning. I'm worried about you, blah, blah, blah. I think you've fallen into some destructive behavior, blah, blah, blah. Is there anything she can tell me to help you? Some way to contact your family?" She snapped her fingers. "It was easy after that. She was so concerned about you, she told me everything I needed to know. Everything."

"Get out of my studio."

"With pleasure." She looked at her watch and gave him a snide smile. "I have a press conference in less than an hour. I figure your career and the careers of everyone associated with you, will be over in less than two."

"Go ahead, ruin me. I deserve it. I don't care at this point, but the people who work here are innocent in this. Leave them alone."

"Even Dante Rizzoli? I highly doubt that. He's your watchdog."

"Especially Dante." If Max was going down, fine. But he wouldn't let this bitch take down his staff. They had families to support. Bills to pay. Dante knew. Of course he knew, but that was one secret Lavender would never dig up. "Dante knows none of this."

"How did you manage to keep it a secret from your own studio manager all these years?"

What was one more lie? "He's stupid…almost as stupid as you. He believed everything I told him. People don't ask questions they don't want the answers to. You fell for it, too. Never batted an eye. You were ready to whore yourself out for me, just like the rest. You jumped at the chance to build your purple-painted empire on the back of my talent. *My* years of hard work. I even tried to warn you off. I offered you the perfect chance to distance yourself from me, but you wouldn't listen. You couldn't see past your own damn greed. Not too smart, Bev."

She took an aggressive stance and stabbed a finger into his chest. Her eyes blazed. "We'll just see how smart I am. I'm about to bury you on live television because I'll be damned if *any* of your shit sticks to *me*!"

Max glared at her. He forced his hands to stay at his sides. "You hurt my people, and I'll make sure you're covered in shit. I'll see to it this whole mess drags you straight to hell right along with me."

"Fine! What do I care about them anyway? It's *you* I'm after."

Max spread his arms wide. "Then take your best shot, lady, but get the hell out of my studio before I decide I've got nothing left to lose."

Chapter Twenty-Four

Emily climbed into her Jeep with a moan. She'd managed to reach someone at Polly's Taxi and get a ride back to the country club. Still in her bridesmaid's dress, she was the poster child for the walk of shame. The cab driver at least had the decency to leave her alone after his initial comment, "Rough night?" was met with a bout of out-of-control hiccupping sobs from the backseat of his cab. Lovely.

Aside from the ache in her chest, she was numb. *Someone wake me up. This must be a bad dream.* How could he have lied to her? After everything they'd done, the cold shaft of truth speared her. How could he have been so calculating? He was Maximo; he wasn't Maximo. He never spoke Italian to her in bed? Did he think that made it okay? They'd spent hours alone together, wrapped in each other's arms, and he couldn't find two minutes to say, "Oh btw, April Fools! You've been falling in love with a figment of my imagination."

She was in shock, but she recognized this feeling. She'd felt this same desperate sense of loss and despair the first few days after her dad died. Struggling through that initial shock and disbelief was followed by the realization she'd never be the same as she was yesterday. As if a part of her would never recover, no matter how much time passed, she would always bear the ragged scar of this on her heart. Always.

Emily took a shuddered breath, pulled down the visor, and groaned at her reflection. *So much for stunning.* She rubbed at the smeared mess under her eyes. Her light plum eye shadow now made her look like she'd been in a bar brawl. She ripped the pink glitter heart clip from where it stuck out sideways from her head and threw it onto the floor mat of her car.

Home. She just wanted to go home. Fumbling through her useless satin purse, she pulled out her keys and recalled a rainy night and the first time Max had broken her heart. Idiot. She'd gone back for more. Was it any surprise he'd crushed her heart again? Swallowing against the ache in her chest, she stabbed the key into the ignition.

All the way home, she tried to come up with what she was going to say to Trixie. What could she say to explain this? Her mother would be devastated. Hell, the woman was learning Italian for him. How was she going to tell her Maximo Vega was a fraud? That he'd deceived the world? She'd sooner believe Elvis was lip-synching. Should she tell her before or after the fact her only daughter had been lying to her for weeks while she secretly had a heated affair with the man? That she'd fallen hopelessly and madly in love and never told her? How did you find the words for that?

Lost in her thoughts, she didn't notice the other vehicle in the driveway until she got out of her Jeep. Her muddled brain registered the huge black truck with the off-road suspension and dark privacy windows. Who? *Wait, I know this truck!* It was covered with the early morning dew. It had been there all night. *Joe Turner? Creepy Joe Turner!*

Bursting through the front door, she called,

"Mom!" The house was quiet. Em started down the hall to her mother's bedroom and stopped. The door was shut. There was no way she was going into that room. Bile rose in her throat. "Mom?"

There was movement.

She marched back into the kitchen. *Let this be a mistake. His truck broke down in our driveway because Trixie's car broke down at the shop and he offered her a ride home but left and walked the eight miles back to his place and he'll show up later to get it....Aahhh!*

"Emily?" Her mother rushed into the kitchen, fumbling with the ties of her robe. "What are you doing here? I thought...oh my God, are you okay?"

"What's Joe Turner's truck doing in our driveway?"

Trixie reached out to Emily. "You look like you've been in a car accident. What the hell happened to you?"

Emily backed away. "Answer the question, Ma! Is Joe Turner here?"

"Yes." Trixie threw her hands up. "Now before you get all crazy—"

All the air left Emily's lungs like she'd been punched. Behind Trixie, Joe Turner came into the kitchen, buttoning the neck of his aqua polo shirt. Emily slapped a hand over her mouth while her body made the frantic choice between screaming and throwing up.

Just then the rooster clock announced the hour, her body made up its mind. In a mad rush past Trixie and Joe, Emily shot out into the front yard and threw up on one of Joe's off-road tires.

Trixie was begging her to stop and "just listen."

Emily jumped into her Jeep and smoked the wheels

getting away. Her cell phone rang before she reached the end of the road. Emily squeezed the Off button and threw the phone into the backseat. She made it to Suzanne's in less than five minutes.

Suzanne had the front door open before Emily made the stairs. "Oh shit. You look like hell. It's all true then?"

Emily covered her eyes as a fresh wave of hysterics crashed over her.

Suzanne ran down the two steps and wrapped her arm around Emily and led her inside. "I've been going crazy. We saw your pictures in the paper first thing this morning."

"Pictures? There are picture of this?"

Suz sat her at the kitchen table and pushed the society pages toward her. "It says Max came to the wedding."

Emily looked at the photos taken less than twelve hours ago. Max was holding her in his arms and kissing her. They were the image of two people in love. It tore at her heart to see. The caption read, "The illusive artist, Maximo Vega adds a splash of drama to the wedding of the season."

Suzanne set a cup of coffee in front of Emily. "I freaked out when I saw it. I mean, Trixie reads the society pages like the Bible. So much for keeping things a secret. Then when that Lavender woman hit the news."

Emily stared at the photo. Suzanne's words didn't register in her brain for a moment. "Wait, did you say Lavender? What does this have to do with her?"

"She's all over the news." Suzanne pointed to the television in the living room. The local station was covering a breaking story. "She's announcing to the world that Maximo Vega is a giant fake."

"Oh my God...how did she find out?"

"What? So it's true?"

"Yes, it's true." Emily pushed away from the table and rushed into the living room. The television was on the news channel. They were showing clips of Beverly Lavender's tearful confession before a room full of reporters. "I am shocked and stunned by what I've learned in the last twenty-four hours. Maximo Vega is more con artist than artist. To deceive his fans, his loyal employees, and representatives is beyond reprehensible. It is criminal. Lavender Blue Art Agency has taken immediate legal action to sever any and all ties with Maximo Vega and Vega Studio." They cut away to shots of the studio, of *Fame*, and a video clip of Max dodging photographers. "Channel Twelve has just learned all upcoming appearances and events featuring the artist once believed to be directly linked to Michelangelo have been cancelled, pending charges of fraud and misrepresentation on the part of Mr. Vega. All attempts to contact the artist for comments regarding today's revelations have been unsuccessful."

"Oh my God, this will ruin him." Emily breathed. "This can't be happening. Everything he's worked so hard for...It's all gone. He must be devastated."

"Why are you defending him? He lied to you. He's lied to *everybody*. I'd think you'd be happy to see him suffer."

"Of course I'm not happy," Emily snapped. "His work is too important. His contribution to the art world shouldn't be dismissed. And...and...I love him."

"Oh, sweetie, you need to get over that. He played

you for a fool, Em. He sucked you in like all the rest. It's okay to hate him."

"I know. Trust me, I know. I wish I could just shut if off like a light switch, but I can't." Emily gaped at her friend. "Last night was m-magical. He showed up and swept me off my feet. It was the best night of my life." She dropped onto the couch and held her face in her hands. "And then I woke up, and my whole world shattered."

Suzanne turned off the television and sat next to Emily. She lifted the fuzzy throw off the back of the couch and wrapped it around Emily's shoulders. "Trixie must be having an absolute meltdown. Have you talked to her yet?"

Emily leaned her head back and squeezed her eyes shut, but it was no use. She'd never get the image of Trixie and Joe out of her mind. Not without bleach, a scrub brush, and a stick of dynamite. "I stopped by, but she was too busy screwing Joe Turner."

Suzanne choked next to her. "Whaaaat?"

Emily curled up in the fetal position and pulled the throw over her head. "I don't want a new daddy," she wailed.

"Ewww, Joe *Turner*? Really?"

"Please, just kill me."

"Oh, honey, I'm so sorry." Suzanne rubbed her back. "And I thought Cynthia's news would be the worst. Boy, was I wrong."

Emily pulled the throw off her head and looked back at Suz. "What about Cynthia?"

"You know." She flipped her hand. "The whole champagne thing."

Em sat up. "What champagne thing?"

"She wasn't drinking." When Emily just frowned at her, she continued with a deep sigh. "You didn't notice? She had a glass, but she never drank it. Oh, jeez, I can't believe I'm the one that has to tell you this on top of everything else."

"Tell me what?"

"Cynthia's pregnant."

****

Max found the small pink Cape Cod house. Emily's Jeep wasn't in the driveway, but maybe her mother knew where he could find her. After the eighth time trying the cell phone number he found in her file, he'd given up. Taking the stairs two at a time, he pounded on the door and pushed at the doorbell. The bell crowed like a rooster.

"You!" A frazzled petite woman answered the door. She looked as if she'd been crying.

"Are you Mrs. Baskins? I'm—"

"I know who *you* are." She tried to slam the door in his face.

Max caught the door with his arm. "Good, then we won't waste time with pleasantries. I need to find your daughter. Do you know where she is?"

"No, I don't. And even if I did, I wouldn't tell you...you...*Il mio portafoglio è stato rubato! Dove posso trovare un agente di polizia*?"

Max frowned. "Someone stole your wallet?"

"I'm only on lesson three. I haven't learned how to swear in Italian yet, you bastard!"

Max sighed. "I deserve that. Swear at me all you want. I'll even teach you how to curse like an Italian sailor, but right now I have to find Emily."

"Haven't you hurt her enough? Leave her alone."

"I can't do that, Mrs. Baskins. I'm in love with her."

Chapter Twenty-Five

Emily towel dried her hair and gave herself a long, hard stare in the mirror. *You stupid, stupid fool.* Her eyes burned from crying and her head pounded, but the hot shower made her feel a bit more human. Slipping on a pair of borrowed sweats and a T- shirt, she joined Suzanne back in the kitchen.

"I made us some tea." Suzanne placed a china cup in front of Emily

"You hate tea, and I'm not a big fan either." Emily lifted the cup and sniffed.

"I know, but isn't tea what you're supposed to offer someone when they're in the middle of a crisis? That's what happens in all those old movies."

Emily replaced the cup in its delicate saucer. It was nice Suzanne was trying, but it was only making Emily more prickly. She was grateful for the shower and the sweats, but what she needed was some alone time to process everything. Unfortunately, Suzanne's caring had crossed over into something akin to a suicide watch as if she was afraid to leave Emily alone for more than five minutes. "Thanks anyway."

"She's called four times." Suz chewed her lower lip. It wasn't necessary for her to say who *she* was.

"Just keep telling her I'm not here."

Suzanne screwed her mouth. "I don't want to tell you your business, but haven't there been enough lies already? You've lied to her, she's lied to you, Maximo has lied to...well *everyone*. Aren't you tired of it? Trixie's your mother, and she's worried sick about you. You don't have to talk to her. Let me just tell her where you are." As if on cue, the phone rang again. Looking at caller ID, Suzanne shot her a pointed look.

"Fine, tell her, but I'm not talking to her. I don't want to talk to anyone."

Suzanne picked up the phone. "Hey, Trix, yeah, she's here. No. I don't think it's a good idea. She's pretty upset. Maybe she should just hang here for a day or two until she sorts things out." Suzanne looked at Em and nodded. "I think she'll be okay. It's just been a lot to take in, you know. I'm sure she'll give you a call when she's ready to talk. Till then, she's here and she's safe. I made her tea."

Emily left Suzanne to finish talking to Trixie and curled up on the couch. Try as she might to block him from her mind, she thought about Max. The local news channel had been on top of the story all day. She couldn't watch any more. His fame was gone. Erased in an instant. The world would hate him for a time and then forget he ever existed. It was all such a waste. While she didn't have it in her to forgive him for what he'd done, she still couldn't rejoice in his demise. It was a fickle world, filled with fickle people, who delighted in cheering someone as they rose to the heights of that great silvery illusion of celebrity only to be the same ones jeering when they crashed back to earth. It was all too sad, and yet it happened every day.

Monday morning, Emily woke on Suzanne's couch in the same position she remembered laying down yesterday afternoon. She'd been covered with the fuzzy throw and had fallen into a deep, dreamless sleep. She stretched the stiffness of her back and wondered what time it was.

The house was quiet. Monday was Suzanne's day off and there was only one thing on Emily's to do list for the day. She needed to face the inevitable fallout from everything that happened this weekend, and the sooner she did it the better.

****

"Madeline?"

"Baskins? Jeez, girl, get the hell in here." Madeline Sullivan move a coiled clay pot from a chair. "Shut the door."

"I'm guessing you've seen the news."

"Are you kidding? I'm still reeling. Talk about dropping a bomb. Daniel Bruce from the Bruce Gallery is a personal friend of mine, and he's been on the phone with me for hours since the news hit. He'd contracted a VIP, three-city tour scheduled for Maximo Vega. To say he's livid is an understatement."

Emily could understand Mr. Bruce's anger. There was a lot of that going around. "Speaking of understatements, I'm in a giant mess now, aren't I? Without the Vega internship, I'm sunk all the way around. The Internship Committee is no doubt removing Vega Studio from the program as we speak. It's too late to secure another for the summer, and without it I won't be finishing my degree on time. Not to mention my behavior was beyond inappropriate. Even if the Graduate Board lets me stay at Stoddard, they're sure to strip me of my scholarship, if they haven't already. You know my circumstance, no scholarship, no school. Either way, I'm out. You've always been good to me, Maddie, but I wouldn't blame you if you showed me the door right now. I was just hoping you'd let me finish up the semester. Then I'll leave Stoddard and maybe this scandal will fade away."

"Emily—"

"No, Madeline, I've been all over this in my head. Maybe in a couple of years, after everything dies down, I can come back and finish my degree. If I get a decent job and can save some money…"

"Or…"

"How is there an 'or'?"

Madeline moved a snow globe of the Statue of Liberty and pulled a thick envelope out of her inbox. "Or, this. It arrived first thing this morning." Maddie pulled several pieces of paper from the envelope and handed Emily two of the sheets.

Emily frowned. She couldn't believe what she was looking at. They were her internship papers. They'd been signed off as complete. "I don't understand."

"'Dear Ms. Sullivan,'" Maddie read from the page she held in her hand. "'Enclosed please find the internship paperwork for Ms. Emily Baskins. Given that Ms. Baskins has demonstrated such an advanced skill level, proficiency, and dedication to craft, as well as providing invaluable assistance to several significant projects within this studio, I am confident she has met and completed all necessary requirements of her internship. Given the speed with which Ms. Baskins was able to complete these requirements, I give her my highest recommendation. Sincerely, Dante Rizzoli, Managing Director, Vega Studio.' It's also signed by Maximo himself. Both were dated Saturday. And there's this." Madeline held up a check. "It's made out to you for the full amount of the internship plus, it says here, a modeling bonus."

"I-I don't understand." Emily snatched the check from Madeline and was stunned at the number of zeroes.

"As I said, it was in this morning's mail. It had to have been mailed before noon on Saturday. So if there's any debate from the committee regarding the validity of your internship in light of what transpired yesterday, this little postmark negates it. It also means your little lip-lock caught in the newspaper happened *after* you were released under the program so there can be no allegations made of inappropriate conduct on your part." She shrugged one shoulder. "Or his, for that matter."

"I-I don't know what to say."

"I'd be singing, Halleluiah, I'm one damn lucky girl." She leaned forward in her chair. "I know the media is taking some serious shots at Maximo Vega right now and he's earned them, but from where I'm sitting, I think he was planning to tell the truth all along." She raised the paper in her hand. "These tell me he made sure you were protected before the shit hit the fan."

A lump in her throat threatened to choke her. Was Madeline right? Did Max know Beverly Lavender was going to expose him or was he planning his own confession? Blinking back the tears she focused on Maximo's bold signature at the bottom her paperwork. "Why couldn't he have been honest with *me*?"

"You can answer that question better than I. Would it change how you're feeling?"

"I don't know." Emily sniffed and shrugged one

shoulder. "I stopped feeling hours ago."

****

Emily balanced her sterling flower vase on top of the rest of her things as she fumbled for Suzanne's spare key. She'd swung by the hotel suite before check out to pick up the rest of her things. The room smelled worse than the men's. Two bridesmaids were still passed out. There were empty champagne bottles everywhere. The after-after party must have been a doozy. She gathered her few things and left them to sleep it off.

"Hello? Suz? I'm back." Em pulled the key with its sparkly teal happy face fob from the lock, closed the door with her elbow, and pushed the key back into her pocket.

"She'll be back in a little while. She ran to the store." Trixie stood in the doorway leading into the kitchen.

Emily slammed on her brakes and tried to throw herself in reverse. "I don't want to talk to you." Her bouquet flowers fell out of her vase and hit the floor with a pink peony splat. She didn't care. She wrenched the door open.

"Emily Louise Baskins, don't you dare walk away from me. I'm still your mother."

Emily spun on her. "Are you? Are you still my mother, because I swear I don't know who you are. It must be a theme, because I don't even recognize myself anymore. Did I fall down a rabbit hole? Did the whole world flip upside down while I was asleep? When did left become right and up become down? When did my life become *The Twilight Zone*?"

"Sweetheart…" Trixie reached out to her.

"No." Emily jerked away. "Maximo's lies and betrayal have destroyed me, Ma, but yours…" She crossed her arms over her chest and dropped her chin. "If there was one person I thought I could trust, it was my mother."

"I was going to tell you."

Emily gave a bitter laugh. "Do you have any idea how many times I've heard those words in the last twenty-four hours? I'm going to have to put that on a T-shirt."

"You know, I could be just as upset with you. You weren't honest with me either. How do you think I felt when I had to learn about your relationship with Maximo Vega from the damn newspaper?"

Trixie had her there. Emily had no good answer to justify her actions. "I knew you'd freak. I was trying to think of a way to break it to you."

Trixie threw out her hands. "Hello. I could say the exact same thing."

"But Joe Turner?" Emily screwed up her face. "Ewwwww. Why couldn't it have been anyone other than him?" She shuddered. "Ew."

Trixie planted her hands on her hips. "There's nothing 'ew' about Joe Turner. He a good, hard-working man."

"But he's so…so slimy…and blond."

Trixie sighed. "You're just seeing his business persona. Joe isn't like that. Not with me. He sells vacation timeshares. He needs to appear sunned and tanned so his customers will believe he's been to some fabulous tropical destination. That's his business face. He's quite successful. And caring and a very generous—"

Emily shot a hand up to stop her. "Dear God, Mother, if the next word out of your mouth is 'lover,' I'm going to puke again!"

"Man! I was going to say *man*."

Emily flopped onto the couch. "I'm going to need serious therapy after this, I swear."

Trixie sat next to Emily and rubbed her knee. "The thing is, he's a great guy who cares about me and wants to see me happy. I didn't tell you because I knew you didn't like him. I was hoping to find a way to get you two together so you could get to know him better. See the wonderful man I see."

"How long has this…this…I can't even say the words." Emily rubbed her forehead. "How long have you been seeing him?"

"We've been dating for a while."

"How long a while? Not before Dad—"

"No. Of course not. I loved your father with all my heart. I was never unfaithful. How could you think such a thing?"

Emily shrugged. "It seemed to me Joe started sniffing around the week after the funeral."

Trixie's mouth dropped open. "You really must have quite the opinion of me. I didn't start dating Joe until almost two years after your father died. He did come by a week after the funeral. Your father had put a non-refundable deposit on a timeshare he couldn't begin to afford, and Joe, out of the goodness of his heart, gave the money back."

Okay, so maybe he wasn't so slimy. "That was kind of nice," Emily said, sheepishly.

"He knew money was tight. He's on the town council, so he knew when I missed the tax deadline on the shop. He offered to write me a personal note, but I said no. That's when he started booking appointments for haircuts and colorings he didn't need. I swear the man would have me wax his eyebrows to give me the extra twelve bucks if I'd let him.

"I should have told you about Joe and me, and I'm so sorry you had to find out the way you did, but you've been struggling so much lately. I've seen how hard things have been for you. You didn't want to move back home. I don't blame you. After Chicago, Stoddard, New Hampshire, is about as quiet as you can get. I understood what a sacrifice it was for you to give up your beautiful apartment and move back in with me. I felt so guilty about it. I didn't want to add my relationship with Joe to your stress. I was trying to break it to you gently."

Emily covered her face with her hands. "I still might need therapy."

Trixie wrapped her arm around her and laid her head on her shoulder. The room got quiet. "Your turn."

"I can't talk about Max. Not yet."

"It might make you feel better."

Em ran her fingers through her hair and gave a slow shake to her head. "Nothing's going to make me feel better."

"Can I just say I'm stunned? Devastated. How could he have fooled everyone? I can't imagine what you're feeling. *I* want to strangle him. Oh, and my beautiful little statue, my pride and joy? I'm using it as a doorstop."

"Don't do that. Don't push aside his talent and skill because he screwed things up. Regardless of the rest, Ma, his work is still his work, and it's still amazing.

Don't be one of those people." Emily's rush into defense mode surprised her.

"Well, I'm just glad you're away from him. He'd have dragged you down too. On the news this morning, they showed a bunch of people clearing out of his studio. Like fleas jumping off a dead squirrel."

Emily hated hearing the studio was in jeopardy. She felt bad for Max, but that didn't mean she forgave him. It didn't mean her pain was lessened or softened. She still loved him, God help her, even with a shredded heart.

"The nerve of showing up on my doorstep after what he did to you."

"What? When?"

"Yesterday. He wanted to know where he could find you. I had no idea where you'd gone. Of course, even if I'd known, I wouldn't have told him."

Emily swallowed the painful lump in her throat. "Ma, can we not talk about this anymore? Please?"

Trixie squeezed Emily's shoulders. "Of course, sweetie. I didn't fall for his 'I'm in love with her' crap, either."

Emily shot her mother a look. "He said he loved me?"

"You don't believe him, do you?" Trixie gawked at her like she was crazy. "The man's a professional conman, baby. If his mouth was moving, he was lying."

Chapter Twenty-Six

Wednesday evening Emily was scheduled to attend the end of semester show at Stoddard. The past few days had been surreal. She'd thanked Suzanne for all the tea and moved back to Trixie's Monday night. After their conversation, she felt as if Max was going to show up again at any moment. Thankfully, he didn't.

Emily had received a phone call from Margo Abbot regarding her show. She was very enthusiastic about featuring some of Emily's work and offered her a wonderful opportunity for the months leading up to it. "I run an artist's cooperative and we have an opening for an artist in residence this summer. It doesn't pay much, but you'd have room and meals and studio space. You'd be required to lead several demonstrations and a few hands-on workshops for our guests, maybe teach a class if you're interested. You can visit our website, and I'll e-mail you some more information."

"Yes, please do. I'm very interested."

"We're pretty remote. But being stuck out in the woods together gives our artists a chance to soak up each other's creative energies and focus on their work."

"Remote," for once, didn't sound like a prison sentence. It sounded like the perfect escape where she could work and disappear for a while. Distance was a good thing, right? She snapped up Margo's offer.

By Wednesday evening, all the details were set.

Emily planned to leave on Friday. She'd already started to pack. She'd been on edge for days, fearing Max would show up. After she jumped out of her skin when the UPS man knocked on Trixie's front door to deliver a package, Em knew this was the best idea. She couldn't keep looking over her shoulder and finding any excuse to run the tiniest of errands, parking her car in odd places, trying to keep one step ahead of him. As difficult as it was, she was forcing him from her mind. Hell, she hadn't thought of Maximo once...in the last ten minutes. That was progress.

Walking into the exhibition hall, what Emily wasn't prepared for was her reaction to seeing her piece again. She couldn't escape its passion or the memories of that night with Max.

The impact of seeing it punched the air from her lungs. Tears threatened, but she refused to allow them to fall. She'd shed enough over her foolishness. She'd make it through tonight, disappear into the woods for the summer, and decide what to do with *Steel Ribbon* when she returned.

People arrived for the show. The hall was soon packed with student artists, professors, friends, and families. Classmates exchanged hugs. Everyone was excited to see and be seen. The walls were covered with artwork, and three-dimensional art stood scattered throughout the crowded room. It was a wonderful display of every genre and level of talent found at the school. And with finals over and deadlines met, the mood of the majority of the students was one of relieved celebration.

Trixie would be by after she closed the salon. She warned Emily she was bringing Joe along. Now that the cat was out of the bag and they didn't have to hide their relationship, Joe wanted to spend as much time as he could with her mother. The town was abuzz. Friday couldn't come soon enough.

"Emily! Great sculpture."

"Jagger! Zee!" Emily hugged her friends Jagger Jones and his wife. Zee was an amazing portrait artist. She'd been in some of Emily's classes at Stoddard, and Jagger Jones was still a favorite model at the school. "How are you two? I haven't seen you all semester. I heard you were moving to London."

Jagger slipped an arm around Zee's waist. "The sooner the better, right lovey?"

Zee grinned at Jagger. They were such a sweet couple. It made the ache in Emily's chest twinge.

Jagger kissed Zee's forehead. "Go on, spill the beans."

Emily frowned at the two of them. "What beans?"

Zee blushed. "We're expecting."

Jagger blurted, "Twins."

"Wow." Emily felt punched again. Suzanne, Cynthia, now Zee? "There must be something in the water here in Stoddard."

Jagger beamed. He puffed his chest as if he was the first male to ever impregnate a woman. Zee laid a hand on his chest. "We were going to wait until the end of the year, but the thought of moving all the way to London with two babies doesn't sound like fun. So Jagger's mom is on her way from Australia, and she's going to help us pack up and be ready to move by the end of next month. That way we're all settled in before baby A and B arrive."

"Wow, babies *and* London. That's incredible.

Congratulations."

"We're still working on wonky names. Kinda a family tradition now." Jagger grinned his crooked grin at his wife.

"No, if they're girls, we're naming them after my grandmother, and if they're boys, after your father. We agreed, no more crazy names. We're not naming our babies Mac and Tosh Jones." Zee shook her head at Emily. "We'll let you know where we end up. You have to promise to come for a visit."

"Absolutely." Emily hugged Zee and Jagger.

The room was warm and hummed with activity. Emily spoke with several people about her work. She received some wonderful comments and was congratulated by several of her professors for a job well done.

Emily paused to take a drink from her water bottle when she saw him. Max entered the gallery space at the south end. Even rumpled and sporting a day's growth of beard, she spotted him the minute he came in. He stood at the entrance and scanned the room.

A war of emotions raged through her. Anger, anguish, hopeless longing. The pinball of feelings made her head spin. It was too soon. She wasn't strong enough yet to pretend his presence didn't throw her. She knew there was a possibility of him showing up tonight, but she'd hoped he'd forgotten. He hadn't. He was there. Emily couldn't face him. Time for her to leave.

Just then, another guest stopped to compliment her. Emily thanked the woman and excused herself, dodging her way through the crowd toward the north exit. A quick glance over her shoulder confirmed her fear.

He'd spotted her.

Into the hallway and through the busy corridor, she made her way out of the building. She couldn't leave, but if she could avoid him long enough, he'd get the message. She cut back around the building and...

"Emily?"

Her heart leapt in her chest. How the hell had he gotten in front of her? "I told you to leave me alone."

Sooty smudges ringed his eyes. He looked as if he hadn't slept in days. "Why did you send back the check?"

"Why do you think?" Emily couldn't keep the anger from her voice. "It made me feel cheap. I don't need your damn money." She crossed her arms over her chest.

"I didn't mean for you to feel cheapened by it. You earned it."

Earned it? "How did I earn all those dollars, Max? By breaking pieces off your statues or by being your whore?"

He jerked back as if she'd struck him. "No! What? You were *never* my whore! How could you say that?"

She held up a hand to stop him. This wasn't helping. "I appreciate your signing off on my paperwork, but keep your money. I don't want any part of it. Please, just go." She turned away from him.

He caught her arm. "I've been searching for you and calling for four days. I'm not leaving until you listen to me."

His hand on her arm wasn't rough or demanding. It was gentle and far more dangerous. It was a tender plea that reached into her tattered heart. If she didn't hear him out, he'd find another time, another place. Emily didn't think she could bear it. She didn't move. She kept her back to him. God help her, she couldn't look at him.

"Em?"

She sighed. "Say what you have to say."

"Will you look at me?"

"I can't."

His hand dropped away. "I'm sorry. I know it doesn't come close to apologizing for all I've done, but you have to know how sorry I am. I never meant to hurt you. I never meant to hurt anyone. This whole business started as a gag. My great-great-grandmother and Michelangelo. High school sweethearts. Florence High School, Class of 1490. It was a stupid joke we told in my family. Some reporter compared how solitary and driven I was to the great artist, one of my idiot brother's told the family tale, and the next thing I knew it had made it into the *New England Journal of Art* article. It mushroomed from there. I didn't take it seriously. It was too ridiculous.

"There's a reason I've been alone for years. I am solitary and driven when I work. More like anti-social and obsessed. That's why my marriage failed. I'm no good with people. Never have been. I have no patience. No filter for what comes out of my mouth. My art was my way to speak to the world. It was my way to communicate, but all of a sudden the media wanted to hear this fantastic story. I denied it all, but they wouldn't let it go. I just wanted them to leave me alone, so I pretended I didn't understand English. It worked. It worked too well. The persona took on a life of its own, and I let it. It was easier to pretend than fight it.

"But then I met you. It was like you breathed new

air into my lungs." His hand was back on her arm.

Emily shivered at his touch.

He stepped closer and lowered his voice. "I thought, at first, you were enamored with Maximo, not me. That's why I pushed you away. I wanted you to want me. The real me. Not Vega. But the more time I spent with you, the more I realized how much I wanted you. You were beautiful and strong. You were so much stronger than I was.

"I can't tell you how many times I started to tell you the truth. Something always interrupted me and then the moment was gone. So, I tried again, and again the words died on my tongue. But I was falling in love with you. I had to tell you the truth. I had to tell the world the truth. I didn't care about the consequences. I couldn't hope to share my life with you if I was living a lie.

"Beverly Lavender did me a favor. It wasn't how I wanted it to happen, but it's almost a relief now the truth is out. No more worrying that someone from Ohio will cash in on their fifteen minutes of fame and expose me. But not telling you—having you find out the way you did. I never wanted that. Not that it changes the facts. Not that it makes any of this less painful, but to see the hurt on your face..." His hand stroked up her arm. "I never wanted to hurt you, I swear."

Emily hadn't realized she was crying until a tear splashed onto her chest.

Anguish and regret filled his voice. Max continued to stroke her arm. "The last few days have been a nightmare, my family is bullshit, the press has been ruthless, the studio is disintegrating, and I've lost most of my commissions. But the only thing I cared about is you, finding you and trying to make it right. I had to explain, to somehow make you understand how sorry I am that I hurt you. I love you, Emily, with all of my heart. I've loved you since the first moment I looked into those beautiful green eyes. I love your energy and your incredible passion. I love that it's making me crazy trying to figure out what flower you smell like. I never imagined I could feel like this about anyone. I love you so much."

He turned her around. "I have no right to think you'll ever forgive me, but I pray you'll try to understand." He tipped her chin so she looked at him and whispered, "I know I don't deserve a second chance. I wouldn't blame you if you never wanted to see me again."

Emily stepped back, breaking their connection and closed her eyes. His explanation grated against her. The wound was too deep, too raw. She didn't know if she would ever forgive him. Her trust was gone. She brushed the tears from her cheeks. "I can't. I *don't* want to see you again. It's too damn hard." She shook her head and stared at his boots. "I'm leaving town in two days. Please don't look for me. Don't try to follow me."

Chapter Twenty-Seven

Months had passed since Maximo had seen Emily, and yet, a day—hell, an hour had not gone by without him thinking of her, loving her, and kicking himself for destroying the best thing that ever happened to him.

His life barely resembled what it had been before the world learned the truth about the great Maximo Vega. He'd lost everything. His employees had walked away. Make that ran away. To try to soften the blow of his betrayal, he'd given them all a generous severance so their families wouldn't suffer because of his deceit. He'd closed the studio and sold all the equipment to pay off his vendors and suppliers. Every single commission had cancelled, deposits repaid. Daniel Bruce of The Bruce Gallery wouldn't even answer his calls. His family was still speaking to him, but as far as the art world was concerned, Maximo Vega was dead.

He ended up moving into an old factory building near Manchester and setting up a makeshift studio where he could work. Dante helped him move.

"So, what are you going to do now?"

"I have work to finish." Max wheeled the last of his marble supply into his new workspace. "I've been scouting cheap gallery locales. I think I have enough pieces for a small showing, as Max Vega this time. If I can sell off some of these abandoned commissions, that will keep me going. Otherwise, the money should last about six months if I don't eat."

"I wish I could stick around and help you." Dante slipped a hand truck from under a wrapped piece.

"No, we've been over this. You need to stay as far away from me as you can. I've convinced everyone you knew nothing about the deception, and that's how it's going to be. The new job is set. You'll do great. You're going to love Arizona."

"What about her?" Dante unwrapped the moving blanket off a stunning piece of pink marble carved in Emily's likeness. "Have you heard anything?"

"No." Maximo stared at the piece. It was his favorite. Even more than *Implorare*, this sculpture was his love letter to her. It was his "Em." Somehow, in this simple pose, he'd captured all her incredible passion as well as her laughter. It was everything he loved about her in that sliver of time when she was his.

"Give her some time." Dante shrugged a shoulder. "Maybe she'll come around."

"I doubt it. She was pretty definite about never wanting to see me again."

"Did you check out the website I sent you about the fresh artist's show at the end of next month? They have her listed as one of their featured artists."

"No." Max ran a hand through his hair and moved a crate of heavy tools against one wall.

"Why not?"

He turned to face Dante and put his hands on his hips. "Because if I know where she is, I'll have to go. She doesn't want to see me, remember."

"It's a shame. You were happy there for half a minute. Walking around the studio grinning like a fool. You really loved her."

"Not loved, past tense. Love. Full, complete, and hopeless. I'll never stop thinking about her and what a mess I made of everything." Max ran his hands over the legs of the statue. "She's an amazing artist and an incredible woman. She sure as hell deserves better than me. We were smart to sign her off before everything went to shit."

"That was your idea. I just signed the papers."

"It was the right thing to do."

"Oh, speaking of shit, this may put the smile back on your face, if only for a minute." Dante pulled a sheet of paper out of his pocket. "I caught this online. There's actual video. Evidently, it's going viral." He handed Max the page. "Our favorite agent, the Lavender lizard ran a press conference for her dearest four-legged client. Seems Babu isn't a fan of the media either. They scared the crap out of him. Literally. Beverly was doing her best to keep things upbeat and went to hug the beast, but he shifted and knocked her back. First, she stepped in a steaming pile of elephant dung in those four-inch heels of hers, then she slipped and landed flat on her back in the muck. You have to see the video. It's priceless. From what I hear, she wrenched her back pretty bad and is now in traction."

"And she was worried about getting *my* shit on her."

"Karma's a bitch."

Max gave a bitter laugh. "Tell me about it."

Another six weeks passed. Scraping together his last few dollars, Max secured a small gallery space on the north side of Boston. It wasn't Copley Place, but it was close enough to potentially draw some wealthier art clients, if he could get the word out. It was to be his comeback show. Maximo Vega was gone, but Max was back.

This was it for him. Do or die. The money was gone. If he didn't make sales, or take in a commission or two, he was done. He'd have to admit defeat to himself and to his family. If he failed this time, it was back to Cleveland to breathe dry cleaning fumes for the rest of his life.

He'd worked day and night, using whatever supplies he had left. He'd given the gallery's cinderblock walls a fresh coat of white paint for a break in the rent, moved in his own lighting, and pasted fliers up all over town announcing his show.

Max stopped at a coffee shop, midtown, to ask if they'd post his flier when he noticed another sat in their front window advertising a Fall Fresh Faces artist's show. He recognized the name Margo Abbot, but what caught his eye first was a photograph of Emily. The poster showed vignettes of each artist. Emily was standing next to the wonderful ribboned piece from her semester exhibit. It reminded him of the night the two of them worked on the piece together, clayed hands on each other's body. Making love to her right there in the studio and carrying her up to his shower. He wouldn't forget that night as long as he lived.

Seeing her name, seeing her face with her beautiful smile, remembering their night together encircled him in an ache that banded his chest like the figure in her sculpture. It wrapped around him as tight as any chain and squeezed the air from his lungs. God help him, his love for her had only gotten stronger as her distance from him stretched past any hope of their reconciliation.

There had been nothing. No communication. Silence. Max had forced himself to stay away from Stoddard. She'd left town for the summer, but she'd be returning soon. His guess was she'd come back after the show. School resumed classes before Labor Day. *If* she decided to come back. Max wasn't sure she would.

The information printed across the bottom of the poster told him the show ran the same week as his, the last week in August. That was good news. If their shows overlapped, he wouldn't have to battle the urge to go see her. Although, to be honest, the urge to see her was getting easier to fight these last few weeks as he struggled to keep going. He didn't want her to see him like this, at his lowest. If and when he went to her, he needed to be back on his feet. He needed to be his own man again. To be a success once more. There was a lot riding on his show.

****

The artwork was set, the signs posted, and the time had come to open the doors. Max was dressed in casual jeans and his lucky shirt. It was the blue button down Emily wore the night he fixed her dinner. He couldn't wear it without picturing her in it, and he wanted her with him tonight, even if it was only in his memory.

He was exhausted. It had taken days to load and place all the larger pieces by himself. But he was happy with the result. It looked professional and his work looked great. He'd even splurged on champagne and some snacks for opening night. He popped a few corks in anticipation.

The doors were unlocked at eight sharp. Max hadn't expected a line waiting to get in, but when he swung open the doors to find no one, his heart sank.

Giving himself a pep talk, he tried to brush his anxiety away. No one was on time to these things. Fashionably late was the way to go. *Don't panic.*

He poured himself a glass of champagne and strolled through the space and waited. Ten minutes eked past. He had to stop watching the clock. It was maddening.

At twenty after eight, he went outside. The streets were busy, but no one seemed to be heading in his direction. Max breathed in the warmth of the August evening and let it out in a slow, prolonged breath.

Back inside, he paced some more and paused before his crowning piece, *Implorare.* He had both pieces displayed tonight; the bisque-fired bozzetto and the finished statue in marble. He studied the expression he'd captured on Emily's beautiful face and felt her pleading reach more than ever. It was eight-thirty, and he was coming to know that feeling of despair he portrayed so well. No one was coming. All the time and effort had been for nothing. It was over. He was over, and he doubted imploring to the heavens would help him tonight.

His failure hit him square in the chest. All these months, all the loss, he had clung to a sliver of hope. Hoping the caliber of his work would see him through the scandal. Hoping his supporters would rally behind him. But no. No one was there. It was 8:45.

For Max, fear and desperation quickly gave way to anger. He poured himself another glass of champagne and toasted himself. His voice echoed off the newly painted walls. "Here's to the art world's former favorite son. Such talent. Too bad he was such an idiot. He might have been someone. Does anyone recall his name? No?"

He picked up a small bust of a woman. It had been the first commission cancelled after the news broke. "Can you remember his name? No? You either?" He stared at where he had signed the piece's base. "There it is, right there. Maximo. Maximo fucking Vega!"

Max hurled the bust toward the nearest wall. It shattered against the concrete.

"If you tell Crystal LeMar I broke that, I'll deny it."

Max spun around. "Emily?"

"Thank goodness you didn't break one of me." She studied the destroyed piece. She was wearing a stunning black dress with thin straps. The soft fabric skimmed every beautiful inch of her. She was sun-kissed and glowing.

"What are you doing here?" Max was afraid to blink. He'd imagined this scene in his head so many times, he was certain his mind was playing with him.

"Trixie told me you were having a show, so…" She held her hands out to her side and shrugged. "Here I am."

"But your show is opening tonight too. Why aren't you there?"

"I was. It started at seven. It was hard to get away. That's why I'm a little late."

Every cell in his body wanted to grab her and wrap her in his arms, but he'd crawled to her before. He might not have anything left, but dammit, he still had his pride. "Have you come to gloat?"

She frowned. "No. I'm here to see the work of an amazing artist."

"Even if he was a fraud and a colossal failure?"

Emily shook her head. "You couldn't possibly be a failure."

"Look around you." He gave a bitter laugh.

She scanned the room. "I am—your pieces are breathtaking."

"It's no use." He threw up a hand. "No one is coming. I blew it. I had it, and I lost it all."

"Not all." Emily was intently studying one of his smaller sculptures. "I'm here." She said the words so quietly, he almost missed them. She still hadn't looked at him.

"And I'm standing here like an idiot trying to figure out why."

She lifted her eyes to his and the jolt of that connection hit him all the way to the soles of his feet. "Because tonight is a very special night for the man I love and it's only right I spend it telling him how wonderful he is. But maybe he needs to hear how I've spent months cloistered away in the woods loving him more and more as each day passed. Perhaps he needs to know I believed him when he told me he tried to be honest with me, and it was the shock that made me walk away from the best thing that ever happened to me."

Emily closed the distance between them. "I'm here because I need to tell you I wear lilac perfume. I'm here because I'm in love with you, and I've never stopped. I believe in you and I'm hoping you'll forgive me."

"Me forgive you?"

She nodded. "I was hurt and I lashed out. I wanted you to hurt as much as I did. All I succeeded in doing was causing us both more pain. You don't do that if you truly love someone. And I truly love you."

"I thought I destroyed all that."

"I thought you did too." She played with the button on his shirt. "But love isn't plaster. Love is stone. Rock solid. Granite. If it's real and true, it's strong enough to weather any storm. It lasts a lifetime." She lifted her eyes to his. "Sometimes it lasts forever."

When her lips met his, the dark shadow of the last three months lifted from his soul. Opening his lips, he groaned as her tongue slipped into his mouth. He crushed her in his arms, grabbing fistfuls of her dress, and pressed her body to his as he returned the passion of her kiss. He swallowed her gasp as he ravished her mouth.

She'd come back. She loved him and she was here. Nothing else mattered. Not the show, not the last few hellish months, nothing. He had everything he'd ever wanted here in his arms.

"So you forgive me?" She held his face. Tears welled in her eyes.

"You did nothing to forgive. I'm the one—"

She stopped him with another kiss. "I understand why. I forgive you. I love you."

His heart soared. "I love you. Not for one second did I stop thinking of you and loving you, and praying someday…"

"Today is someday."

"*Hey,*" a gruff voice called to them from the door. "If you two are done, can we come in now? The natives are getting restless out here."

Chapter Twenty-Eight

"Dante?"

Emily broke away from Max and smoothed her dress. "Yes. Come on in."

Max stood there in amazement as a crowd of more than fifty people poured through the doors into the gallery with Dante leading the pack. The man crushed him in an embrace. Men and women began shaking his hand and thumping him on his back, congratulating him on his comeback, complimenting his work. Emily hugging them each in turn, thanking them for coming, and apologized for making them wait.

"You brought them here?"

"Invited. They wanted to come."

Another man pumped Max's hand and expressed his appreciation for his work when Emily grabbed at his elbow. "Oh, there's someone you have to meet."

She dragged him toward a towering man wearing a very expensive suit. When he saw them approaching, he gave Max an appraising look and Emily a courteous nod.

She shook his hand. "Mr. Bruce, I can't thank you enough for coming."

"Mr. Bruce?" Max stared at her in surprise.

The man before him held out his hand. "Mr. Vega, I'm Daniel Bruce of the Bruce Gallery."

"I know who you are." Max shook the man's hand.

"It's nice to meet you. I have to tell you, I'm more than a little surprised to see you here."

"I'm more than a little surprised to be standing here myself, but this young woman can be very persuasive when she puts her mind to it. Relentless might be a better word. There's an old saying about a dog with a bone." He shook his head and glanced around. "You really threw yourself in front of a train by hiding behind that ridiculous persona you created, Mr. Vega. What the hell were you thinking?"

Max shook his head. "I don't think I was."

"That's obvious. I have to ask, are you done with all the grandstanding and ready to get back to the important things, namely your work and promoting your career?"

"That's what I've been doing."

"Good. Know this, Mr. Vega, I *never* give second chances. They have a habit of biting me in the ass." He stared down his nose at Max. "But, I have been enamored with your work since I first laid eyes on it, and I was devastated when the scandal ruined my chance to showcase you. Furious, but devastated none the less." His eyes roamed down the length of the gallery. "Then I got a call from my good friend, Madeline Sullivan from Stoddard, and she threw me into the ring with Ms. Baskins here."

Max frowned at her. What had she done?

"Emily reminded me your work was still your work. She refused to take no for an answer and asked me to reconsider your tour. You have quite the champion." He pulled a business card from his jacket pocket. "Now, I'd be an absolute fool to reinstate a three-city tour to someone as risky as you, but a little bit of scandal might work to our advantage. I'm thinking we start with one. San Francisco doesn't mind the odd scandal and they love an underdog. They just may embrace you wholeheartedly. We can start there, see how the numbers run, and who knows."

Max took the card and looked at it like it might be made of flash paper and disappear in a puff of smoke. "You mean it?"

Daniel Bruce raised an eyebrow. "Do I look like a man who jokes?"

"No, sir."

Bruce kissed Emily's cheek and shook Max's hand again. "Good. Get in touch with me at the beginning of the week and we can put something down on paper." He started to leave. "Oh, and I have to say, if this whole mess did anything positive for you and your career, it rid you of that odious woman, Beverly Lavender. If I never have to deal with her again, I'll die a happy man." He pointed at Max. "Don't lose my card."

Max slipped it into his shirt pocket. "I have no intention to."

"Or that one." He pointed to Emily and winked at her.

Max slipped an arm around Emily's slender waist and pulled her tight to his side. "I don't intend to do that either."

Daniel Bruce joined the crowd milling through the gallery.

Max leaned toward Emily and kissed her. He whispered against her lips. "What did you do?"

She shrugged one shoulder and grinned. "I made a few phone calls to the man. A few dozen. Madeline helped."

"Remind me to thank her later, too."

More people were arriving. The gallery was full of neighborhood people, art people. He caught Emily waving and saw the newlyweds, Jeremy and Cynthia arrive.

"You don't mind me inviting them, do you? Given your jealous streak where Jeremy is concerned, I hesitated."

"You love me. I'm not worried."

"Good." She patted his chest. "They're going to have a baby. Jeremy is having sympathy morning sickness and has already gained eight pounds."

Max laughed when he spotted another group coming through the door. It was a man and a woman he remembered as Trixie, Emily's mother. Trixie was helping an older woman… "Nonna?" He shot a look at Emily. "You invited my nonna?"

"I invited the whole Vega clan, but they couldn't leave the shops. Did you know they're opening a third dry cleaner? Your grandmother insisted on coming, though. Your brother Nick was coming with her, but she said no, she could make it on her own. She flew in just to come tonight."

"*Maximo, il mio Maximo!*"

"Nonna!" He hugged the woman as tight as he dared. He hadn't seen her in a few years. She looked like he remembered her. "How do you stay so young, Nonna?"

She swatted at him. "How do you stay so fresh?" She turned to Emily. "Where are your manners, Maximo? Introduce me to your girl."

"Nonna, this is my Emily. Emily, this is my grandmother, *Michelangela Raffeala Innocenti Vega*."

Emily's eyes opened wide. "*Michelangela*?"

Nonna Vega rolled her eyes and raised her hand. "*Si*, my family, they have *one* joke." She poked her index finger into the air.

Emily laughed and hugged her.

Max watched the two most important women in his life embrace for the first time and felt a rush to his heart.

Nonna shook her head. "She's pretty, *si*, but too skinny." She pinched at Emily's side. "You don't eat? Don't you like Italian?"

"No, I love Italian." Emily's eyes held his over the silvery head of his grandmother. "But I haven't had any for months."

There was no double meaning in her gaze. She loved him, and she missed being with him.

Emily smiled back at Nonna. "Maximo cooked for me, though, a delicious meal. Your recipes."

Max's memory flashed back to feeding her honeyed oranges in bed. He caught Emily's eyes again. Was she remembering the sweet oranges too?

Nonna missed nothing. She caught the exchange between them and nodded. "She is the one." She elbowed Max. "*Si*?"

"Yes, she is."

Trixie and her date had been waiting behind Nonna. Max shook the man's hand when they exchanged names. Trixie's welcome wasn't as warm. "Mrs. Baskins."

"Mr. Vega." Ice dripped from every syllable.

"Vega? No, it's pronounced *Bastardo*." He smiled. "Lesson four."

That earned him a forgiving hug.

Max watched Trixie and Mr. Turner join Nonna in their walk through the gallery. Max wrapped his arms around Emily. "You got my grandmother to come? It's a miracle. She never leaves home. How did you do all this?"

"I was properly motivated." She kissed him. "She's here because she loves you. It's another thing we have in common."

Max swept his fingers over Emily's beautiful face. He missed this face and wondered if a man could die feeling too much love in his heart. He lowered his mouth to hers.

Behind him he heard a horrified gasp. "Emily Louise Baskins! This is *you!*"

"*Damn!* I forgot to tell her..." Emily slipped from his embrace in a panicked rush. "Ma, I was going to tell you…"

****

The morning's sunlight filtered through Venetian blinds to stripe the bed and their entwined bodies. Max slipped Emily's pale hair behind her ear. His fingertip played with the curve of its lobe.

"You're so beautiful." He moved to kiss her and she stopped him by laying two fingers across his lips.

"No, that's not how you say it. Just for me, when we're alone, in bed like this, and you're kissing my neck and running your strong hands over my body, can you call me *bella*? And say my name the way I love?"

He held her gaze as the sun's kiss played across her cheek. "And you won't forget who you're making love to?"

"It's only ever been you, Max. I love *you.* Every part of you."

He copied her and laid a fingertip against the soft pillow of her lip. "No, that's not how you say it. *Ti amo*, remember?" He moved his finger away and watched her mouth.

"*Si. Ti amo*."

Maximo moved over her and ran his fingertips down over the slim column of her throat. The beating of her heart met his touch. Reaching lower, he cupped her breast and teased its tip with a sweep of his thumb until it tightened and peaked. Emily pressed into his hand and whimpered.

Max laid a line of kisses down the side of her neck. "*La mia bella, Emily, ti amo, ti amo*."

She shivered in his arms and sighed. Pulling back to gaze into her eyes, there was only one more thing to say. "*Mi vuoi sposarmi?*"

Emily gave a slight shake to her head. "I don't know what that means. You've never said that before."

"No, I've never said it before. Not like that. Not to anyone." He took her hand off his chest and kissed the backs of her fingers and opened it to lay a kiss in its palm. "It means, will you marry me?"

A word about the author...

Lisa is an artist/writer who lives in her dream house nestled among the lakes in New England. She is married to her best friend and is thankful to him for putting up with all her craziness and for giving her the chance to be who she's called to be.

She loves getting lost in a good book, finding the perfect pair of fabulous shoes, and hearing the laughter of her sons.

Her faith in love and grace has carried her through many things. Her deep spirituality shines through in her work, and she believes in ghosts, silver linings, and happily ever afters.